THE GALILEO

Nathan H. Green

The Galileo

First Canadian Edition

www.Authornathanhgreen.com

Cover designed by Rob Joseph

Library and Archives Canada Cataloguing in Publication information is available upon request

ISBN: 978-1-7780553-1-7

To my wife.

who supported me as I practiced.

It takes vision to believe in something grand,

it takes love to believe that something can become grand.

CHAPTER 1 - 87 Days from TR-583

PANIC WILL MAKE any emergency worse: Chetan Gonzales panicked.

Physically his mission was simple. The Galileo had detected an asteroid in the void of interstellar space.   The three-kilometer-long hunk of rock was primordial, lifeless, and had travelled undisturbed for billions of years. In other words: boring.

After three years in deep space with nothing but vacuum for company, even a boring rock was rarer than diamond and impossible to ignore. Ensign Gonzales was to perform a spacewalk to the asteroid's surface, collect several samples, and return them to the Galileo for analysis. The mission had been planned, debated, rehearsed, and approved before the twenty-three-year-old Ensign had even opened the airlock, though that is exactly where things began to go wrong.

The Galileo had five airlocks – one on her belly, two on her port and two on her starboard. Naval ships of old used rudders for navigation and, as most navigators were right-handed, it was easier for rudders to be mounted on the right hand side of the ship. To prevent the rudder being crushed by docking at ports, the "port" or left side was used to load cargo.

Chetan Gonzales stood in the forward port airlock. His armored space suit emitted a short rhythmic series of test thrusts, and he triggered the airlock doors. Four staggered airlock doors slid open and a whiff of residual moisture in the air condensed, froze, and then sublimated into a gas as it was sucked out. Chetan didn't miss a beat. He jogged forward and jumped through the airlock and into space. He used his hands to push himself down, off the top lip of the outer airlock door just as he cleared it. Before he could go to the asteroid he needed tools kept in a storage hatch on the Galileo's belly.

Any first-year physics student will tell you that space most perfectly demonstrates the laws of physics. But for a human being, evolved to expect gravity, air resistance, and friction, no environment feels more like the laws of physics have been abandoned. Chetan had taken care to launch himself out of the airlock at an angle so he traveled across the hull, towards the belly of the ship even as he moved away from it. It was a sign of practice that this motion did not send him toppling end over end or twisting around like an off-balanced top.

There are two, and only two, ways for a person to move effectively in space. They can move like a dim-witted robot, giving five seconds of conscious thought to every motion, or they can move with the grace of a synchronized diver. Ensign Chetan Gonzales dove through the heavens.

He was not tethered to the Galileo. His suit could literally fly. Thrusters scattered over its surface could tap into the oxygen normally reserved for breathing and, mixed with a small amount of hydrogen, produce a powerful rocket fuel. Electromagnetic plates in the sole of the suit's boots could also be switched on to grab any magnetic surface.

Allowing his momentum to carry him away from the ship's hull, Chetan activated the magnetized plates on the bottom of his boots and felt a gentle tug as lines of magnetic force connected him to the Galileo's skin and superstructure. His boot's magnetic pull slowed his speed away from the ship, but not his speed across the hull. By pulling his legs closer to his body and away from the hull he decreased the magnetic force and by extending his legs he could increase it. Chetan balanced, by feel, his momentum away from the Galileo with the magnetic pull from his boots. The result of this tug of war of physics was that Chetan glided across the surface of the deck twenty meters before his boot's magnetic pull finally won and he touched down just a few yards from the storage hatch that was his objective.

Instead of climbing out of the airlock and taking slow, magnetically locked steps, as called for in his mission plan, Chetan had saved a minute and a half by grace. He was equally adept at retrieving his "mission package", the technical term for a toolbox, from its storage hatch. The title "mission package" might seem grandiose but, for fifty times the price of a toolbox, a grandiose name is the least Earth's government could get in return.

Mission package retrieved, the Ensign took a moment to fortify himself for the next small step. The Galileo was under his feet. Technically he was standing on the belly of the ship and thus 'upside down', but the hull represented a convenient reference for 'down' and thinking of oneself as hanging from the roof by your feet was a sure ticket to nausea. The asteroid he would be 'walking' to was 'above' him, directly under the Galileo.

Had the Galileo remained stationary Chetan could have stood where he was for the rest of his natural life and the only sound he would hear would be his own breathing, and the only motion he would see would be his own limbs. The stars did not twinkle, an optical effect caused by variations in a planet's atmosphere, they stared at Chetan, unblinking, unwavering, eternal.

While beautiful, any illusions about the safety of his environment were cured by looking 'up' at the asteroid two kilometers away. The Galileo had stopped in the emptiness of space between solar systems because an asteroid was interesting in the relative sense of the word. Like an abandoned gas station along a deserted highway, it would have been passed without thought at the start of a long trip but, after three years of travel, without anything to see or do, it couldn't be ignored.

In the absence of a solar system's star the asteroid was visible only because it blotted out the stars behind it. What ought to have been a sea of stars had a giant hole of utter blackness. The Galileo had turned on her exterior lights, but the depth of darkness seemed to drink in the light as soon as it left the hull, and the asteroid was invisible, except for the hole it left in space.

When the asteroid had been detected, the Galileo's commander, Captain Peter Grey, had awarded naming rights to the crewman with the best performance review. The Corporal who won named the asteroid "Jennifer's Tear" after an old flame who he assumed would eventually be sorry for ending the relationship. A frozen tear forever drifting through the heavens to commemorate a broken heart; or so Sergeant Daniels had described it, her face turning red as she choked back laughter.

Jennifer's Tear loomed as a vortex of nothingness, a hole in the heavens. Chetan couldn't help but think that Jennifer, whoever she was, had gotten the better end of the name: an ex-lover desperate for her to regret ending the relationship vs. her, a bottomless pit of blackness and indifference, so deep it could only be seen from the gap it left in the background of the universe. Daniels probably would have lambasted him equally ruthlessly for the thought, but she didn't have to fall through space towards a hole in the sky.

Chetan bent his knees into a deep crouch, pulled the toolbox - mission package - close to his chest, switched off his magnetic boots and pushed off, hard, towards nothingness. Even jumping required a checklist.

As soon as he cleared the hull Chetan activated the thrusters on his suit giving himself a tiny burst of additional speed towards the rock that must be above him. Technically he was not supposed to have used additional thrust but increasing his speed even slightly on the journey there would shave minutes off the mission.

The plan was for Chetan to land on Jennifer's Tear, on his feet, and let his legs stop him. In order to do that he would need to spin his body around; a task for which two precious bursts of thrust had been budgeted (one to start him spinning and another to stop him in the correct position). Having used one of the thruster bursts to speed his approach, he had a different plan. Extending his mission package in front of him so that its length was aligned with his body he spun the box sideways, end over end, like a baton.

The torque he applied to the mission package applied an opposite torque on him. Even though he was heavier and thus moved more slowly, his body began to rotate in opposition to the box. Newton was very much correct. Eventually, his feet reoriented themselves "down" towards the ground that must now be rushing up towards him. To stop his spinning motion he simply grabbed the toolbox and both man and mission package were none the worse for wear.

It wasn't that his suit didn't have enough fuel; he could have used his thrusters much more liberally if his only concern was how much he had in his tanks. But everything was rationed and recycled on the Galileo. The oxygen he breathed could be reclaimed from the CO_2 he exhaled. The water he drank at lunch was recycled in the evening. But when oxygen and hydrogen were mixed, burned, and vented into space they could not be reclaimed. So thrusts were rationed like everything else.

By the time twenty minutes had ticked by on the mission clock Chetan was forty minutes into the scheduled mission plan and had excess fuel to show for it.

Stars below Chetan began to disappear into a growing horizon of nothingness as he approached Jennifer's Tear. His suit's laser range finders told him that he was two hundred and twenty meters above the surface, but he could see nothing. Lights from his suit ought to illuminate the surface before he crashed into it, but depending on how reflective the surface was, he could have as little as a half a heartbeat between seeing the ground and impact: if the lights were even working.

Instruments, machines, software are inherently unreliable in ways that humans are not. They cannot be hungover, have a bad day, or be preoccupied. Absent an excuse, a human's senses might be imperfect but if they say something is thirty meters away you can be sure it is not three meters away. When a laser range finder says the ground is, now, twenty-five meters away the mind silently adds "probably". Instruments break, go wonky one time in a thousand, and can be absurdly wrong. One relies on instruments over their own fears only when trained to, yet never trusts them. Chetan used his thrusters to slow his descent. Three long seconds later his suit lights caught the surface. It took a half second to judge the distance, but it was enough, and he landed, on his feet, without breaking anything. Neil Armstrong had been more graceful in his first step, but Chetan hadn't bungled the most famous quote in history, so he called it even.

From there his mission was less astronaut and more geologist. The toolbox / mission package contained a number of drills, excavating explosives, and sample containers. Chetan was to gather and label a dozen surface samples, drill and take samples of the subsurface and, after carefully positioning a half dozen bore holes, attempt to blast a car sized segment of the asteroid away so that he could sample the bottom of the crater.

The scientific value of the work was, virtually, non-existent. Jennifer's Tear was three light years from the nearest solar system and the Galileo's destination TR-583, unimaginably farther from Earth's solar system, and given its speed and course, navigation indicated that it had been five billion years since it had last been anywhere but interstellar space.

Thus, it was preposterous that Jennifer's Tear had ever contained life. Perhaps one day mankind would encounter enough bodies like this that a meaningful statistical analysis could be conducted and something interesting deduced about the primordial makeup of the galaxy. That task would take lifetimes and the data collected from Jennifer's Tear would simply be the first entry. Science was about surprises, and the difference between virtually useless, and actually useless, was large.

Chetan easily scooped up handfuls of the asteroid into sample containers. From fragments of ice that shattered at the slightest touch, to desiccated rocks and dirt, Chetan collected everything within arm's reach. There was no reason for him to move from the spot he landed and, in any event, Chetan didn't want to spend the time doing so.

When he had filled a dozen sample containers and returned them to their slots in the mission package, Chetan retrieved the small drill he would be taking deep surface samples with. The two-foot-long drill bit chewed into the asteroid's crust. It easily cut through ancient stone, ice, and dirt as though they were Styrofoam.

He was careful with the drilling even though he probably didn't need to be. His space suit was closer to a knight's armor than the tailored foil-balloons worn by 20th century astronauts. The suit consisted of three layers: an inner layer of tough, skintight, polymer that created a positive pressure against the body by squeezing it tightly. The material was engineered at the molecular level to loosen when the external environment was high pressure and tighten when the external environment was low pressure. The second layer was made up of paneled electrical components each the size of a man's hand. They were spread over the suit to allow radio communication, telemetric data collection, and a host of other useful functions. The outermost layer was titanium plates jointed, fitted, and individually machined. The titanium plates covered 90% of the suit's exterior surface so, even if the drill slipped, it was unlikely to penetrate the suit. Oxygen and hydrogen were stored inside hollowed segments of titanium outer plates. The suit didn't distinguish between oxygen for fuel and oxygen for occupant. This eliminated the need for bulky tanks and any physical damage would only compromise a small portion of the suit's fuel and air.

On the Galileo there was a constant hum, the resonance of a hundred systems acting in unison to produce a unique and, hopefully constant, sound. As he worked, Chetan could hear only his shifting footsteps on the ground, the brittle ice and dirt that shattered under his feet, and the whine of the drill conducted through his arms.

***

THE HUM ABOARD THE GALILEO permeated even the bridge. Captain Peter Grey wore a suit identical to Chetan's, save the quadruple bars of captain's rank painted in gold on the black titanium of his left shoulder plate. On the bridge everyone wore the suits. This was protocol in case of a sudden decompression.

"Let's say I had a rod thousands of miles long, but very light and very strong. If I started swinging it like a bat, could I get the end of that rod to go faster than the speed of light?" Grey asked.

Corporal Tsang worked to keep his face passive, despite the fact it was concealed inside his helmet. It had been foolish of him to think that the Captain wouldn't know about his latest physics test results.

"No sir. You can't go faster than light using conventional methods," Tsang replied.

"That is the obvious answer, Corporal. What would happen if we tried to do this? Why wouldn't it work?" Captain Grey let the other crew on the bridge listen in to the conversation and Corporal Tsang wanted to sink into the floor. There was only one reason the Captain would be grilling him on physics and everyone else on the bridge knew it.

"Well to begin with Captain I would challenge the assumptions. A rod thousands of miles long would have an enormous mass. You couldn't simply start swinging it like a baseball bat."

Grey's head ticked up in approval. "Alright, so say we had a giant machine do the swinging. Where would our next problem be?"

Each member of the bridge's crew was locked into chairs at their control panels. They all wore armor and their chairs, extra-large to accommodate the bulk of the suits, had locking mechanisms that grabbed the suits' titanium plates to hold them secure. No seatbelts or harnesses aboard the Galileo.

Though the bridge was small the lack of free motion made it feel more spacious, and even at that it was significantly roomier than any other compartment on the Galileo.

"Next would be strength, sir. Even if the rod were stronger than titanium matrix composite, over dozens, or hundreds of kilometers it would be about as rigid as wet spaghetti." Tsang took a breath, "and to answer your next question, sir, if the rod were infinitely strong then as it approached the speed of light it would effectively gain mass and it would take more energy to speed it up. It could gain an infinite amount of mass and so would take an infinite amount of energy to reach light speed."

Tsang left a great deal to be desired as a person but as a professional his redeeming quality was a refusal to fail twice. "Very good Tsang. If only you studied civics as seriously. Alright, enough with that, where are we with Mr. Gonzales?"

***

ON THE SURFACE OF JENNIFER'S TEAR Chetan had drilled a dozen holes for his sub-surface samples. Each borehole was a point on the perimeter of a circle roughly two meters around and all angling towards the center. After he had drilled a hole, he collected a small sample of material from the bottom using a scooping drill bit, and then carefully slid a small detonator into the hole.

He held the detonators as he would a live cobra. In theory the devices were safe; a point their civilian sales rep had blown her right arm off trying to demonstrate. She had been the first person, but not the last, to die in training on Earth. As much as he had to rely on his equipment and team, Chetan knew that often one tiny thing, a frayed wire in the case of the civilian rep, could mean life or death.

Nearly an hour early, Chetan set the last of the charges, and cleared the blast site with a very long, careful, jump using the tiny gravity of Jennifer's Tear just as he had his magnetic boots on the Galileo's hull. As soon as he was thirty meters away the charges automatically detonated in unison (this time working exactly as their manufacturer said they would). A car-sized chunk of dirty ice separated from the asteroid.

Chetan had one final task to do. Once he collected a sample from the bottom of the crater he was free, for exactly sixty minutes, thanks to the time he had shaved off from the mission plan.

With the help of his suit's electronic suite, and one giant leap, Ensign Gonzales flew sideways into the hunk of ice and rock. With a liberal use of thrusters, he sent it on a slow path into the blackness of space. This cleared the blast site for him to take his sample and sealed his own fate.

With the final sample retrieved Chetan stood back and looked into the night's sky like he had as a child.

Looking out into space from the inside of a starship is a little like laying on a hammock in your backyard looking up at the stars. You are surrounded by the familiar noises of home, the light pollution of civilization, and the silhouettes of neighboring houses, all obscuring the view.

Gonzales had been raised in Nebraska. His parents had always understood that he was a free spirit and though they must have known that he snuck in and out at night they never commented or tried to stop him. Not every night, not most nights, but some nights, something would grab Chetan. As soon as his parents had put him to bed, he would climb out from his window and walk as far as he dared away from the lights of houses into the endless fields of the agriculture conglomerate. It would take hours but eventually he always found a spot that just seemed right. He would stand in the fields, above him nothing but the stars, and if he was lucky, catch a fleeting feeling of falling off the world into the sky above. Standing on Jennifer's Tear, not a sound to be heard, not a thing but his suit separating him from eternity was like inhaling and exhaling the essence of those moments. He smiled at the irony of reminiscing about the child who would have given anything to trade places.

Very slowly in the reduced gravity, Chetan dropped to one knee and scooped up a handful of dirt. Touching it felt like touching something from a museum. He was holding something unconceived, unseen, unknown for billions of years. Jennifer's Tear was so far from the light of any star that its temperature was only nominally above absolute zero. The simple act of rubbing the dirt between his hands caused it to dissolve, the molecules disassociating from one another, perhaps even the molecules themselves being broken down into atomic components so weak were the bonds holding them together at that temperature.

Chetan stood, closed his eyes, extended his arms, and tried to inhale the vastness of space one final time before returning to the confines of the Galileo for years more.

He had traded his life for this moment. After three years in space they were three months from their first stop, TR-583, but with no official end to their mission the Galileo could be in space for a generation. If they did make contact with intelligent life, it would be the senior officers enjoying the thrill, and history, of making first contact. It was entirely possible he would never again have more than a few cubic feet of space for himself. But for one moment the universe was his.

Chetan was the first human being to stand on a body and look out on the stars not knowing which was home. He might never eat another steak, have children of his own, watch the sunset with a lover, or drink another beer, but he had something that no one else in human history had or would have. Jennifer's Tear was his. She was something everyone aboard the Galileo would understand without a word, and almost no one back on Earth ever could.

The car-sized block of ice Ensign Gonzales had sent flying had not been sent off with enough velocity to escape the gravity of Jennifer's Tear. Though the force of gravity pulling it was small, the block of ice had so much mass that it would have been wasteful to accelerate it to escape velocity. Chetan had given it enough speed to allow it to avoid falling back down, but not enough to have it escape the asteroid's gravity completely: the definition of an orbit.

This had been planned for. The mission had been scheduled so that blasting the rock free was the very last thing to happen, with the Ensign returning to the ship immediately after. Since that was the plan no one had bothered to ask how long it would take the rock to orbit back. The answer to that question was exactly 54 minutes, 43 seconds.

For all the vastness of space there is also exactness. High school physics classes almost universally begin with the phrase "in a frictionless vacuum". While the orbit of the massive, car-sized chunk of rock and ice had been slightly altered by gravitational fluctuations in the asteroid, it returned to its point of origin give or take two inches.

The massive rock caught Chetan square in the back. It was like being hit by a very slow truck. It knocked the air out of him, and his head slapped against the back of his helmet, blinding him.

A small outcropping on the rock struck Chetan's ankle, bending his leg forward and shattering the bone. More seriously though, the outcropping connected with a soft point in Chetan's suit. It sliced through the polymer underlayer, his skin, and an artery in his leg. Arterial blood, aided by the beat of his heart, and the suction of space's vacuum, poured from the wound.

It took nearly fifteen seconds before Chetan was conscious enough to realize what had happened, and his situation. Suit breaches were serious matters but not nearly as serious as they had been when space suits were foil birthday balloons. The suit had no atmosphere to vent, it could not pop, and while skin exposed to vacuum would die, the extent of the damage would depend on how long the exposure. Even several minutes of hard vacuum would not result in permanent injury to a small amount of skin.

That he was bleeding from an artery was far more serious. His blood could literally be sucked out of his body and that would be fatal in seconds. Gonzales remembered his training and did exactly what he should: he abandoned the mission package, pushed off Jennifer's Tear, used his thrusters liberally to accelerate towards the Galileo, and sent a rapid distress message. Abort, thrust, mayday – ATM – even disasters have checklists.

***

ONBOARD THE GALILEO SEVERAL THINGS HAPPENED AT ONCE. The rock's impact on Ensign Gonzales's suit triggered an automated emergency signal. With over a thousand separate sensors on a space suit, and space being a little more rough and tumble than the suit's manufacturer had expected, false signals were common. All that Captain Peter Grey knew with certainty was that he was already dangerously close to a poorly surveyed chunk of rock. Micro-asteroids could well be in random orbits around it, or thrown up by the force of Gonzale's excavations. So, he had to wait for Chetan's mayday, if he sent one. When it did come through, twenty seconds wasted, Grey acted at once.

"EC 3!" Grey commanded. They had drilled for this, and it showed in his voice. With the simple command every system on the ship powered up. In seconds the Galileo was bathing Jennifer's Tear with four million watts of radar energy and had plenty more left in the tank if needed. The Galileo's sensors were powerful enough to microwave a full-grown cow at twenty miles and avoided that only to spare Gonzales.

Of course the Galileo could be commanded like any other ship through history, with her Captain barking detailed orders. But she was also programmed to automatically respond to several types of emergencies and an injured crewman in space was one of them, the third as a point of fact. It took the Galileo's crew a few precious seconds to process the situation but when the order was given things happened quickly, efficiently, calmly.   Back on Earth, in some planning department, there was a file imagining this exact situation written by the smartest, calmest, minds after being given abundant time for consideration. So far it was all going according to their plan.

The computer took over thruster control for the ship, and networked with Gonzales' suit to take over his thrust control as well. It accelerated Gonzales on a collision course with the forward port airlock, and the forward port airlock on a collision course with Gonzales. Captain Grey and Ensign Gonzales had spent their entire adult lives navigating space, yet neither could plot accelerating intercept courses as quickly and accurately as the computer. Thanks to the computer, what had been a twenty-minute journey to Jennifer's Tear would be a two-and-a-half-minute return trip.

For most people aboard the Galileo if they were given this situation as a hypothetical and asked what the Captain should do next, the answer would be "nothing." Two and a half minutes wasn't enough time to double check the computer's math, and there was little point as the computer was certainly correct in its courses and thrusts. Life for the crew aboard a ship was about trust: trusting your fellow crewmen and women, trusting your equipment, trusting your commanders, trusting your training, and trusting the computer.

Command was about doubt. The days of the captain being more knowledgeable about navigation than his navigator, or knowing more about his ship's engines than his engineer were long gone. When nuclear reactors and computers were installed on ships, the old arbiters of fate, waves, winds, and the gods were replaced by experts.

Grey wasn't a savant who could run equations in his head, he just had a near perfect sense for guess work, and there was something very odd about the intercept the computer had plotted. The computer had Chetan accelerating towards the ship at nearly full thrust, yet the ship was to accelerate towards Gonzales using less than 10% of available thrust.

Even with the best computers, all the automation in the world, this was why human beings could never be removed from command, and why Grey had spent years studying the Galileo's systems and programming.

"Mr. Tsang. What is MSD for Jennifer's tear?"

Tsang tapped on his console, pulling up the answer. MSD was one of a handful of factors the computer might be zeroing out against. When Jennifer's Tear had first been identified one of the routine orders of business had been setting a minimum safe distance that the Galileo could close to within.

There were a host of dangers in approaching an asteroid too closely: small micro-asteroids could be in orbit which could have enough energy to damage sensitive instruments. It was possible for there to be mountains on the asteroid that could be hundreds of meters high. Without a full survey – which hadn't been done – caution was the watchword.

"One point five kilometers, sir!" Tsang reported back.

A nice round number. That was a guess not an assessment - probably.

"Reset MSD to 1 - 0 - 0 meters. We are *not* going to lose Gonzales," Grey ordered.

Tsang's hand hung over his console. Grey could see the wheels turning inside his helmet. Tsang cared about Tsang. One hundred meters was too close. It put the ship at risk, which put Tsang at risk. But if he refused the order, or waited much longer to make a decision, he would be relieved of duty and the MSD would be reset regardless. He tapped the console.

The effect was immediate.   The Galileo's computer recalculated the intercept before Tsang had time to pull his finger back from the keystroke, and the ship's thrusters fired at full power, hurtling the ship towards Jennifer's Tear. She would thrust at full power for half the distance, and then reverse thrust for the final half the distance coming to a stop a hundred meters from the surface.   One point five clicks had been a guess, but it had been a safe guess, and Grey's heart thumped in a silent prayer for everything to be ok. The Galileo crossed an imagined threshold in space and plunged towards the asteroid.

***

IT'S CALLED THE TRIPLE POINT. Any chemistry student who was more interested in chemistry than tests, could lovingly tell you about it.   Water, or in this case blood, can exist in three states: solid, liquid, or gas. At one atmosphere of pressure blood boils at 105 degrees Celsius (water's normal boiling point raised slightly by the dissolved salts, sugars, and other minerals in the mixture).   Blood freezes at negative six degrees Celsius, again thanks to the minerals in the mixture. If pressure drops, as it does in the vacuum of space, the range of that temperature gap narrows until there is a point where blood can exist as a solid, liquid, or a gas in a near vacuum. A degree of temperature, or a micro-Pascal or two of pressure, determines which of the three states wins.

The exact physics is horrendously complex. One might think high blood pressure would raise the pressure at a wound making it more likely for blood to exist as a liquid or solid. But higher blood pressure means the blood moves more quickly when it "hits" the wound.

A hundred years after man's first trip into space NASA realized the importance of the very question Gonzales faced and sent a dozen piglets into space for slaughter. Animal rights activists were incensed, and it was the last time NASA ever carried out live animal testing, but it provided the answers needed.

Chetan had only one job, to stay calm. At the lower end of human heartbeat, blood pressure, and body temperature Chetan's suit could keep the relative temperatures low enough that blood would flash freeze and sublimate away from a wound – the next best thing to clotting. He would lose blood quickly but might be able to last ten or twenty minutes before he no longer had sufficient blood volume for his heart to beat. An elevated heartbeat, heightened blood pressure, raised body temperature from exertion, his suit's ability to cool would be overwhelmed and Chetan's blood would not freeze but be sucked out as a liquid aided by the vacuum of space – a process that would take seconds.

Despite Chetan's heritage, meditation was a skill he had never attempted, let alone mastered, and he focused on taking long, deep breaths trying to remain calm. His head-up display provided him a wealth of information about his situation, all of it bad. He tried to tune it out and breathed deeply willing his heart to slow just as he had been trained.

The Galileo's computer had been given a number of variables: the fuel/breathable air available in Ensign Gonzalez's suit, his speed and position relative to the Galileo, and his medical condition. As his situation deteriorated the computer dynamically changed the plan, rebalancing for the new reality. One minute out, and the computer determined that the best course of action was to use all of Chetan's fuel and oxygen to get him back to the ship as quickly as possible. The bulkhead on the back of the airlock would do the work of stopping him.

Essentially the computer decided that saving five seconds was worth a truck hitting Ensign Gonzalez at 20 miles an hour, after a minute of suffocating him. There was no human in the loop for the decision. By the time a human could be given the relevant information, process it, make a decision, and enter the orders, the opportunity to influence events would have passed.

Chetan was in mid-breath when the computer, with the twist of a valve, cut off his air supply, saving it for propulsion. Without being able to hyperventilate Chetan's heart rate began to tick up, and blood, oozing from his wounded ankle, began to stream out.

His head-up display bombarded him with automatically generated instructions:

Warning: Planned High Speed Impact Approaching – Relax and DO NOT BRACE

Warning: Suit Breach Detected – Relax to Control Blood Loss

Warning: Air Supply Terminated – Relax to Control Oxygen Use

Warning: Planned Hypoxia and Rapid Pressurization - Risk of Embolism

Forty seconds from impact Chetan made a choice. Hundreds of millions of years of evolution told Chetan to fight for his life, to press ahead no matter how hopeless things looked, not to give up, ever. Chetan's rational mind told him to step back, accept he might die, and leave his fate in the hands of a computer and his crew. Relax, and accept death, to avoid it.

Evolution won. It wasn't a conscious decision, but whether the choice came from his mind, or his body, a choice was made. As adrenaline flooded his system, his heartbeat ramped up and literally pumped his life away.

Ensign Chetan Gonzales died, fighting for his life, twenty seconds before his body slammed into the back of the Galileo's airlock.

CHAPTER 2

THE GALILEO'S BRIDGE WAS SMALL by science fiction standards; though compared to the bridge of a destroyer, or aircraft carrier, it was spacious. There were stations for five crewmen: the captain, a helmsman, a sensor officer, and finally two empty stations that could display and control any of a thousand ship systems should a specialized need arise.

Captain Grey was sweating. Under his suit cold perspiration collected as a thin sheen on his forehead, chest, and arms. It was squeezed down over his skin by the suit, its direction chosen by the Galileo's artificial gravity. There was simply nowhere for the water to go but down, progressively soaking him and pooling in his boots and gloves. For all the material's wondrous properties the comfort of its occupant left a great deal to be desired.

"Biometrics on Gonzales just flatlined, sir!"

"If there's a surface anomaly on the other side of Jennifer's Tear how much warning will we get before we hit it?" Captain Grey asked his helmsman, thankful his voice stayed flat. Grey had rolled the dice blind and it was time to find out whether he had won or lost.

A hard pause of three seconds followed the Captain's question. With a fifteen second countdown on the screen three seconds spent waiting was a luxury they simply did not have. Grey knew it and Tsang knew it. "I don't know how to check that, sir."

"Rotation speed of the asteroid Corporal. Figure it out."

A warning flashed onto the display: 'Thruster Fuel Consumption Critical – 2%'

Ensign Gonzales hit the back of the airlock before Corporal Tsang had pulled up the data he needed. Medical teams were waiting and, while the official word would take a half an hour to come, Captain Grey put his concern for the Ensign aside. Chetan was aboard, Grey had done everything he could, and now he had a ship to think about.

Though the Galileo's maneuvering thrusters fired at full force in opposition to the ship's motion, she still skidded towards Jennifer's Tear. According to the computer, she would come to a stop one hundred meters away from the surface of the asteroid, assuming there were no mountains or debris in the way to shorten the journey.

The warning flashed again on the display: 'Truster Fuel Consumption Critical – 3%'

"Sir, permission to power main engines?" Tsang asked, voice fast.

The Galileo's main engines were meant to produce significant thrust and propel the ship. They ran on electricity, and so long as the nuclear reaction that powered the ship ran, the main engines would run. The maneuvering thrusters on the other hand ran on a chemical reaction and were meant for quarter second bursts to reorient the ship. Firing continuously at full power guzzled a limited supply of fuel.

Grey searched his memory for any information about the computer's emergency algorithm; had it considered using the main engines to arrest their fall towards Jennifer's tear? It must have. A moment of mental relief at the realization freed up enough neurons that he realized his mistake. The computer wasn't worried about micro-asteroids; it wasn't worried about surface anomalies above a hundred meters; it wasn't worried about saving thruster fuel. He had told the computer up to a hundred meters was safe and it accepted that without question or apprehension. He had activated emergency protocols and, in an emergency, efficiency was ignored.

"Ready main engines," Grey ordered.

This was a task Tsang did know how to do and had practiced a thousand times. "Main capacitor 1% charge; Reactor at 5%; Engineering board is yellow for full power; thrust stabilizers out of alignment; reorienting, sir."

"Bridge to Engineering," Grey hailed over the com, "prepare for 50% on the reactor."

Deep inside the Galileo a magnetic valve expanded allowing antimatter to flow from its storage tank at half its safe maximum rate.

The air inside the Captain's helmet mixed with his sweat, fear, and stress to form an almost acidic fog, yet he kept it on. "Sound decompression warning, all compartments." Klaxon warnings blared through every compartment on the Galileo, except the bridge. The whole crew, or at least those not already suited, would be running to don their helmets, and then armor, in that order, in case the Galileo hit a micro-asteroid that pierced its hull.

The official standard was fifteen seconds. In theory Grey owed his crew fifteen seconds warning before a decompression, and in theory his crew owed him the ability to be vacuum ready in fifteen seconds. In reality at any given moment a third of the crew were sleeping, and from waking groggily to pulling on suit, helmet, boots, and gloves forty-five seconds would have been tight. The consensus among the Galileo's seventy-four crewmen was that it would be preferable to die in vacuum than sleep in their uniforms. As much as he would like to order otherwise, even Grey didn't sleep in his uniform and wouldn't be a hypocrite on that point.

Another third of the crew would be performing duties that practically required them to have left their helmet and gloves somewhere other than where they worked. This fact had come as a rude surprise in the first three months of their journey.

The majority of the crew had heads large enough, or hands small enough, that both armored gloves could fit inside their helmets and the bundle could be carried one handed. The rest of the crew needed both hands to carry helmet and gloves; and so they didn't. In either case most tasks required both hands free, so very few could spare a hand to carry their suit, even fewer actually cared to do so. Instead, almost all of the crew left their helmet and gloves at their duty stations.

If there was a decompression within two minutes of the warning, people would die.

Even though her skin was titanium, and nearly a centimeter thick, the Galileo was vulnerable to debris. It was simply a question of speeds. A wad of wet paper could punch through a centimeter of titanium if it was going fast enough, and in space there was no reason why a wad of paper, or realistically a rock, couldn't travel fast enough.

That was one of a dozen reasons shields were a prerequisite to any kind of serious space travel. They were down at the moment and wouldn't have done any good had they been up.

The Galileo's shields worked in only one direction, directly forward, and did so by generating powerful gravitational fields so strong that even light would be bent out of the way. Even if they had been pointed towards Jennifer's Tear the only effect of turning on the shields would have been to pull the asteroid towards them and speed up their fate.

As the Galileo skidded towards Jennifer's Tear, Tsang read out engine data "Capacitors at 75%; engineering board is green; thrust stabilizers are aligned."

The Galileo's exterior lights caught on the surface of Jennifer's Tear at two hundred meters distance. Compared to the asteroid the ship was small, and the surface of the rock looked like a solid wall.

The ship slowed and finally came to a stop exactly a hundred meters away from the rock. Captain Grey had won his roll. Not even professional gamblers got to wager seventy-four human lives.

"Capacitors at 100% Captain. Main engines at your command."

A hard three seconds of self-recrimination later and Grey answered. "Move us back out to two kilometers Corporal." The air inside his helmet was suffocating and a pressure was quickly building up in his chest now that the danger had passed.

***

THE FORWARD PORT AIRLOCK wasn't far from the bridge. By the time Grey arrived, two medics were assisting the DOCTOR as it worked on Gonzales. The DOCTOR was a case, the size of a small footlocker, that magnetically attached to the metal deck. A dozen mechanical spider-arms extended from the box stripping pieces of armor off Chetan, injecting him, cutting into him to repair internal injuries. They all worked rapidly, all independently, and all completely autonomously following their programming. Sensor data being collected from scanners inside the DOCTOR's case guided their motion, and bathed the Ensign in blue laser light. Chetan was ashen and didn't respond even as the DOCTOR stabbed a laparoscopic probe into him and, with a sickening crack and shift of Chetan's chest, set a snapped collar bone.

DOCTOR stood for Direct Operation Care and Treatment autOnomous Robot. With its mechanical arms extended it looked like a giant spider, overturned, but struggling to attack its patient. The comparison was uncanny, and Grey had to fight the urge to recoil as two robotic arms rose up high into the air, exactly as a spider preparing to strike, and then stabbed into the center of Chetan's chest. The two arms delivered an electric shock trying to restart the Ensign's heart. His body trembled once, a second time, a third time. Grey lost count after a dozen and eventually the DOCTOR seemed to lose enthusiasm, its arms relaxing and then slowly retracting and returning to their case.

One of the medics, still wearing his full armor, looked up towards Captain Peter Grey and shook his head.

Grey looked from the medic to Chetan and then back. His muscles tensed ready to fight, and his stomach churned ready to vomit. "Turn that fucking robot back on! You keep trying until Chetan is alive or that thing runs out of batteries!" The medic nodded and turned the DOCTOR back on. Scanning beams began criss-crossing Gonzales' lifeless body. The second medic stood up and removed her helmet. Her brown hair looked dark with moisture and she walked over to her Captain and placed a hand on his arm "Peter…" He pulled his arm away and pushed his chest forward crowding Sergeant Daniel's space. His fists clenched into titanium hammers and his arms tensed inside his suit. She took a half step back, looked down, and turned to obey her orders.

For all the technical wonder of the DOCTOR some things, life and death information, can only be accepted if it comes from a person. Daniels and Grey had talked about the issue at length over the past years. Truly, her job was simply to transport the DOCTOR and then be the human who broke the bad news. But in this moment Grey wouldn't have accepted bad news had it come from God himself; and like all men confronted with the unacceptable, there was a part of the brain that knew he could beat the world into submission.

The DOCTOR didn't run out of batteries. Instead, a programming block came up that had been inserted by an ethics board on Earth. The irony was that the medical community, who would practice on cadavers, believed that death and life were binary states without soul or transcendental spirit, also felt that at some point "care" meant stopping and allowing a body to lay in peace. Grey had always suspected this has more to do with doctors' egos than knowledge or philosophy: if they couldn't decide between life and death for a patient, they could at least pretend to have some special knowledge as to the morality of death and human dignity.

**

THE CAPTAIN'S PRIVATE QUARTERS were the size of a small meat locker and had a similar aesthetic. As soon as the metal hatch locked closed, Captain Peter Grey ripped his helmet off and smashed it into the wall, scratching helmet and wall, and sending reverberations through the cabin. "Fuck!"   He slammed the helmet into the wall again imagining he was beating the DOCTOR, tiny mechanical bits flying from it in all directions. His helmet came off worse than the wall. By the time he had run out of energy and stepped back, breathing hard, raw titanium glistened from deep gouges in the helmet.

With his helmet off, Grey's youth was apparent. The Captain of the Galileo was just thirty-two years old, three of which had been spent in deep space. His cropped black hair was matted down to his head and his skin was pale, clammy. His gloved hands were clumsy and disengaging the gloves from his armor was a five second task that took thirty.

Grey crumpled down onto the small cot that was his bed, his body trembled as he tried to pull off his boots. A quarter cup of perspiration spilled out of each as he dropped them to the deck. The sweat spread slowly over the patterned metal of the deck. It was an artificial act, in an artificial world. On earth soil, wood, wool, even desert sand, would have absorbed the moisture. On the Galileo it was only the air, parched of moisture for just this reason, that would act to restore balance. In an hour, salt stains would be all that survived the spill, that and the acrid smell of sweat that filled the cabin.

The rest of his uniform stripped off quickly and Grey tried to catch his breath. It didn't work. He rubbed his heart and stumbled to his cabin's head, the bathroom. The automated shower activated as soon as he stepped inside it, and with the wave of a hand the water turned ice cold. The water cut through the stink and grime that clung to his skin. He crossed muscled arms over his chest and stood in the cold for ten minutes, the shower's timer keeping an exact count.

The shower walls were completely bare, with one exception. There was no soap dispenser, shampoo, or any of the thousands of possible lotions and potions that might be found in a shower stall on Earth. The Galileo's water reclamation system couldn't handle the chemicals traditionally associated with showers. Had the Captain wanted to wash, a cleansing scrub deposited in a special processing system was the answer. The one flourish on the blank shower walls was a timer showing how much budgeted water a crewman had.

Grey's read negative eighty-three minutes. His was the only one on the ship that would allow a negative balance. A thermal camera, hidden behind the shower wall, identified each crewman and automatically tracked their water use. The time to feel self-conscious about cameras seeing everything had passed a generation before. If god was all seeing, what did that say about the computers that also saw all?

The backs of Captain Grey's hands were deeply scarred. The scar tissue was old, ragged, overlapping. While his flesh stretched and reddened from the cold water, the scar tissue interrupted the process and blown blood vessels gave the back of his hands a blotched appearance. When he leaned forward, bracing his hands on the wall, the extra extension caused scarred skin to stretch and tiny fissures opened and wept yellow blood plasma.

Uncommanded, the shower shut off. The Captain swore it back on, and fire hot water drenched him as the shower reactivated. To Grey, his skin chilled, it was too much. He lashed out at the shower wall with a closed fist punch that took a chunk of scarred skin off two of his knuckles before he thought to say 'off'.

***

WITH THE ANNOUNCEMENT OF CHETAN'S DEATH, Captain Grey's two senior officers were summoned to his quarters.

Major Benjamin Williams reported promptly, having expected the meeting. Major Katherine Bakker, Grey's chief engineer, had not, and ran late.

When Williams arrived he was greeted by his Captain in a fresh uniform, but haggard face. Grey was a child compared to his fifty-six-year-old second in command and executive officer. A tall, thin man, Williams was a career naval officer. A lifetime in the military had seeped into every atom of his being. His posture, his hair, his leathered skin, and sharp, unblinking eyes, all resonated with a lifetime of hard duty.

After a combat tour soldiers will often describe civilian life as having its volume turned down; as though they had gone from university back to kindergarten. For Williams the volume had been on full blast for three decades. He was a ball of knots, tightened pull by pull, over a lifetime, and then wrapped in stone.

Without a word, Williams took a seat at Grey's table, sat straight, face hard and fixed. Grey could see that he had been through this particular experience many times before.

The two waited three minutes before the high frequency tone of Major Bakker's voice cut through the bulkhead and announced her imminent arrival.

"No. No. No," she said with a metronome's regularity and the increasing pitch of an explosive countdown. "That's number sixteen on our to-do list today and we are going to be lucky to get the first five done. I don't want you wasting your time on it." She opened the Captain's hatch and walked in. She held her helmet in one hand, raised up to her mouth to talk over its radio.

Grey was just older than his chief engineer Major Katherine Bakker. Katherine was physically slight. Her body had none of the hardness that seemed to make every inch of Williams a knot of muscle, tendon, or bone. Instead, she was delicate, her features bone china, her skin porcelain from years without sunlight. She moved to the Captain's table and wound up her conversation with a "just get it done".

"You really screwed me powering up the engines, Captain." She said before she stopped, surprised at the silence in the room.

"Sit," was his reply.

Captain Grey looked from one officer to the other, and began by setting a freshly bandaged right hand, on the table. "Ensign Gonzales… Ensign. Was twenty-three-years-old. He didn't go to some topflight university or read physics textbooks for the fun of it," Grey gave his chief engineer a knowing look. "He trusted us, and we killed him," the Captain pressed his left hand, scarred but unbroken, down on the small table and gave a cold stare to Major Benjamin Williams and Major Katherine Bakker in turn. The table barely seated the three of them. It was closer to a high school desk than a kitchen table.

Major Williams' well-earned wrinkles covered his face and grey hairs his crown, sat silently, statue-like, as was his nature. Even tragedy could become routine. Grey wondered for a moment what it would take to pry Williams' true feelings on Gonzales' death from him. Retirement, a bottle of scotch, and another Major, seemed to be the only answer. More likely than not his feeling amounted to 'shit happens'.

"We all knew that people were going to die on this mission. The Galileo's a new ship, her engine is the first of its kind, we are the first crew to ever leave Earth's solar system, and we could have grandchildren faster than help could get to us," Grey pressed on.

"Three years ago I asked you both a question when we first met: when someone dies under your command will it be so you could learn a lesson that care, and forethought, could have taught you."

The Galileo was never really silent. Her life support, propulsion, power, and water systems were all constantly running, and the ship had a distinct low frequency hum as a result, however at that moment Captain Peter Grey's personal quarters were as quiet as it ever got aboard.

Major Bakker sat with her arms crossed over her chest and her jaw clenched under paper thin skin. The most serious chewing out the twenty-eight-year-old blonde experienced prior had probably been over an unmade bed.

The nose doesn't so much detect smells, as it detects changes in smell. For civilians going about their daily life every room, office, house, and city has a different scent, each duly observed, and remembered, by the nose-brain sensory tag team. The Galileo was a closed system. Air circulated through the entire ship, filter systems scrubbed and recirculated it infinitely. So, aside from the crew, there was little change for the nose to notice. Grey noticed Katherine's smell.

Grey knew it was a mistake even as he did it, but he wanted a fight, if he couldn't fight death, he could fight his engineer. "Major Bakker, you have something to say for yourself? Speak freely."

The Captain's voice easily filled the tightly packed room with one of the most ironic phrases in naval parlance. There was no speaking freely on a ship. A Captain couldn't un-hear words. Like a platter of ribs at a cocktail reception; it was an invitation to demonstrate imprudence.

"Yes sir, I do. The mission plan I approved was safe – as safe as anything can be in this death trap. If Gonzales had followed procedure instead of racing ahead to play hooky this never would have happened. Yes, in future we need to anticipate when crewmen might deviate from our mission plans, but I don't appreciate the implication that this is somehow my fault. Sir."

"I am sorry if you misunderstood Major. I wasn't implying this was your fault I was saying it outright. Chetan's death is your fault, and Major Williams, and mine. On this ship if you could have saved someone but were too stupid to have realized it then you killed them."

Katherine's face didn't redden with emotion, her jaw didn't clench in anger, she didn't huff nor puff. Though never married, she gave her Captain a look that ex-wives reserve for ex-husbands.

It was almost physically pleasing to finally let the self-loathing that burned through him out and direct it at someone else. "Major this is not a union operation. We do not have a specific list of tasks to be done and, once every box has been checked to some reasonable standard, if something goes bad the blame falls on someone else. For us the job is the result. We failed," Grey's hands tightened on the table into fists, his skin cracked, and a drop of fluid darkened his fresh bandage.

Major Bakker tilted her head, a long strand of blonde hair falling out of place as she did so. "Do you have any idea the hours I work, the time I put in to make sure we will get through this alive? It's a miracle this is our first casualty. This ship has too many interdependent systems, too many things being done for the first time, too many lines of code, all of which were built by contractors more skilled in navigating appropriations contracts then delivering product. Chetan will absolutely not be the last death, and there is absolutely nothing we can do to guarantee otherwise. Despite my best efforts. Sir."

"I don't want to talk about your best efforts, Major. I want to talk about results."

"You know what I want to talk about? Sir. I want to talk about why the Galileo was 100 meters away from Jennifer's Tear. I want to talk about why this whole ship was put in danger to shave a few seconds off recovering Ensign Gonzales. I want to talk about why we burned 4% of our thruster fuel," Katherine's voice could have cracked ice.

You could never tell with Williams. Sometimes, behind his grey eyes, he was plotting murder, other times he could have been meditating for all he moved. "I can't believe they gave you a commission," Williams ground the words out at Katherine.

It took the engineer a moment to realize Williams was referring to her rank, and she shot him a venomous "What?"

"I'm sure you had a lifetime of talking back and because you're smart, and beautiful, no one ever put you in your place. But your duty is to this ship and your loyalty is to your Captain and if you don't understand that you shouldn't be here, never-mind a senior officer."

"Stand fast Williams! I don't need my honor defended," Grey snapped.

"Bakker, I took a calculated risk. It might have meant the difference between saving Gonzales or not."

"You took a stupid risk that could easily have gotten us all killed... Sir." Katherine squared her shoulders off against Grey's as she said it.

"That is your opinion Major and when it comes to this ship there's only one opinion that matters."

Captain Grey took a ragged breath and carried on "Now, what do we tell the crew?"

Williams answered quickly, almost shouldering his way between Katherine and Grey verbally. "They are going to be angry, hurt, and scared. All those old feelings of fear from the first year of the mission will be back. If we don't focus that on something it is going to turn on us. So, we blame Gonzales. Last thing he would have wanted was for this to sow doubt in the crew."

Williams carried on, "Captain... As I told you, there's more to duty than the numbers. You were right that anyone could "win" a competition for EVA rights, and it would give the crew something to bring their performance numbers up for, but the result was that the person who wanted off the ship most had his own plans."

He was right. He had been right. Grey had been too focused on numbers to appreciate it at the time, but he could admit his guilt in this at least. "Agreed. Let's change that policy. Bakker I'll leave it to you to put together some recommendations for how we can incentivize top level performance without this happening again."

Katherine brushed a lock of blonde hair behind her right ear deliberately, too casually. "So, after all this talk of honor and personal responsibility we are going to blame Chetan. Ok. And I'm supposed to clean up the mess on performance reviews? What was it Churchill said about naval tradition: nothing but buggery, drunkenness, and hypocrisy?"

"You're both dismissed!" The two senior officers rose and left in silence.

Katherine's scent lingered in the small room and Grey tried, unsuccessfully, to ignore it.

***

THE CORRIDOR WAS EVEN MORE CRAMPED than the Captain's cabin. It was wide enough that Williams and Grey might have stood shoulder to shoulder, or perhaps three times Katherine's width. The walls had been designed to be smooth and conceal the wires, ducts, and conduits that wove through the ship, like vines through a jungle. It had quickly become apparent this design also conducted noise as though the ship were a giant trombone. Over the years panels had been strategically removed, where nothing behind them was especially dangerous, to dampen the noise. The sound of footsteps was no longer at concert hall levels, but it gave the ship the feeling that it was still under construction. Almost like an antique luxury watch, smooth and clean in most places, with windows into the mechanical madness beneath the skin.

"This whole thing is disgusting," Katherine spat the words at the wall.

Williams considered the young chief engineer, "Katherine... No denying you're smart, but you think like a little girl. Two things hold a ship together: professionalism and honor. The crew needs to see that at the top, and lord knows the Captain has enough on his plate just keeping this ship running."

Katherine flushed and took a slow breath before responding, "explain to me how this is about either of those things. The crew knows it's dangerous out here, they know that small mistakes and deviating from procedure can be dangerous, and they know their officers are just humans and make mistakes. Tell them the truth! And for that matter how does blatant sexism fit into honor?"

Williams exhaled and lowered his voice. "It's just an expression..." the word "relax" formed on his lips but, knowing exactly one thing about women, he stopped it before it left his mouth and switched tack. "I have a small bottle of something I've been saving. Let's have a drink, I'll tell you some old Navy stories. You're a great engineer, but you have some work to do to be a good officer." He tilted his head a quarter of a degree and inhaled as though he were about to do something that took every ounce of self-discipline he had, "it isn't your fault that you don't know what you're doing." He exhaled and carried on. "You've had your bars for three years. Most officers spend as long in OTC without giving a real order. That's why they stuck me on this ship – to give you and the Captain the benefit of decades of service. So, I called you a little girl, I would call any man a little boy, if the situation called for it."

Katherine seemed to rise beyond her full height and looked up into Major Williams' old eyes, the frustration of the day reaching a crescendo, "if you're right then a little girl shouldn't be drinking!" without pausing for a breath she turned and stormed off down the hall.

Major Williams glanced quickly down both ends of the hall, and found it blessedly empty, "God help me with the women…"

CHAPTER 3

GREY HAD BIGGER PROBLEMS than women. In the days and weeks after leaving Earth the crew had almost universally worn their armor when inside the ship, their helmets always within arm's reach. Fear of sudden depressurization weighed heavily against chafing, clammy, suits.

Confidence and training, or perhaps laziness and complacency, had slowly whittled that habit away. After their first year in space wearing the armor had become a sign of insecurity: though helmets and gloves were still a common sight. After two years it was a sign of paranoia. Fashion however is cyclical, and after Chetan's death titanium was the new black.

The walk from the Captain's cabin to the bridge was too short. It was over almost before it had begun. Grey paused only a heartbeat at the bridge's hatch before he turned and walked away, headed for the mess.

Crewmen moved to the sides of the corridors as Grey approached. There were no salutes, another naval tradition indoors, but making a hole for their Captain to pass unobstructed was meant much the same way.

Being Captain of a ship shared much in common with being a plague victim. Everyone on board physically avoided touching you, they were all nervous to speak with you, and the closer you got the more anxious they became. It had been three years since Grey last spoke with someone who wasn't his subordinate. Without shore-leave, vacations, or time off, the Captain was always the Captain.

During an eight-month tour on Earth, a Captain might join the crew in the mess a handful of times. It was not strictly a faux pas, but it was something done sparingly, and mostly to show the crew that their Captain was keeping tabs on the quality of the chow.

For Grey, taking a meal in the mess was an indulgence that felt more like an addiction. The majority, the vast majority, of his meals were taken in his cabin, like a good Captain should. Bakker's and William's duty schedules prevented them from joining him, assuming Bakker was on speaking terms with him. Which meant he ate alone.

Had his steward delivered two meals without an obvious companion, rumors would have run wild. Of course the alternative, a meal for two, with Daniels in open attendance, would have been even worse. But a man can only be alone so much.

The Galileo's mess hall was the size of a coffee shop. A dozen tables were scattered about as if deliberately trying to defy military orderliness. Three large food dispensers dominated a corner of the room, and a dozen crewmen stood in line to draw food. As Grey entered, the volume of conversation dropped by a third but began to recover when he joined the line for the dispensers.

He didn't cut in line. He could have, but that would have defeated the point.

It only took a minute for the volume in the room to tick back up, and two of the crewmen in line ahead of him returned to their conversation. Both were Corporals, double silver chevrons adorned each of their armored shoulders. It had been over a year since Grey had seen anyone in the mess wearing titanium. Each man held their helmet and gloves in their left hand, and each held a mess swipe card in their right.

The Corporal nearest Grey, Corporal Rowatt, was pudgy for a Galileo crewman, which was to say, pudgy for someone who had been eating precisely rationed food that was not particularly appetizing for the past three years. His red hair was cut close, but it was just long enough to hint at tight, wild, curls. The further crewman, Corporal Franklin Macko was thin, Grey made a mental note to have a medic check his weight. Macko looked as though he had shed ten pounds in the last year. With seventy-three crewmen, after three years, Grey knew them all in the biographical sense of the word.

"I'm telling you this is stupid. You should just, politely, say it isn't working and move on," Rowatt yawned out the words with all the force of advice that had been given a hundred times before.

"Yeah, yeah, but I'm not going to. I love her, she loves me, and we're going to make this work. So… what do you think she meant?"   Macko shifted his grip on his mess card and a communications slip, folded over itself, came into view. Macko unfolded the leaf of paper delicately, using a single free finger from his left hand, the other four clutching the safety of his helmet. "I mean why is she talking about this friend of hers so much?"

"She's getting you ready for the big news… that she can't do the long-distance thing, the one 800-character-a-year letter thing, the not knowing when you're getting home thing. And she met someone new. You'll see. One year from now you're going to get that letter."

Macko gently refolded the piece of paper and said nothing, face tight.

Rowatt, sensing an opportunity, pressed forward, "you know... Corporal Montgomery just ended things with Jack. You two could hit the gym together."

Macko's face bunched for just a fraction of a second, "Montgomery could bench press me. Not my type."

"Well unless your type is men you might have to expand your horizons a wee bit. The count stands at 11 right now and Major Bakker probably isn't interested. I am pretty sure Serana and Mally are getting together. So that's eight single females left aboard the ship."

As Grey eavesdropped, the deck under his right foot surged up two inches and he had to press down hard to keep his balance, almost stumbling to his left in response. His head snapped down hoping to finally catch the effect. Katherine outright denied there were any fluctuations in the ship's artificial gravity. He was sure the sensation wasn't just in his mind. He'd never felt anything like it on Earth.

Macko reached the food dispenser, made his selection, and swiped his card. He had punched the key for corn, a popular choice as the flavor was pretty close to the real thing. The machine made a noise between a fart and a splurt and, one handed, Macko retrieved his tray. A pancake sized globule of yellow paste sat in the tray's center, slowly spreading under its own weight. He stepped aside and allowed Rowatt to make his choice.

"What about Daniels? She's cute," Macko asked, and Grey stiffened.

Rowatt scoffed, pushed the button for green beans. The machine dispensed a serving of green paste with an auditory flourish. "This is why you shouldn't play cards; you love the long odds too much. And I'll tell you something else Franklin, you drain the swamp with Montgomery, get that evil out of your system, and you won't be into Tsang for four months of produce."

Macko reddened at that, and his features hardened despite the blush, "screw you. It's just a bit of fun to pass the time. It has nothing to do with the swamp being backed up. Which I'm not... It isn't."

"Pass your time with Montgomery, not cards. We can talk about the swamp after it gets drained," Rowatt said, and the two men headed to a table.

The mental note to have Macko checked on by a medic was amended: a medic other than Daniels.

There were four "lunch" items on offer, always on offer: corn, Crème Brule, pork, and green beans. Grey hit the button for pork, swiped his mess card, and the machine whirred for a second and then splurted a serving of "pork" onto a tray. A slightly lopsided globule of pink sludge slowly spread out towards the tray's raised edges. The machine's display flashed a digital 2 at him, and he rolled his eyes in reply. He had been over-indulging in the 'pork'. Only two servings were left on his budget for the next ten days.

What would he have said to Macko if he could have? He'd never had the choice about keeping a relationship during the Galileo's journey.

***

GREY'S APARTMENT, HIS FORMER APARTMENT, had been an hour outside Boston. You join the navy for the adventure, not the pay, and it showed in Grey's "bachelor pad." That's what Sarah, his girlfriend of ten months, kept calling it.

His couch was second hand. It was dark purple, "velvet" the ad claimed, and had faded yellow patches in the center of each cushion where body touched fabric.

Why sell a cheap couch that will last, when you can sell an even cheaper one that won't? It was a philosophy shared by both the manufacturer, and purchaser, of most of his furniture. The only redeeming feature of his decorating philosophy was the scarcity of its application. With six hundred square feet to his name, which included his proportionate share of the hallways, reception, laundry room, there wasn't much space left for bad furniture. After a desk, couch, bed, and dining table, the space was filled.

The apartment had two virtues. It had fit his budget, and it was rented by the week. Sarah had known exactly one of those things.

Their relationship had ended with him in the shower. In retrospect the apartment had three virtues.

"How …. Cat…… Lout," Sarah's voice barely cut through the torrent of cold water that cascaded over Grey. A handful of valve, old fashioned and color coded, and the flow slowed enough to hear over.

"What?" Grey called back out.

"How did that job interview turn out?" Sarah shouted through the bathroom door. Light footsteps shuffling through the apartment. She was a good woman. He was sure she was making someone a good wife by now. Go through a list of good qualities in a person and Sarah had them all. She was bright, she worked as a dental hygienist. She was pretty, honest, loyal, and she had a plan in life: husband, then condo, then baby, then a second baby, then a third... then death. She always referred to that last step as "growing old together".

"Yeah... No idea. You know I can never tell with stuff like that."

"You should apply outside of the military. My boss knows a guy with a construction company that needs a foreman." She was a good woman. After the Gazer she knew his career was over and she pushed, just enough to show she cared, for him to get back on track.

He never actually lied to her: as though that mattered. He still didn't know why he'd done things that way. On one hand, there must have been thousands of candidates. No need to start a fight over such a remote chance. On the other hand, after the Gazer he didn't trust his own feelings. Sarah was perfect in that there was nothing wrong with her. Given time, that might have been the basis for a real life.

Twisting the valve back to full force, feeling metal grind against metal under his hand, the shower responded as only mechanical valves can. The water was ocean cold and numbed his skin, washing away every hint of tingle.

Sarah was strong for such a petite woman. That, or the bathroom door was as well made as his couch, and with one good shove she shouldered the latch right out of the door. Flecks of particle board slowly settled to the floor in her wake. "What the fuck is this!" A data pad slapped against the shower's glass wall; the glow of the screen cut through the mist that obscured the rest of the room. Grey couldn't see the delicate hand that propelled it, but the screen was legible 'Final 5 Galileo Captain Candidates Announced."

***

THERE ARE CERTAIN MOMENTS WHEN GROUPS HAVE A HIVE MIND. Something instinctively social kicks in. Over the dozen tables in the mess hall there were seven empty seats. Three scattered randomly about the room, and four at a single table left empty for the Captain. Grey had never been the kid to eat alone in high school and while the crew meant well, ostracism out of respect was still ostracism.

The centerpiece of the tables were cutlery stands holding spoons. The spoons were not the circular devices common on Earth. Rather they were elongated and almost flat on their edges. They had been designed specifically to scrape and scoop the Galileo's edible slurry off its mess trays. Setting his helmet on the table beside his tray, Grey took a spoon and started eating.

From a flavour perspective the difference between the meal choices came down to the basic flavour groups. Corn was sweet, Crème Brule even sweeter, pork was salty, and the green beans were bland. A chemical flavoring agent added a whiff of the original food to the mix, but, as a person can taste the difference between sugar and artificial sweetener, it was clear "pork" was not pork.

At the table across from him Grey watched as a Sergeant and Ensign huddled over a ripper and swiped their mess cards. Capitalism, for all its advantages, and all its evils, was alive and well on the Galileo.

Back on Earth ID cards had been standardized decades before. The card itself was simply a serial number that referenced an entry in a central database. If you swiped the card, the reader took a biometric scan of you and sent it, together with the ID number to the government database. The government's computers did a security check comparing the biometric information of the person who scanned the card with the biometric information in the database, and then returned the requested information to the scanner if the biometrics matched. On a police reader they got a picture, address, outstanding criminal matters, arrest history, and so on. Swipe the card at your doctor's office and they get your medical records. Nothing was stored on the card. Taking someone else's card was meaningless because the biometric check would fail when you swiped.

The mess cards on the Galileo were different, intentionally. The card itself securely stored information about the number of credits on it. A ripper could transfer credits from one card to another, after a biometric test was passed. As a result the Galileo's crew had a form of currency.

Of course, credits for the automated slurry were of limited value. The real money was in the form of each crewman's weekly credit for a hydroponically grown fruit or vegetable. Those were a hot commodity.

Grey finished his meal, bussed his tray back to the machine, and left the mess hall. He felt better, as though he had opened a valve and let off just enough pressure to take the edge off.

***

THERE WAS ONLY ONE WAY on, or off, the Galileo's bridge: a double titanium door. Each segment was a meter wide and weighed a thousand pounds. The seam between the two doors was rippled with fist sized interlocking teeth all the way down to the deck.

One of the crew had painted a mural that covered almost the entirety of the doors. It showed a sagging, wooden, bridge as though one could step into the door, and onto it. Whoever the artist was, they'd used the teeth of the door as breaks in the painted bridge's planks so that, for the instant the door opened, it looked as though the bridge was being split apart.

The drawing had appeared overnight a year into their journey, and since then almost a dozen other paintings, some large and others small, had appeared throughout the ship. At the time Grey had considered doing something about it, but the paintings were well done, ironic in their own way, and provided the crew with a mystery to discuss. Most importantly though, he liked them and couldn't bring himself to order them scrubbed off.

He pressed his gauntleted palm onto the security panel controlling the doors. The console flashed yellow twice, "Jesus Christ," Grey muttered and pressed his hand again into the console, this time his fingers spread slightly wider. The console flashed yellow again. He pulled his hand back and slammed his palm onto the console's surface. The console shrugged off the hit, and this time flashed green to the Captain's throbbing hand. A dozen soft mechanical clicks followed, and the doors parted, sliding on precision milled guides.

The bridge had been designed to be an oasis of calm and protection. A solid meter of titanium completely enveloped the room. If solid metal were not enough, gravity dampeners reduced the feeling of impacts and acceleration within the bridge. The Galileo could be rocked with explosive decompressions, internal detonations, and small arms fire, and the only indication on the bridge would be through the instruments.

There would be no falling ceiling tiles or beams, no overloading display panels, no crewmen being knocked out of their seats. The bridge crew would be able to issue clear headed orders until well after there were no crewmen left alive to carry them out.

In spite of that design objective, the bridge was no oasis. It seemed to radiate its own weight on those who manned it. Captain Grey preferred to command from the ship's different departments. A trip to stellar cartography told him more about navigation and the state of that department than a helmsman could from a bridge panel. Likewise, meeting with Major Bakker in engineering provided a far more useful update about the ship's mechanical status than could be garnered from a readout, or briefing, on the bridge. Thus the bridge was only employed for its intended use on special occasions such as the launch of the ship or transitioning in or out of FTL. Mostly the bridge was used for training simulations.

Today Ensign Mindy Arnold sat in Grey's command chair and attempted to decipher orbital data from the bridge's main display. He could have interrupted, but that would have been cruel. Ensign Arnold was three hours into her test and had spent the last year preparing for it. Having already failed once, two months before, she had a lot to lose.

Every simulation on board was graded, recorded, and had real consequences to a crew member's duty status and fitness reports. Fail three times to qualify in an area, and entire lines of career advancement were forever cut off.

The bridge's main display did not show an image of space outside the ship. For all intents and purposes such a view would be useless. The only things visible at even extremely close distances, say five thousand miles, would be planets and moons. For those, where their atmosphere began, and whether there were satellites in orbit, was far more important information than whether the planet was pretty.

The main display showed Captain Grey everything he needed to know about the young Ensign's simulation. The Galileo was hiding behind a planet's moon. A satellite between the planet and the moon received the majority of the ship's sensor attention and was thus either an early warning satellite or a weapon's platform: either way, the target. The Galileo was moments away from coming out of the shadow of the moon and into line of sight with the satellite.

"Mr. Tsang please have missile tubes one and three loaded with one megaton charges. Helmsman come about to heading 2-7-0 by 0," Arnold ordered, voice tight.

Grey watched the display as the Galileo reoriented itself facing back towards the path it had taken in its orbit around the moon. She was now sixty seconds away from coming out of hiding and had her starboard broadside to the enemy satellite – the perfect position for her to be seen and engaged.

"Mr. Tsang, is missile tube one ready to fire?"

The Corporal tapped quickly on his console and furrowed his brow before answering, "ready to fire but the computer cannot verify a firing solution."

The Ensign was sweating now – the computer was telling her one of two things: that the Ensign's math didn't work, or that a billion-dollar computer couldn't anticipate what a junior officer was going to do. Forty-five seconds. Ensign Arnold was hard working, and decisive, but not a natural navigator. Grey imagined her pouring over the plan she was now trying to implement making sure every maneuver, every turn, was perfect. Two months of every free moment she had consumed by this one problem. Yet she knew she couldn't navigate on the fly. Even though the computer was telling her something was wrong, if she left her plan she wouldn't be able to get back on it and could lose everything.

"Override fire control and fire missile one."

She'd decided. Damn the torpedoes. The Galileo would be coming out of cover in twenty seconds. There was no sound, no shudder, just the appearance of another object on the display as the Galileo fired its first missile.

On Earth the difference between a missile and a torpedo was that a torpedo was fired and traveled underwater, and a missile was fired and flew in the sky. Both had a propulsion system (some missiles used propellers, and some torpedoes used rocket engines), both had a warhead of explosives, and both had guidance systems. Ultimately it was a missile's reputation for speed that made it the preferred term for the Galileo's rockets.

"Bring us to heading 7-9 by 0. Expedite!" Ensign Arnold ordered and again the Galileo rotated on the display so its nose was facing the edge of the moon, seconds from having a clear line to the satellite.

"Is missile three ready to fire Mr. Tsang?" a bead of sweat dropped from her nose onto the inner surface of her helmet as she asked.

"Yes sir! We have a firing solution and are ready to fire."

"Fire Missile Three. Status of forward railguns and laser charge?" With five seconds before it exited the moon's shadow the Galileo fired another missile. This one would skirt the edge of the moon carried sideways by the Galileo' momentum and, according to Mindy's math, would hit the satellite thirty seconds after that. This was an elegant maneuver. Firing while still in shadow allowed the missile to do most of its acceleration hidden which was a significant advantage: the math on this would have taken Grey a full day, Mindy must have spent a month.

"Rail guns and lasers ready Sir, full charge," the Corporal reported.

"As soon as we acquire the satellite, fire all forward railguns and lasers, don't wait for my command," Arnold ordered.

As the Galileo cleared the moon she fired four forward rail guns and two forward laser arrays at the satellite. The laser beams traveled at the speed of light and covered the ten-thousand-mile gap almost instantly. The rail gun rounds traveled a small fraction of the speed of light but still carried an impossible amount of kinetic energy. The railgun slugs only weighed twenty-five kilograms and were not much bigger than a man's forearm. But, because of their speed, they'd strike with the force of a small office building going down a highway at fifty miles an hour.

"EMF pops," a crewman reported. Grey watched the rail gun rounds making their way across the emptiness of space, and then wink out of existence as they reached the satellite.

"EMF aspect change," the crewman reported. Arnold bit her lip; her wildcard might decide the day. The Galileo' sensors were extremely sensitive to EMF – electromagnetic fields. Alien technologies might vary wildly but would all cause electrical or magnetic disturbances in their operation. A "pop" in the EMF field meant that there had been a very sudden change in a target's magnetic signature. It had either just done something abrupt like fire a weapon or had taken damage that destroyed a system.

Since the EMF pop coincided with the laser strikes it was almost certain the lasers had hit and caused damage. The EMF aspect change was more interesting. A more gradual change in a ship's EMF, an aspect change, meant it was doing something, but there was no way to know what.

That the display showed the rail gun rounds arriving at the satellite, but it did not show an explosion into a billion pieces, implied a shield.

"Any further change in EMF?"

"No sir."

Mindy sat ramrod straight in the command chair. Missile three was closing with the satellite quickly. She decided to wait and see the result. Five miles from the satellite the missile exploded. Like all nuclear weapons it was breathtakingly powerful, simple, and maddeningly difficult to perfect.

The antimatter payload released the same amount of energy as a million tons of dynamite. By all rights everything within a hundred miles should have been obliterated: the satellite survived.

"EMF aspect change," Tsang reported.

Ensign Arnold was quickly running out of cards to play, "shields up."

"Shields responding, and at 50, 70, 90, 100%," Tsang reported.

"Mr. Tsang give me a position on Missile one."

"Missile one not detected."

Captain Grey wondered if anyone else on the bridge knew why not. Ensign Arnold sat a moment contemplating her situation and gave the Captain a nervous glance over her shoulder before issuing an order, "give me another two missiles, tubes 2 and 4 one megaton charges each."

A half a thought after issuing the command and the Bridge's display snapped off from the navigational map, "Simulation Failure" filled the screen.

"Crap," she pulled off her helmet and pushed aside a soaked lock of hair from her face.

Ensign Arnold gathered herself up, tucked her helmet under her left arm like a football, and started past Grey for the door. A gentle touch on the shoulder stopped her withdrawal. Lowering his voice so the rest of the bridge crew wouldn't hear him, the Captain leaned towards the Ensign. "Major Williams is going to downgrade you for that sim. Come see me in a day or two when you've had a chance to clear your head, and we can talk about how to do better next time."

Shoulder released, the Ensign walked off the bridge likely not having even heard his words. He regretted making the offer instantly.

The Captain took his seat, his armor plates shifted under him as the chair locked them in place. "Mr. Tsang, let's clear this simulation from the display and put up E-1."

The screen snapped over to an engineering display of the Galileo. It was difficult to actually read the numbers. After three years of watching them all slowly change every day his brain rebelled at the attempt to think about them. It took an effort, but he forced himself to focus and, satisfied that all was well with his ship, he addressed the Corporal again, "ship-wide broadcast."

The communications system chirped in obedient reply and throughout the ship crewmen stopped at the sound of the address.

"Now hear this. Yesterday at 07:57 Ensign Chetan Gonzales died from vacuum exsanguination. My report to Earth will indicate that it was an accident. When I write to Chetan's family, I'll tell them he was a hero, and that he had a good death doing what he loved and furthering humanity's legacy in space. I will say that because their son worked hard on this ship. He was a good man, a good friend to many aboard, and his death was ugly and unfair."

"From the first round of interviews for a posting on the Galileo any one of you should have known the answer to whether or not you can vary your mission plan. Every procedure, order, or mission plan has gone through a dozen levels of review. This is not because we are bored bureaucrats looking to feel important, but because everything around us is deadly serious and this is how we stay safe. We trust our training, we trust our crewmen, and we trust our procedures. It was a stupid way for Ensign Gonzales to die, but none the less we owe it to him to learn from his mistake."

"I want you to all ask yourselves a question. What if Ensign Gonzales made it back but someone else had been killed because he broke protocol? What if someone else died because you broke protocol?"

Grey tried to shift in his seat, a futile motion for a man locked in place. "But this was also a failure on my part. Ensign Gonzales died to teach me, and all of us, a lesson that we could have learned by thinking ahead. And that is a sin I have to live with. I failed him, and we failed him."

"In three months, we become the first human beings to visit another solar system. We could well become the first human beings to meet alien life. We've all made sacrifices to be here but now, one way or the other, we change man's understanding of our universe. To do great things requires great sacrifices, sacrifices that no one before was willing to make. Remember that, remember your duty, and remember that your work keeps your shipmates safe, and they're work keeps you safe."

A tap of the console at his left hand, and the communication system shut off.

CHAPTER 4 - Two Months from TR-583

"JESUS!" GREY RIPPED off his soaked sheet and sat up. He cradled his hands together against his chest. The motion of scarred skin shaking itself hurt, but less than it had in his dreams.

His feet found the cabin's cold metal deck, and drops of sweat joined them there, falling from his chin and elbows. His beddings was thin, worn, and soaked. The cheap fabric had been made for military barracks not the multi-year use of space travel, and it bunched and clung like wet rope. He should have known this would happen.

Stress condensed in his stomach into a toxic knot. Adrenaline pumped through his veins in equal measure with blood; but for that, he would have thrown up. He was twice damned now.

In Greenwich England it was 2 am. This fact ought not to have meant anything billions of miles away from Earth, but it did.

Deep breaths helped. Both the adrenaline in his blood, and the bile in his gut, slowly responded. It was a matter of discipline, he told himself. The demons in his head told him it was his fault, they terrorized him with guilt. Discipline would let the rational side win, he hoped.

He was sick, that was all, and that knowledge should be enough to overcome it.

There was no shame in having post-traumatic stress disorder. There was even a cure. Two years in therapy, a few thousand dollars' worth of medication, and he would have been fine. With a mild case he might have even been done treatment in eighteen months. But even that delay would have taken him out of consideration for the Galileo.

The ISC didn't discriminate, it was just a question of timing and availability. Grey's choice had been to toughen up and be a captain who had the occasional nightmare, or sell patio furniture along route 85. A captain had a very specific set of skills. After the Gazer his career with the Navy was over, and his skills had no commercial value outside of that. His ex-girlfriend back on Earth, Sarah, could have gotten him a job in construction. He could have worked his way up to foreman, and at the end of a long career, had a nice small house, a few kids, and a couple of slightly better built buildings as a legacy. He was less afraid of vacuum than that life.

It took several minutes but eventually he managed to close his hand over a single piece of his suit's armor; a silver segment designed to wrap around his left forearm from wrist to elbow. The silver metal responded to his touch, and black letters appeared as though they had been etched into its surface.

The small device cycled through a series of menus before the night's duty roster appeared. Grey tried to put the list to memory. It helped push other thoughts aside, and few things are as important to morale as having the Captain pat you on the back for a good performance review. He couldn't give his crew fresh food, much contact with home, or even time off, but he could give them that.

Dried, dressed, studied up, and fractionally calmer, he stepped into the hall and felt his blood pressure drop, a first in several days. Someone had dimmed the corridor's lights. Without the normal hustle of the crew, and the lights dimmed, the ship felt exactly like how a night ought to feel. The ventilation system worked more efficiently at night. Without crewmen filling halls, moving panels, or blocking vents with cargo, the system had free reign to do its job. The result was the slightest of breezes, a sensation that tickled every nerve on his exposed head.

He decided he'd begin his rounds in engineering and found himself trying to step lightly as he made his way through the ship. The halls were completely empty, and he felt like his breaths were deeper, more filling.

He passed a porthole, a window to space beyond the ship, and looked out. There was nothing. No stars, no reflection from external lights, nothing. Travelling faster than light meant that anything that touched the ship would hit with the kinetic energy of a faster than light impact. From a lone atom, to a small rock, even the energy from starlight would have been enough to vaporize the Galileo. And so, shields were a requirement. The shields diverted everything around the Galileo's path, everything. So, faster than light, there was nothing to see.

He missed the stars, or perhaps the feeling of depth they gave.

Halfway to engineering one of the ship's mysteries grabbed his eyes. The same artist who had painted the bridge door had painted a bird, some sort of songbird, wearing a 1950's space helmet, on a communications system access panel. How much paint could they have? The Galileo had a certain pallet of colors. The ship's stores contained the sharp red, white, blue, green, black, and yellow paints which made up the vast majority of highlights, and a large quantity of the navy grey that was ubiquitous throughout the ship. This work used none of those. The bird, its wings extended in flight, was free, even chromatically.

He would have had to turn sideways to extend his arms fully. What would it be like to be outside again?

It hadn't been a fair trade for Chetan. But he had still gotten something wonderful in return for his life.

The port airlock that Chetan had wound up in was only a deck up and a few corridors over. Grey found himself walking that direction and away from engineering; his duty as appealing as the mess' food.

How was he supposed to live with Chetan on his conscience? The mistake was so obvious now, and even if he hadn't known the specifics, why allow a crewman to spend an extra minute in space? It was courting disaster.

He couldn't tell himself it wasn't his fault, he couldn't tell himself that Chetan had died for a worthy cause, he couldn't tell himself that he had spent Chetan's life and sometimes that is what command requires. He fucked up and Chetan died because of it. The only consolation possible was the truth: that it was a dangerous mission and men were expected to die from his mistakes. Katherine's point. How was anyone supposed to live with that?

The inner doors of the airlock were open as Grey approached. It was an odd breach of protocol as both doors should be closed when not in use. The airlock connected at a right angle to the hallway which obstructed his view of its interior. He slowed as he approached, each step carefully placed, toe to heel, deliberate and slow, though he was unsure why. Perhaps the low lighting gave the corridor too much mood.

Grey glanced to the airlock's control panel. It was simple; at the top of the control panel a pressure gauge showed internal airlock pressure. Just below that was a Christmas tree of buttons. At the apex a single green button flashed. This button controlled the inner airlock door. Press it and the door would open. Just below the green button were two orange buttons side by side. These should have been illuminated and they were to close the inner airlock door. Press them both simultaneously and the inner door closes, and the buttons flash orange, caution. The final row was three red buttons side by side. Those controlled the outer airlock doors. Press all three simultaneously and the airlock would depressurize and open its outer door. Exiting the airlock was as simple as 1, 2, 3. Entering through the airlock was the reverse sequence.

Grey tried not to peer, but he couldn't help himself. He leaned around the edge of the airlock to see what was inside. Major Katherine Bakker sat, her back to him, wearing a threadbare shirt and a pair of tattered jeans. Flecks of paint splattered her clothes. Her left hand held a plate with a spread of paints. Large globs of red, blue, and green, waited at the edge of the plate to be mixed, the center filled with a commingled rainbow. In Katherine's right hand deft fingers guided a brush. Katherine slowly painted on the outer airlock door, oblivious to her observer.

The technical term for her style escaped him. Could there be a landscape of space or did land make the landscape? Perhaps Jennifer's Tear, prominently featured in a funerary grey against a deep blue and purple field of stars, qualified as land to the art types. While he couldn't name the style, he could name the emotion he felt looking at artist and painting. It made no sense, like a sailor longing for the sea, yet it was longing.

"I never would have suspected you," he said.

To her credit, Katherine didn't react. Perhaps she had heard his steps or had just expected someone to find her eventually. Either way she ignored him and applied another stroke of paint.

An impossibly dark line of blue mingled with deep purples that warmed the void of her painting. He entered the airlock and sat down, back against the inner airlock`s frame. The ship's deck was metal cold.

The Major was a beautiful woman. She still had the energy of youth. Her porcelain skin and blonde hair spoke of a European ancestry. "Is this for Chetan?"

Katherine exhaled slowly and set down her easel. "I work sixteen hours a day in the same room with the same people. When I get up in the morning Ensign Waters climbs into my bunk for her 8 hours of sleep and when I get off shift my bed is still warm from Ensign Jenkins. I shower in the morning in a bathroom I share with six other women on my deck in water that has been drunk, pissed out, and purified a hundred times already, and for which I get a purity report every morning right after my shower. And we're two months from getting our first hint whether it was a big waste and I'm going to spend the rest of my life in this box going from one lifeless planet to another. Is it asking too much that this one thing in my life be private? Respectfully Captain..."

He considered arguing. He considered staying. He considered taking the young woman in his arms. Instead he stood up, wincing as he scraped his spine against the airlock wall's rivets. "There is something ironic about an artist who paints in public spaces but wants her work to be private."

"I am glad I amuse you."

Sometimes retreat is the prudent maneuver "Good night, Major."

"Good night, Captain."

CHAPTER 5 - One Month from TR-583

"GOOD MORNING, PETER. You had a tough time last night," Sergeant Rebecca Daniels looked very un-sergeant like in a soft blue undershirt. Her hair was untied and flowing, the loose fabric of her shirt hinted at what was beneath. She was soft, warm, human, and intoxicating.

A kettle of hot water screeched, demanding attention. Grey took over and poured its boiling contents into two large mugs adding the last of his tea. "I'm sorry about that..." he lifted the mugs and examined the contents, his eyebrow raised in disapproval. "You're going to have to give this a bit to steep... This tea's been used about a dozen times, and it's just about given up the ghost."

The medic shrugged and began to pull on her uniform, "so what do you have today?" her boots put up a struggle as she asked.

"I need to give some serious time to the Katherine problem." Grey gave his razor a shake and flipped it on. Inside the small silver device micro-lasers powered up. Grey slowly passed the machine over his chin and followed it with a swipe of the hand, and then another pass of the razor over the same spot, and another. He should have learned to use a straight razor when he had the chance.

"Demote her," Rebecca said for the thirtieth time, "honestly I don't understand why you haven't already."

After the fifth pass still left stubble, Grey had to set the device down to avoid smashing it to pieces; there'd be no replacement if he did. Before he could manage a rational reply to Rebecca, he took a deep breath, "you can't fix trust issues with a closed fist. Besides, I need someone who's going to be a nerd. Someone who'll study and think about every system on the ship, every minute of the day. Someone who'll think of things no one else would, or could. That's who Katherine is right now, and if I can get her to trust me, trust her people, and inspire that trust in turn then she'd be the perfect officer."

"Train someone else to be a nerd," Daniels said.

"I can teach command skills, at least I hope I can, I can't train someone to be an engineering nerd."

"And you're Mr. People-Skills aren't you," Rebecca flashed him her perfect teeth. "Ok. Technical skills are important. But what about loyalty and respecting authority? She's insubordinate, and the stories about her are unbelievable. She won't let nuclear physicists handle a wrench. She personally watches everything that happens to 'her' engines."

Grey took a long sip of hot water. The flavor of water was unadulterated by the old tea leaves, Elvis had definitely left the building. He looked down into the cup and wondered whether the last time he had tea was the last time he would ever have tea. "I need obedience from people who don't have enough information to judge the logic of my orders. I need a chief engineer who's going to point out errors. If I can trust her to obey in the end, it'll be fine."

Grey looked at the mug in Rebecca's hand. It was white, ceramic, a coffee mug in the most stereotypical sense of the word. The yeoman who cleaned his quarters would also see that there were two of them today, that there had been two mugs each morning the week before, and sporadically for the last six months before then. Rebecca's bunkmates would have noticed her absence. They'd wonder why she didn't volunteer who she'd been spending her nights with. Which was a question that answered itself. How long before the crew started talking? Maybe they were already. Would Williams have passed along rumors? He wouldn't approve, Grey knew that much. The regulations were clear, and more than that, they existed for a good reason.

"You're the Captain... sir," the Sergeant said as she took a sip of her hot water. "But I'll tell you, when things heat up you don't like having your orders questioned, even when it is by someone who knows better." At that the warmth drained from her face and she waited, expecting him to get the hint.

"How many times do I have to say sorry for that?"

"At least once more it seems..."

Hoping to get some caffeine at least Grey poured the last of his "tea" into his mouth and thought a long second. "I am sorry. This whole thing, it's just not right, it's not fair to you."

Rebecca pulled up her uniform's zipper to her neck, ready to confront the day.

It had started if not innocently, then perhaps understandably. Grey had been lonely, and Rebecca hadn't shied away from his rank. A half joke had made her light up, which led to a conversation, which led to another, and another, and then a rendezvous. He had to be honest with himself. As much as she was a friend, things crossed the line because of loneliness, because of weakness, because he wasn't as strong a man as he needed to be.

"I think this needs to be the last time for us Rebecca," Grey was on his feet facing her as she grabbed the last of her armor segments and attached it to herself.

"And now this again? Ok, fine."

"I'm not just saying it. I mean it. It isn't fair to the rest of the crew. I'm not in love with you Rebecca."

Sergeant Daniels took Grey's arm and gave it a squeeze. "And who said I love you? Do you think you would risk being unfair to the crew, to me, without having some feelings for me, sir? But I understand. Men are the biggest fools when it comes to their own feelings..."

Daniels walked to the hatch and turned back, looking at Grey, "when you're ready, I'll be waiting. Maybe," she smiled like a woman with a secret and closed the hatch behind her as she left.

His uniform half on, Grey sat at his table and looked at the two empty cups. Aside from the Galileo's buzz the room was silent. Until he invited someone into it again, it would remain silent – forever. As much as he wanted to tell himself he wouldn't; if they didn't find anything at TR-583; if they were ordered to spend another three years going to the next candidate world; if he was supposed to spend the rest of his life alone: he couldn't.

CHAPTER 6 - Two Weeks from TR-583

"THAT'S TWICE YOU'VE KILLED US all," Major Williams stated flatly and drummed his thumb against his calf at a slow cadence, matching the slow pulses of the ship's hum. Then he waited, his grey eyes fixed on the young woman. The seconds ticked away and social pressures the Major didn't feel, built up on the Ensign.

Ensign Arnold stood at attention in the Major's cabin, a handful of tablet computers tucked under her arm, and managed to look even more rigid than the Major.

"I've been over my maths three times. Was Missile 1 a simulated dud... did the computer figure it had malfunctioned and I shouldn't have pinned my hopes on a single missile?"

Williams rolled his tongue over the dry interior of his mouth. For a half a second he looked like a dead-eyed cow chewing cud. "We don't know what kind of technology aliens might have. So, the only safe assumption is they have better. What we do know is that weapons are not kept ready to be used at a moment's notice; that's true of bows and arrows, or nuclear weapons. We also know that defenses cannot always be kept on at their highest level. So, if we're smart, and sneaky, we can get the first shot. That one shot needs to be big, it needs to be fast, and they can't see it coming."

Williams sat down on the edge of his bunk, exhaled, and with effort, managed to slouch, slightly. This was now as informal a conversation as the man was capable of.

He motioned towards his desk chair, "take a seat Arnold." He gave the young woman a second to consider, resist, and then sit. A personal chair in a cabin was a luxury and a symbol of the Major's rank. That it had a plastic seat and a frame made of roughly welded steel tubes was irrelevant to that. The Major might have forgotten sitting in an identical chair in his high school years, the Ensign had not. Mindy's brown hair was tied back neatly, computer tablets stacked on her lap tentatively.

"You're like a monkey with a rock, fighting a tank. You watch, you wait, and when the tank commander climbs out to stretch and take a piss, you sneak up behind him, and club him on the back of the head. Unless you see the enemy's dick in their hands you don't attack," his voice stayed flat, no excitement or displeasure. War was methodical, not exciting.

"Which is why I fired lasers. I used the moon's shadow to conceal firing heavier weapons and softened the target with lasers as soon as we cleared the moon. If I'd waited for the heavy weapons it would have only given them more time with us in the open."

"Using the moon to hide the launch of missiles and EM fluctuation from firing rail guns was proficient. But when you announce your presence and hostile intention with laser fire you gave the enemy time to get its shields up and then the rail gun rounds you fired were useless."

"I did land two laser hits."

Williams pursed his lips and exhaled slightly, cutting off further argument, "your lasers proved to be as useful as spitting in a tiger's eye." He looked the young officer over and waited to see if she had gotten the message. She said nothing.

"When my daughter was... oh twelve, thirteen... What are kids in the 4th or 5th grade? Doesn't matter. I came home from a tour, and she showed me this medal she had won in track and field. It was for participation," the last word was said as though it were rancid.

"She was so proud of it, she didn't realize it was a stupid, insulting, award. But because it was important to her, I taught her how to actually run... to earn something real. We trained our asses off together."

Williams' face broke into a rare grin, "I was humping a hundred-and-fifty-pound pack to slow down for her, and had her humping a thirty-pound pack after a few months. Next time she came in second and nearly blasted her heart out of her chest doing it." His smile faded, replaced with a hard pride of a job well done. "I told her that second place was respectable but that sometimes you can't be the best unless you're naturally blessed."

"You're a superb weapons officer Mindy. You are the best. You don't take chances. You respect the weapons without being afraid of them. And you're hard-working, no denying that. But you don't have a head for orbital dynamics. Why do something you're no good at when you already have something you're the best at?"

"Isn't life about trying to improve? Trying to be the best we can be? Sir, to be honest the antimatter weapons come easily to me. Everyone's terrified of them, but I know if something goes wrong it would be painless. If I've done my best, and lead a good life, I'll be with God in heaven so there's nothing to fear. But I want to grow."

"No one knows their place anymore," Williams ran a hand through what was left of his grey hair. "Mindy, I'm not a priest or a therapist. But I am trying to do what's best for you."

Major Williams straightened, stood, and was back to business. "You've failed twice so far and one more attempt is all you get. Make it count. I hope you'll pass, but I doubt it. Command positions on this ship are not here for your feelings. You want it, you earn it."

Williams considered a moment and added, "you know what would impress me? Be excellent at your current job – don't try to become a mediocre bridge officer."

Mindy`s face contracted, her eyes narrowed, her lower lip quivered a whisper. Major Williams' eyes went wide and he took up, not for the first time, a look every man knows.

"I am not mediocre," her voice trembled. Then more firmly, "permission to carry on?"

Ben hesitated a half a second wondering if he could put the genie back in the bottle; but, as he had never previously succeeded, he quickly mumbled "granted". Ben Williams looked at his cabin's hatch and asked himself the same question he had asked a thousand times before. 'Why were all the women in his life crazy?'

CHAPTER 7 - One Light-Hour from TR-583

THERE WAS NO SIMPLE ANSWER. Major Benjamin Williams marched back and forth in front of his desk, as though the single sheet of paper sitting on it were inspecting him. The paper's corners were dog-eared and a well-used crease ran across its waist.

The single autumn leaf of paper was roughly the size of a man's hand and aside from the header "Personal Communication – Priority" contained only a rectangular grid twenty by forty boxes, enough room for exactly 800 characters. It was the Major's most valuable possession. The first eleven boxes were filled with the words "Dear Julia," and the last nine boxes were filled with "Love, Your Father" the remaining 784 boxes were blank.

It was possible for the Galileo to transmit and receive messages from Earth. Deep inside the ship, shielded from magnetic, physical, and thermal interference, was a single proton and the summation of five Nobel prizes for, a system the press dubbed, 'the biggest loophole in quantum mechanics'. The math of it was beyond Williams. Something about lowering the entropy of a quantum entangled system. The takeaway was that a signal could be transmitted, instantly, across the galaxy.

The only problem, aside from the seven-billion-dollar price tag, was speed. For the tiny size of a proton, and the massive computer and laser apparatus to isolate and manipulate the system, the signal was more probability and less 1's and 0's. Over a long enough time, one minute for the Galileo's equipment, a statistical model could be built and a 1 or 0 inferred.

A single letter contains 8 bits of information. Each bit needed to be transmitted separately, 1 or 0, one minute per bit, eight bits per letter or 13 hours for a single eight-hundred-character letter. Taking into account regular status updates and reply letters, each crewman was allotted one letter sent, and one letter received, every year.

In addition to that, if a crewmember could simply not wait a year to send a message, each was allotted a single priority communication sheet that could jump in line and be sent immediately. The Galileo's journey had no fixed return date and that single priority message sheet was each crewman's only lifeline home.

Major Williams paced the four-step width of his cabin wearing boxers and an undershirt. His bare feet landed hard on the frigid deck with each step. "I love you and I miss you?" he said to the riveted metal walls as he paced, and the words appeared on the sheet of paper. Three steps forward, turn, three steps back; the length of his cabin. "I love you, and I'm sorry..." He exhaled deeply, as though his emotions could be blown out of his chest, and stopped pacing long enough to address a deep, old, ache in his back. He braced the palms of his hands on his lower back and stretched his chin towards the ceiling. "I'm proud of you. I regret that I wasn't there for you... Dammit. Delete," he said to the roof of his cabin, and the paper on his desk wiped itself clean.

He looked at the sheet, "you're all I have left, and I want to be part of your life. I'm sorry I came out here. I am sorry I left you. I just never realized how much you'd mean to me." Williams shuddered and rubbed his head slowly.

The com system chimed with a programmed time reminder. "Wonderful, just when I start to make some progress..." he closed his fist around the fabric of his jump suit and lifted it from his cot. The fabric was always strangely cold to the touch when first worn, something about the macro properties of pressure sensitive molecules that he couldn't have cared less about. He clamped the various armor plates onto the suit in seconds both indifferent to the comfort of the fit and deft at the task.

A ship ran on discipline as much as it did fuel. To have discipline, a clear chain of authority and command was necessary. To make that chain of command perfectly clear the trappings of power were important. Major Williams and Major Bakker had the same rank, but Williams was the XO, second in command, and so had a private cabin while Bakker had crew quarters she shared. Williams had a chair, a desk, trappings of his office as the ship's executive officer. Grey had no desk; Grey wasn't expected to need it. He was the ship's father, the heart and compassion, the "old man" who the crew felt care from. Williams was the closed fist. He was the one who cracked the whip, the one the crew feared as well as respected. At least that was the job description.

Helmet propped under his left arm, exactly like the manual depicted, Williams took two steps towards his cabin door and stopped dead. He turned, looked at the sheet of paper sitting on his desk. A private cabin in naval parlance was not private in the way civilians would understand it to be. A knock and waiting for an "enter", or "leave", was as close to privacy as it came. Any one of a dozen crewmen would pass through the room each day to drop off reports, requisitions, ration cards, and so on. Any of them could see the sheet. The Major leaned over, swept the com sheet into the top desk drawer, and then slammed it shut. "Women…"

***

CAPTAIN PETER GREY STOOD IN THE CENTER of the bridge. The room was empty and silent save the constant hum of the ship, which managed to penetrate even the thick titanium shell and gravity dampening systems that protected the bridge.

Only the Captain could order the bridge cleared and it was something he avoided doing. As the bridge door slid open Grey turned his head towards Major Williams. "Couldn't wait either Major?" he asked as the man marched into the bridge with a metronome's cadence though his footsteps were muffled on the thick titanium floor.

The hatch sealed with a series of mechanical clicks behind Williams, "respectfully, sir. Bullshit – if you're not nervous about this you aren't human."

Grey looked at the long list of data displayed on the main view screen, "not many people get to feel the hand of history on their shoulder."

"You know, I was with Admiral Hood when he intervened in the Sea of China War," Williams said. "I was younger than you at the time, just twenty-one, a freshly minted Ensign. I still remember the XO reading off range findings as the Chinese and Russian fleets came at us. Hood just stood there saying 'hold'... right until the first missile hit."

"Worried I'll be another Hood?" Grey asked.

Williams wrinkled skin cracked as he grimaced, "worried you won't be. Hell, I'm dying out here one way or the other. I have thirty years on you. I'll get cancer or pneumonia in this icebox, and we won't have the drugs to fix it. I'm worried you won't take the first hit because you don't want the crew, or Rebecca, to get hurt or killed."

And there it was.

"You know about Rebecca," Grey closed his eyes, exhaled slowly, then turned to face his XO.

"I stopped a few rumors," Williams said.

"I ended things." Grey offered.

"I'm not the equity officer. So long as it doesn't affect your duty, you won't hear about it again from me. My job here is to watch, advise, and my advice is that I have seen better men than you ruined by various combinations of dick and heart."

Grey looked down at his hands, scarred skin stretching as he flexed them. "One thing I know about myself is that I'll do the right thing when it comes to it." Lighting on the bridge was always low, it was supposed to encourage calm thought. Grey found nothing about it calming.

Williams looked at his Captain's hands, "I'm sure that's what those bureaucrats on the International Section Committee figured when they picked you. But they didn't know the difference between doing a thing, and living with it. I doubt those ISC paper pushers would have thought you would reset the MSD on Jennifer's Tear to a hundred meters... I also bet they didn't know you have trouble sleeping through the night."

Before Grey could formulate a response, the bridge doors opened, internal locks unfastening with the precision of a watch. Four crewmen entered, taking their stations, ready.

Captain Peter Grey donned his helmet and felt it lock tightly in place around his head. A second later he, and the rest of the bridge crew, save Williams who stood, were locked into their seats. After a thousand practice runs the Galileo was about to begin doing her job.

"Mr. Tsang, position, heading, and astrometrics."

"Sir, our current course is tangential to the TR-583 solar system. Most recent observations show six planetoids in orbit of TR-583 and we are one A.U. beyond the orbit of the sixth planetoid."

The practice helped. It was surprisingly easy to set aside the Major's words and put himself fully into the moment. The routine was drilled into everyone and it freed Grey to notice the details. The way Tsang's shoulders rose and fell as he breathed quickly, the slight buzz reality seemed to be coated with in times of stress.

"Major Williams, please have stellar cartography plot a display to the main screen."

The bridge's main display almost instantly flashed from an engineering and system summary of the ship, to a map of the TR-583 solar system. The crew was responding quickly, faster than they had in simulations. Eager, excited, and fully engaged in the task.

It was no accident that Earth's solar system was roughly a flat plane, the planets all rotating about the sun like they were marbles rolling around on a plate. Over the tens of millions of years it takes a solar system to form, the clouds of dust which planets condense from settles into its lowest possible energy state, a flat plane.

The Galileo approached the TR-583 system along this plane and travelled just outside the orbit of the planet furthest from

TR-583's star. Another hour at faster than light speeds, and the Galileo would have been well clear of the system, having just grazed its edge.

"Major Williams I believe this course and position comply with the Fermi Protocol. Do you concur?"

Williams, predictably, actually considered the question fresh and, twenty seconds after being asked, responded, "I do, sir."

"Very well, Major, take us to sub-light speed."

The transition to normal space was imperceptible aboard the ship. Theoretically a ship transitioning to normal space would look like it suddenly winked into existence. The mathematicians who worked with FTL fields claimed that there shouldn't be any optical effects lasting more than a trillionth of a second, however no one had actually seen an FTL transition. The Heisenberg uncertainty theory dictated that an object can only be observed with a certain degree of accuracy. The more precisely you know an object's speed the less precisely you can know its location, and vice versa. For a spaceship travelling at orbital speeds Heisenberg's equation means you could, with a perfectly designed rocket and perfect knowledge, probably hit a space station's airlock, but not a button on its control panel.

The Galileo was on a completely different scale. Orbital speeds are on the order of 7,000 miles per hour. The speed of light is just under 670 million miles per hour. The Galileo could travel nearly thirty times that speed, or 18 billion miles per hour. When dropping out of FTL the Galileo would come to a stop somewhere in a sphere with the volume of Earth. In other words, there is no way to catch the Galileo dropping out of FTL on camera to know what it looked like.

"Major, drop shields and have communications begin an EM frequency scan of the system."

"Yes sir. Coms estimates fifteen minutes for a preliminary frequency analysis."

The Galileo' delicate antennas began collecting every stray photon that collided with them searching for active frequencies. Fifteen minutes, and for all intents and purposes they would know if the system was inhabited... probably. Presumably any reasonably advanced alien civilization would emit some kind of electromagnetic radiation; the more people, the more technology, the more electromagnetic noise to detect. If the detector in coms didn't light up like a Christmas tree at some point on the EM spectrum it was unlikely that a more detailed review would detect anything of note.

If this system was empty the Galileo would go to the next, and the next, and the next until someone decided it was a waste of time. It could take decades and there would be no other ship like the Galileo built without reason. Returning the Galileo to Earth would waste decades and so, they wouldn't. This could be the first of a lifetime of disappointments for Grey and the whole crew, and they would have spent their lives, given everything up, for nothing.

Fifteen minutes, after three years of waiting and it might as well have been a week. The Captain needed a distraction before his apprehension manifested itself.

"Mr. Tsang. What is the difference between a radio wave and a beam of light?"

Corporal Tsang began the journey as a twenty-two-year-old Private and had been diligent in applying himself but, with a liberal arts degree, physics was his weakness. Add the stress of the moment and it would be as good a time as any to see how the man thought on his feet and what he had learned. Grey thought of Tsang as a long-term investment. The man was far from perfect but had real potential if he could find his honor.

"Sir, the difference is frequency."

"And why are some frequencies more interesting than others?"

"Some frequencies occur naturally and so are difficult to work with due to natural interference. Other frequencies penetrate better than others, some reflect better than others. 2.4 gigahertz is a special frequency because it penetrates better than most, and doesn't typically occur naturally."

"What is light made up of?" Grey asked.

"Photons, sir."

"And radio waves are made of?" This caused the Corporal to slow, "also photons, sir."

"If radio waves and light are both photons, why can I get radio through a brick wall?" Grey pressed.

"It has to do with the frequency, sir. Light waves are fatter and can't fit between the gaps in a wall's atoms, radio waves are narrower, lower frequency."

"If frequency is how fat waves are, what's amplitude?" Grey watched the back of the Corporal's helmeted head as he puzzled that out. He knew he had made a mistake. Amplitude was how "fat" waves were, but as soon as he said that Grey would ask why frequency mattered for waves passing through walls, and not amplitude.

"Sorry, sir. I need to hit the books on that one."

Grey smiled enjoying the privacy his helmet offered – the Captain couldn't smirk at the crew when they didn't know something. There was a reason Tsang had been promoted so quickly. He was honest when he was out of his depth and proposed solutions not excuses. Ambition however comes with a price. One day, if he became a better man, his Captain wouldn't smirk when he tripped him up, though for Tsang's benefit he would still try. "Let's change gears for the moment. The Fermi Protocol – why did we drop out of FTL on a tangent to the orbital plane?"

This was a topic Tsang knew, and he was eager to show off. First rule of leadership: don't tear a man down if you don't build him back up. "It's part of the Fermi Protocol's attempt to hide Earth's location. For the same reason, Earth's coordinates are only known by a handful of crewmen. The assumption is that exiting FTL along the system's plane would obscure transition to normal space from observation."

"I was under the impression that it was practically impossible to observe a re-entry to normal space visually. What do you say to that Corporal?" Grey asked.

"It is, sir, but there's a burst of radiation released when the transition occurs. It affects a large area of space forward of the ship's path and could, in theory, be detected and a relatively accurate return vector calculated."

"Correct. And what do you think of the Fermi Protocol Corporal? Good idea, waste of effort?"

"Not my place to say, sir."

"It is when you're asked. Everyone has opinions."

"It's worse than a waste of time, sir. There's absolutely no point in hiding Earth's location because there's no point in attacking Earth. There's a million, a billion, closer and easier places to harvest raw materials. There're probably tens of thousands of easily habitable planets out there where you wouldn't have to fight the locals for the land. I just don't see a motive for an alien to come to Earth and do us harm – movies notwithstanding, sir."

"What happens if we encounter aliens who don't reason along the same lines as you do Corporal?"

"Logic is logic, sir. It applies just as much to us as to aliens."

"Have you read any Hadfield? He argues that conclusion is not necessarily reliable."

"No, sir. I'll add him to my reading list. There's a larger issue with the Fermi Protocol. Only a handful of crewmen, almost all of them in astrometrics, actually know how to plot a course to Earth. If something were to happen to them, and our comms, we'd never be able to find our way home."

"I think homework in physics and philosophy is likely enough for one week: radio waves and Hadfield. We can revisit this next week when you rotate back to bridge duty."

"Yes sir."

Out of distractions the bridge's walls seemed to pulse closer and closer with each passing second. Grey wasn't claustrophobic, none of the crew were. Back on Earth he had never understood claustrophobia. After three years indoors he did. The walls were both safety and prison. If they found nothing, all the mystery, the magic, would disappear from the ship and the walls would just be metal, the ship no more majestic than a fishing trawler.

Finding nothing was almost never talked about openly. It was too horrible to even imagine. The Galileo's crew was the best of the best, who were also willing to gamble their lives for the chance at making history. If they lost that bet...

"Sir! Coms reports multiple interfering signals at 2.4 gigahertz!" Corporal Tsang almost shouted it out.

"Give me a ship wide address!" Grey couldn't have held back his own excitement had he tried.

"Now hear this. Comms has not yet finished its scan, but we are picking up multiple signals at 2.4 gigahertz. It's going to take days to confirm and make our approach, but you all know what this means. Congratulations ladies and gentlemen."

Grey wished he could have simply enjoyed the moment. His brain wasn't wired that way. A second of exultation and then the clouds appeared. Barring a surprise, it was now more likely than not that the name Grey would be carved into history. Columbus had been celebrated for centuries, debated for decades, and then cursed in perpetuity.

CHAPTER 8

IT TOOK THE GALILEO A WEEK to complete a detailed electromagnetic survey of the system. The conclusion was that the second planet from TR-583 was radiating signals. The frequency spectrum being emitted from the planet was even more crowded than that of Earth. Slightly off-axis signals, signals originating from the space around the planet, were almost certainly from satellites in orbit.

The content of the signals was completely indecipherable. There are two forms of radio signals: digital, and analog. None of the TR-583 signals were analog (meaning using the simple wave form to convey information) instead they all appeared to be digital and either encrypted or conveying a form of information that was not readily decipherable. For humans, audio, video, or text-based signals were all based on discrete units, a tone, a pixel, a letter. Break a signal down tightly enough and it was just a matter of guessing the correct color, tone, or letter, and the signal makes sense. The signals that the Galileo was processing didn't contain those tiny repeating pieces.

And so, Captain Peter Grey, on behalf of all humanity, had a choice.

Despite years of thought and planning it was a choice that no one on the Galileo, or Earth, had ever considered: just leaving.

The question of whether humanity, life itself, was just a fluke in the universe had just been answered. The philosophical, political, and religious ramifications of this could take hundreds of years to settle. That life had been found at the first likely system visited meant it was plentiful. The Drake equation would be revised up several orders of magnitude and humanity faced heavens crowded with life.

With a handful of digital signals, the Galileo had fundamentally changed humanity's understanding of reality. No one stopped to ask whether this was enough knowledge for one century.

So many fundamental discoveries and steps forward are made by the young, the reckless, the dreamers who moved without consultations or debate. Gutenberg, a man in his thirties, invented the printing press and began the age of enlightenment. His only moral authority for doing so, that he was first.

If Gutenberg's contemporaries had formed a committee to debate the merits of his invention, what would have been the result? They would have been men, only men, of the 1400's who were religious fanatics, merchants of grain or slaves, and Kings who would make warlords look civilized. If these men came together to debate the printing press, something that was fundamentally beyond them, what would have been the result?

As terrifying as it might be that a single man had the power to change humanity's course, there were worse options.

So, Captain Grey made the only decision he could comprehend making and ordered the Galileo to approach the planet for first contact.

The Galileo came to a stop just outside the orbit of the planet's single moon. The thought was that the lunar orbit of a planet represented the furthest realistic threshold which permission to pass should be sought. If aliens ever came to earth, stopping outside the moon's orbit and asking permission to visit, seemed the least threatening way to do it.

The request to approach had been pre-made by a team of scientists on Earth long before the Galileo had set off on her voyage. The message took twenty minutes to broadcast and, freed from the constraints of quantum broadcast, was massive.

The Galileo repeated the signal continuously for 24 hours. It was written in math. Formulas showed an approach into a low orbit, along with what was supposed to be a language key and information about humans and the Galileo's mission. Finally, some masterpieces of art and music were included to show the human soul; or so Earth's scientists had calculated.

There had been great public interest in contributing to what made the cut of humanity's most important art. The Mona Lisa made the list, but so did the Wizard of Oz and select episodes of Doctor Who. The last entry had caused joy on the internet and consternation among the rest of the population. Humanity had still not learned its lesson about internet polls.

For all that, Grey thought it would take months, if ever, for a reply to arrive. Even if the planet's inhabitants heard their broadcast, and were interested in it, it would take weeks to decipher the message and even longer to form a coordinated, global, reply. So, two weeks after transmitting their greeting message, Grey decided action was needed.

***

GREY FOLDED HIS PILLOWCASE TO MILITARY SPECIFICATIONS, two inches of slack at the end of the case before the excess was folded over and tucked under the pillow. His bed sheets had razor-sharp hospital corners. The rough weave of the cotton sheets caught on his scarred hands as he tried to smooth out imagined wrinkles, doing as much harm as good.

Satisfied with the bed, his attention turned to the table setting. Ever since Captains had private cabins, they'd had tables and, occasionally, hosted meals. From Columbus' Santa Maria, to 20th century US navy destroyers, tucked away somewhere aboard was a single set of good china, silver flatware, and crystal wine glasses.

Grey immediately spotted a problem. The Yeoman who brought him his meals had become too used to simple place settings. After years with a trowel as his only cutlery, the crewman had forgotten which side of the plate the knife and fork went on. Grey corrected this. The easy rule was that a table should be set in preparation for combat: knife ready at the right-hand side, blade in.

Being a good host meant extending courtesy to guests, which returned dignity to the host. It didn't matter that Katherine wouldn't care about wrinkles in his sheets, or which side of the plate a knife went on. He knew, and was out to do his best.

From the cabin window a field of stars greeted Grey. Travelling faster than light had meant years of utter blackness from the windows. The stars were stark, and beautiful. He could, however, do better. Grey tapped the silver armor piece on his arm and his comms unit beeped to life. It was the only piece of armor he was wearing over his black and gold uniform. "Bridge. Give me a 1-7-0-degree longitudinal rotation."

The Galileo rotated about its length; the Captain's window rotated towards the planet below. A blue and white orb the size of a softball rose into view and came to a rest near the top of the window.

Grey spoke again, "bridge, now give me negative 1-5 degrees of yaw". The Galileo rotated again, and a silver moon in half eclipse joined the view. Because the Galileo was much closer to the moon than the planet, the moon looked like a beach ball to the planet's softball. Van Gogh would have had trouble doing better.

When invited to the Captain's table, one was punctual and at exactly 1700 Greenwich Mean Time Grey's cabin door chimed. Katherine wore her uniform, slightly unzipped at the neck. A mile of fastened zipper stood between the edge of her barely revealed collarbone and her bust. This 'relaxed' look was common. The uniform's material, though remarkable, didn't breathe. Without a hint of collar bone the suit quickly became stuffy and humid. Katherine's blonde hair was half pulled back and tied. She wore exactly enough makeup to say that she was wearing makeup. It took more mental energy than he would have liked to meet her eyes and smile.

The young woman's eyes locked on the view the instant greetings had been exchanged. "My god. It's beautiful." She walked past him to the window, and Grey caught her scent dissolving into the cabin air.

The two stood silently for a long minute, staring out at their life's work. "What are you hoping for with them?" she asked, past disagreements forgotten for the moment.

The only honest answer was something Grey couldn't bring himself to say aloud. Three years of nightmares, three years of loneliness, three years of living the job as 'Captain', and now his one goal was to make sure his conscience was clear, whatever happened.

"I hope, even though there is no reason we should, that we have enough in common to build on. You?"

Katherine leaned forward and rested the side of her face on the window. A strand of hair drifted down, across the glass, and her eyes reflected the moon and planet ahead of her. "I never gave it much thought beyond fantasy. I imagined playing an alien sport on the backs of dragons, but I never expected that. My focus was on getting us here. The last three years I thought of as my job. This is yours."

"Speaking of your hard work... I hear you and Major Williams are talking about taking main power offline for a few hours to do some repairs. You could have brought that to me tonight."

"I didn't think you'd be interested in the technical details. Was I wrong?" She asked, arching an eyebrow in challenge, then shrugged, and went ahead, "how familiar are you with the secondary antimatter vent?"

Grey closed his eyes for a moment and mentally reviewed the engine schematic, "it's supposed to be completely automatic. If we have an antimatter leak, or potential leak, the computer should divert the antimatter flow out of the ship, hopefully safely. If the primary vent fails there is a secondary vent, and then a third and fourth backup. As I recall, if they all fail, we'd have about enough time for a warning light in engineering to blink before we were blown straight to hell."

"That sums it up. Know how the secondary vent works?"

"No idea. Do I need to?"

Out the window the planet slowly rotated. It was a blue and white orb, the Galileo still far too far away to visually see land. As meaningless as its appearance was on the bridge, here it was the main feature and Katherine's eyes reflected every color in creation.

"No. It was probably omitted from training because if something ever went wrong, no one would live long enough to regret their ignorance. Anyways about one time in ten it would malfunction and kill us all."

"What are the odds of us needing it? The primary vent's an emergency system anyways and this is the backup's backup?" Grey asked, interested and concerned. There was more to know about the Galileo than any one person could hope to, though Katherine was putting that to the test.

"Over the course of a twenty-year mission this would save our lives one time in a thousand," she said.

"You had me worried there."

Katherine was a poker player, and her expression was locked. She showed nothing she didn't intend to. "It's a cumulative problem. We have seven hundred critical systems on board and if each one has ten faults like this then there's a 70% chance one of them will rear its head over a twenty-year mission."

"So how did you spot it?" Grey shifted a half an inch closer.

"I've been reviewing the design of the ship in my free time looking for issues. This is the thirtieth I've found so far,"

Katherine's eyes sparkled and her posture hardened as she shifted forward slightly. Dominance of the space between them not to be yielded.

"I hope Earth's learning from the work you're sending them."

At that Katherine laughed and backed away running a hand through her blonde hair and pushing it back over her ear. "Should I have been sending it to them? I just let them know I found a fault in their system and they're idiots. That tends to get the desired result. They found another hundred or so faults looking for the ones I found."

"That's... aggressive."

Katherine looked Grey square in the eyes, delicate jaw set hard, "It's taken us from a 70% chance of death to a 57% chance, and that's just so far. I want them intimidated. I want them to tear the designs apart while I'm sleeping. I want them to know that they don't know what they're doing. I want someone there to understand that I'm keeping this ship together with *my* two hands." She raised her pale hands at that, holding them at waist height before dropping them to her thighs.

"I'm sure they know that; and if they don't: I do."

She twisted to the left and exhaled sharply before leaning back on the window, "please. No one appreciates how much work it takes to keep something working the way it should. Even you have no idea what it takes to keep your own ship running."

"You don't think I see the work you put in?"

"You see it, and you don't. You want to believe we can control what happens out here, and acknowledging how much blind luck has kept us alive so far would make that impossible. You see what you want: hard work, but no miracles."

"I do believe that we're each responsible for our own choices and, allowing for chance, we control our destinies. Isn't the alternative too depressing to be true?"

The cabin grew noticeably warmer as they talked. The Galileo's ventilation system was designed to accommodate a single person in the Captain's cabin. Two, standing, talking, and the air noticeably warmed. Or so it felt.

"My parents felt the same way as you, Captain. My brother was…" she looked up searching for the word "… impulsive. He wasn't evil. He just couldn't stop himself when he got a 'good' idea. When he was young he'd steal bikes, shoplift, anytime some 'good' idea popped into his head, he just had to do it. My parents punished him, took him to therapy, they did everything they could do. But he still wound up in jail again, and again, and again."

"I'm sorry."

Katherine shrugged. "Machines at least have a reason. They can be fixed and designed into obedience. They don't reset minimum safe distances because it pops into their head that it would be a 'good' idea."

"Ahh… That." Grey tapped the control on his arm. "We'll talk about that. But let's eat first."

Announced by the click of the hatch unclasping, a Yeoman entered the cabin. He carried a large tray with two small china plates, "dinner, sirs," he said and set the plates down on their larger cousins already on the table. The plates clinked together merrily with a sound that plastic could never simulate.

"Thank you, Yeoman, what do we have tonight?" Grey asked, knowing the answer.

The plates gave off no smell, and the food, two clumps, one brown, one white, could have been, literally, anything from engine degreaser to frozen yogurt.

"Sir, hydrated mashed potatoes, and the chef's dinner protein mix. I believe this one is number sixty-five. He calls it *Tuscany*."

Katherine's face contracted and her lips curled into a tight line before composing herself and smiling softly.

"Thank you, Yeoman, that will be all."

Cabin clear, Grey took a seat at the table. Katherine joined him, tilted her head to the right in thought, and then spoke "I'm really not hungry, sir."

"Eat anyways. The mashed potatoes weren't cheap and mess credits don't grow on trees."

A globule of what would charitably be called mashed potatoes hung from the Captain's silver fork. "I swung by the forward port airlock the other day. I like it, the completed work I mean."

Katherine took a long breath, closed her eyes, and rolled her shoulders. "I'm just amazed it took you so long to figure out it was me. I went to art school; it should be in my personnel file."

The food sat on the plates indifferent to the passage of time. 'Equilibrium' would have been the term in chemistry. It was room temperature, didn't steam, didn't lose its moisture, didn't run or contract. It simply existed, passive and waiting to be eaten. The only grace in its total passivity was a lack of smell to intrude upon those pleasant moments between bites.

"I read through those when screening candidates but haven't opened them since. I don't care what a person was like before this mission started – just what they do on this ship."

"You don't think there's relevant background... whether they're sloppy, impulsive... that helps you manage them. I used the personnel records a lot the first year or so."

"People change. This is an open-ended mission, and, as you say, a dangerous one. I don't think anyone who signed up necessarily planned on making it home. That takes something special – dedicating yourself to your job for the rest of your life. For example, were you a secret guerilla artist back on Earth?"

"No. I was not," Katherine truly smiled at that, and ran a hand through her hair, leaning forward. "Something I've always wanted to ask... Why didn't you have them scrubbed off? I thought you would."

Grey considered the question and picked up his wine glass. The pristine crystal caught the cabin lights, and the water in the glass reflected the moon and planet out the cabin's window. The water in his glass had been drunk, and pissed, by every member of the crew more than once by this point. Every drink was a toast to the power of technology. He took a small sip and let the water move around his mouth before swallowing slowly. "The first time I saw one, something about it hit me. Every inch of this ship is military issue. And here was this painting that wasn't just warm, but poking fun at all of it. It made me feel happy."

"It is nice to be appreciated... So, Captain, why did you volunteer for this mission? You obviously have a sentimental streak in you for home."

Grey set down his fork and traced the edge of the plate with the palm of a scarred hand. "I joined the US Navy because I wanted an adventure. This command though: I needed a purpose in life. I asked myself what the best thing I could possibly do with my life would be, I saw the job opening, and I knew. You?"

The young woman swallowed a small bite of protein paste. The chef's sixty-fifth attempt at mixing protein slurry into a palatable blend was a slight improvement over his sixty-fourth. "I always assumed you read my personnel report..." She pushed back a loose strand of blonde hair and glanced out the window. "You said you wanted to talk about the MSD at Jennifer's Tear."

His plate scraped clean, Grey set his fork down.

"On a ship one person, and one person only, has to take ultimate responsibility for everything. Everyone else has to defer their judgment to him, or her. You can advise me, you can lead your own department, but this is my ship, not yours. That means it's my judgment that matters, not yours."

Katherine rolled her eyes. Grey rose from the table. With three steps, he walked across his cabin and retrieved a holstered MX-3 from his locker. He drew the gun, confirmed it was loaded, and passed it to Katherine, grip first. The motion was routine, gun handling a practiced skill. "Stand up and hold this," he said and tossed the holster onto his cot. Katherine took the weapon, but her entire posture recoiled from it. She held the gun in front of her with three fingers, her pinky and ring finger raised off the handle.

"Have you ever murdered someone Katherine?"

"Of course not!" The immediate reaction was followed a moment later with a more considered reply, "I know what guilt feels like if that's what you're getting at."

"Moral responsibility is what I mean. I murdered my last crew. I thought something else was more important than their lives, than mine. So, I traded. I killed them. Everyone onboard has hopes, dreams, a great accomplished, rich, life ahead of them, or at least the chance of one. I did it again trying to save Gonzales. 1.5 kilometers was murdering Gonzales through over-caution. 100 meters was a risk, but that was the number in a split second that balanced my duties."

"That isn't murder. There's a difference," she said as her grip on the gun's handle tightened to a proper four finger grip, trigger finger resting along the edge of the weapon.

"Maybe you think murder means some drunk who gets in a bar fight or beats his wife. But cold, premeditated, murder means that the murderer thought it was the right thing to do. They have a moral code that compels them to act. Whether that code is egocentric, about killing their daughter's rapist, about pride and killing their daughter because she had sex, or something external like the borders of a nation, or civil rights. Killing isn't an accident, it is something that was considered, accepted, and then carried out." Grey looked up to the cabin's overhead, "I spent a long time asking myself why I felt so dirty about what I'd done. I had saved lives. Thousands of them.

But I'd also formed a resolve to deliberately end the lives of the people under my command. That's what command really is, and it's murder. So, we're going to settle our little power struggle right now."

His eyes turned down, on the gun, as Katherine considered the comment.

"If you really think I'm reckless, a danger to this ship; if you think you're right and you're willing to take moral responsibility for the choice, then you take that gun, point it at my chest, and pull the trigger."

Katherine looked down at the weapon in her small hand. Grey could see the wheels turning in her head. He prodded further, "you won't be punished. They need you too much to do that. And for me, in honesty, it'd be a relief."

"And what if I refuse, just hand the gun back?"

"That's a choice too. That's you choosing to defer your moral judgments to mine. That's you choosing to accept my command."

Katherine's body tightened, readying itself for whatever came next.

"How did you ever get through psych screening with such a sense of arrogance?" She asked, almost spitting the words.

"Arrogance is our job description Katherine: a thirty-two-year-old Captain, chosen at twenty-six, to be humanity's representative to the galaxy with virtually no supervision or oversight. To represent all of mankind, including the 99.999% who had no say whatsoever in who their representative was going to be. I'm charged with the lives of a ship full of people, many of whom will die by my, or your, command. That's not a job for the humble."

With an explosive exhalation, Katherine handed the gun back to him.

"Every time I think I have seen a new depth of stupidity on this ship…"

The conversation was cut off as Grey's armband chimed. 'Captain to the Bridge. Surface ballistic launch detected.'

"Navigation: time to intercept!" He turned to Katherine, "can we go to 100% power?"

Katherine gave her own armor segment a half a glance, then tapped it, "engineering prepare for 100% on the reactor, and charge shield capacitors."

Katherine, without a word more, sprinted out of the cabin on her way to the rest of her armor in engineering. Light footsteps echoed down the corridor behind her. Captain Grey clasped on his own armor, cursing himself for having ever taken it off.

The comms chimed back online, "Sir, navigation reports no intercept vector. Vehicle has entered orbit and is moving to pass behind the planet. It does have an intersecting orbital plane with our position."

Armor on, Captain Grey walked to the bridge, hand jammed into his helmet. Fear was contagious on a ship and a seemingly confident leader its vaccination. He entered the bridge and took his seat like a king taking the throne then donned his helmet.   Ensign Arnold manned the bridge's engineering station; they had been caught on a training shift.

"Navigation, let's see where she is," he said.

The view screen shifted to a render of the planet below and two orbital paths, the Galileo's just beyond the moon, and a small object orbiting just above the planet's atmosphere, about to pass out of sight. "Has she stayed ballistic Ensign?"

For all the effort that had gone into making the bridge a calm oasis, Grey hoped his voice stayed as flat as Arnold had managed during her test.

"Yes sir. We observed an initial surface launch, it appeared to be two stages, and then an insertion burn but nothing else. Classic orbital insertion."

Grey considered the plots: of the responses he had expected, this was not one.

"Ensign Arnold. You've been brushing up on orbital tactics. If you were our contact, how would you be planning an attack right now?"

As the reactor moved to 100% power the noise of the ship shifted. Systems that had been in low power modes came up to full function. The ventilation system cycled up to circulate and remove the excess heat these systems generated.

It wasn't just the ship that had moved to full power. Grey felt his hot breath bouncing back onto his face after each exhalation inside his helmet. His heart thumped faster in his chest just as his ship's engine did. A buzz of adrenaline slowed down digestion and poured the saved energy to his muscles, sharpened his vision, and peaked the primal parts of his brain.

"Sir, I see two options. First, if they had enough power they could overcome the orbital dynamics of the situation and come out from the planet's shadow virtually anywhere at any speed. But why give us the kind of notice they have? If they have that much power why not just blast off from the planet straight for us before we have any time to react? Unless of course it's some kind of bluff or there're technical limits we don't know."

"Let's assume for the moment that their launch gives us an honest estimate of their technological sophistication. Multiple stage rocket engine – technically impressive but technologically inferior. What then?"

"In that case sir, option two. Use the planet's gravity and the time in shadow to thrust unseen and sling shot out from behind the orbit faster than we expected. As you say they don't know our level of technology and might think they have a chance of taking us by surprise with those kinds of speeds."

Captain Grey considered through a haze of adrenaline. It would have been so easy to let the unthinking part of his mind take over. It wanted to. But the man forced the beast back. Neither option sounded correct. They knew the Galileo had come from outside their solar system. That meant technology superior to their own if they were using rocket engines, which meant a simple gravity slingshot maneuver would be unlikely to get the kinds of speeds necessary to tip the scales in combat.

"How much 20th century Apollo history do you know, Ensign?" it was a rhetorical question, and Grey didn't wait for an answer, "when man was first attempting to land on the moon the Apollo rockets could have simply launched straight for their target. Instead they always completed an orbit of the Earth before thrusting towards the moon. It let them do a shakedown on the ship, make sure she had survived launch. What if that's what they're doing?"

Major Williams marched onto the bridge. Grey couldn't hear his breath, but the man's shoulders, slightly rising and falling, could usually be used to level a shelf.

Grey tapped his console and activated the ship-wide intercom. "Communications – Bridge. Send a priority message to earth. Message reads, 'making contact.'" Grey could only imagine the commotion in the ship as he addressed the crew.

"Moments ago we detected a ballistic rocket launch from the planet. We suspect their next stop will be here. We're going to attempt peaceful contact." The intercom fell silent, and Grey turned his attention back to the display.

Over-pressured heart beats thumped in his jaw as Grey watched and waited. If the ship had accelerated while behind the planet, and emerged from eclipse sooner than expected, it was almost certainly a sign of hostility. Almost. Of all the myths of science fiction he most wished that hailing frequencies and universal translators were a reality.

"Corporal we do have all sensors on their maximum gains, correct?"

"Yes sir."

"Bridge to Navigation: make recommendations on improving sensor resolution." Not that there should be anything.

Navigation reported a moment later. They must have known the question was coming or had been thinking along the same lines themselves. "Navigation to Bridge: advice coming about to 9-0 by zero by 1-5." The comm line clicked off and Grey winced. Navigation had suggested pointing the ship towards the planet, which it had been until he ordered a change to improve the view from his cabin.

"Make it so Corporal." The Galileo rotated towards the planet, bringing its most powerful sensor arrays onto a clear line of sight. Grey didn't breathe until his display continued to show no contacts. He could have just lost the ship trying to impress a girl.

If the alien ship hadn't accelerated, it was thirty seconds from exiting the planet's shadow. Grey counted down the time and tried to will the display to stay clear. The only thing worse than the ship appearing early, would be it appearing late. Putting a ship into orbit was hugely energy expensive and slowing down, or worse, stopping, meant they were significantly more advanced than they appeared to be.

As the final three seconds ticked down, Captain Grey strained to see the individual pixels of the display along the planet's edge. The countdown hit zero, and there was nothing; Grey inhaled to begin issuing orders when a ship appeared on the display. The radar signal that should have first detected the ship had been slightly distorted by the edge of the planet's atmosphere, delaying identification for a fraction of a second.

"Ensign, confirm course and speed is unchanged."

Titanium encased, delicate fingers tapped the diamond console surface with sharp clicks. The fingers of the gauntlet had been handmade, a rubber pad tapered off to the edge with titanium forming a fingernail.

"Sir, no change in course or speed, however the ship has now reoriented itself."

"Alright. They might initiate a burn towards us. If they do, I want to know their intercept time immediately."

Major Williams more turned than walked to the set of computer terminals at the back of the bridge and began tapping at them slowly. "Captain... that ship didn't come from nowhere. We've been having a devil of a time getting surface pictures that make any sense. Some fool forgot to give us the right software to compensate for atmospheric distortion and planet rotation. But, with the launch coordinates..." Williams' voice trailed off and the main display switched over to an aerial photograph of an empty field. A road ran to its center, cutting a path through golden grass. For nearly two kilometers in every direction the ground looked flat, manicured almost. At the apex of the road, in the middle of the field, there was a structure of some sort, the view from directly overhead provided almost no information about its shape.

"This is the launch site? When?" Grey asked.

"The day we arrived, sir... Let me check the logs... Yes, we have photos of these coordinates on four different days. This image is from three days after we arrived."

A new image filled the screen. This one was virtually indistinguishable from the first except for its angle. It must have been taken slightly later in the day as the structure in the middle of the field was captured at a twenty-degree angle and was obviously a launch tower. Scaffolding extended upwards with horizontal arms to hold a rocket vertical for launch though there was no such rocket.

"And this is a week after we arrived..." The next image to flash on the screen was useless. There must have been cloud cover and the image was just a grey blur. Grey could almost hear Williams grind his teeth in frustration as he tapped the console for the last image.

"This one was taken a week and a half after we arrived."

"Jesus," Grey said reflexively. The image couldn't have been more different. The launch pad was surrounded by hundreds of black blobs of various sizes, the entire image fuzzy and out of focus. "The day's take was corrupted by a software bug. But you can tell they were doing something – probably building a rocket."

That explanation made sense, in an abstract way. There was far too much activity evident for them to just be putting together a vehicle fabricated somewhere else. But no matter how simple a ship, no one could build a spaceship in a few days.

"Major, on Earth what do you think it would take, to design, fabricate, test, and launch a simple ship, assuming you had designs that only needed minor mission modifications?" Grey asked.

Ensign Arnold interrupted the answer, "sir! Alien ship initiating a burn. Accelerating on a direct course towards us. Intercept in 30 days, 20 days, 10 days, still accelerating, 1 day to intercept, 10 hours to intercept, 4 hours, 2 hours to intercept. Acceleration stopped, intercept in 1 hour 48 minutes."

"They don't waste much time do they?" Major Williams commented over the open channel.

Corporal Tsang, his voice rising, "sir! Alien ship is radiating on the same frequency we broadcast our introduction on!"

Grey's breath caught, "put it through to comms. See if they can make something of it."

"No need, sir. It's an analog broadcast, too little bandwidth to be video, probably audio, we can try playing the signal directly."

Three pulsing heartbeats later and Grey realized he was holding his breath. He forced himself to exhale and then take a slow breath in. The audio systems switched on. Everyone jumped out of their skin. Anyone who had an AM radio would have known what to expect, but the Galileo's crew were all born too late for that, and the loud burst of static caught them off guard. When the system was tuned, Grey's brain refused to process what it was hearing. Of everything he had expected, this was the last thing. Grey and Williams exchanged a glance, the old man equally caught off guard. The alien message repeated. It was a voice, a woman's voice speaking English, British English. The message repeated a third time over the speakers and Grey was still at a loss for words.

"Are you a good wolf, or a bad wolf?" The message asked. Even the inflection of the question was correct.

Major Williams was the first to talk. "Tsang, if this is a joke I am going to personally throw you out an airlock."

Ensign Arnold laughed, "it is a joke, sir! We sent them Doctor Who and the Wizard of Oz and they are making a Doctor Who meets the Wizard of Oz joke!"

"I'm a bit behind on my Doctor Who, Ensign."

"They are asking if we're good, or bad, sir."

"How do we say we're good?" Ensign Arnold reached for the control to reply and hesitated, her hand hovered over the console, "may I, sir?" Grey nodded and gave first contact to his junior officer.

With the tap of a finger Mindy Arnold activated a simple radio broadcast. "But I'm not a wolf at all," she said softly.

Mindy held her breath as a few seconds ticked by, nothing but static on the channel. Then the woman's voice returned, "my name is Dorothy. Welcome to Kansas."

"My name is Peter Grey. I'm the Captain of this ship, called the Galileo. We come from a planet called Earth and we want to peacefully learn about you, your people, and your world."

The alien, Dorothy, had a musical voice. She jumped from tone to tone with gusto, as though she were playing with the British accent she wielded so perfectly.

"We're eager to meet you. But before we invite you to bring your ship closer, we'd like to come aboard."

The com line silent, Grey turned to Major Williams, "thoughts?"

"I imagine we'd want the same if someone showed up to Earth. We can't quarantine the whole ship though," he said.

The seconds ticked by. Some decisions, life altering decisions, have to be made from the gut. There was a moment to act if the invitation was to be credibly accepted, and there was not enough time for Captain Grey to reason out his options. So he went with his gut. "Dorothy. We'd welcome you aboard, however our ship is not always safe. There are many areas that are dangerous. We were planning to wear special suits when we visited your world that would protect you from any diseases or microbes we carried."

The radio cracked back, "that's kind of you, but we've had germs dealt with for some time. Myself and my ship are free of them, and my immune system will protect me from any of yours."

Grey tried to shrug but found his shoulders held fast by his chair, "in that case it would be our pleasure to have you onboard."

"Thank you. I look forward to it."

The radio clicked off and Major Williams, be it out of mercy for his Captain, or genuine shock, asked the question. "Ensign Arnold what the hell just happened?"

"Sir, did you watch the videos in the first contact package? We sent hours of Doctor Who and the Wizard of Oz," she said.

"And their message was some kind of reference to that?" Williams asked.

While the two talked Captain Grey used the time to think. It didn't really matter what the content of the message was. The format was the important thing. The aliens had made a joke, a play, a twist on Earth's own popular culture, and that meant something. He had a few seconds to figure out what.

"... she tells them she isn't a witch at all."

"Ok. Hilarious. And the bad wolf?" Major Williams pressed on.

"In Doctor Who there was a recurring message for the doctor calling him 'Bad Wolf.' It was funny because he was a good person and not wolf-like at all."

"Alright, also hilarious. Say the only reason they haven't attacked is because they want to see whether we are a threat or not," Williams said.

"And that'd be a bad thing?" Grey asked, "if we were in their shoes we'd want to take a look around an alien ship before it closed in on Earth. If you think about it, it would be kind of rude to land in Washington, roll down the ramp and demand to see our leaders." Grey tensed at another obvious truth, "but... Major, if we were on Earth, and an alien ship showed up, and we sent a mission up to have a look, what else would we do?"

Williams looked at the track on the view screen as he would a viper snaking towards him. It was easy to imagine his face harden inside his helmet as he realized. "I'd also send up my biggest nuke and if anyone twitched, or my boarding party thought they posed a threat, I would blow them straight to hell."

"So, if there is no bomb on that ship?" Grey asked

"Then they're more trusting than I'd be."

Grey considered for a moment, "Bridge to Engineering – prepare a shuttle for immediate launch to escort the alien ship in and perform a close scan on route."

"Engineering to Bridge: the shuttles are both being prepared to land on the planet. They're half apart on the cargo bay floor. I can have them for you in two days," Katherine's voice cracked back.

"They don't need to be perfect Major just get them flying."

"Yes sir. Thirty minutes I can give you two big fireballs about fifteen seconds after launch. Who should I have pilot them? I'll make sure they know to get goodbye's sent."

Grey rolled his eyes.

"Fine. Let's make it easy for her to dock at least. Corporal, come to heading 2-7-0 by zero. Ensign Arnold please have the aft starboard airlock illuminated and outer doors opened." The Galileo rotated to show its right-hand side to the approaching craft and activated external lights around the open airlock. She rolled out the welcome mat as it were.

"Major Williams, Major Bakker, my cabin," Grey ordered, then disengaged himself from his seat and led Major Williams off the bridge.

His hair was slick with sweat, as he removed his helmet. He hadn't realized he was sweating and was going to need a shower before meeting an alien.

Katherine jogged up to Grey's cabin as he arrived. He made a mental note to talk to his senior officer about the need to project calm.

Inside the cabin all three began stripping off their armor pieces acutely aware the clock was ticking.

"We're exactly seventy-eight minutes away from having a guest, or guests," the Captain said, eyes flashed up from his arm's display. "Has anyone ever given any thought to what protocols we have for aliens coming up to visit?"

Williams and Katherine returned blank looks.

"Fine. Let's take ten minutes and see what we can come up with. Suggestions?" The biggest decisions were left to those bold enough to simply be first.

"Need to know," Williams fired back at once.

Katherine wiped her brow with a finger, clearing a stray, blonde hair, "partial disclosure. Nothing technical, nothing about our capabilities or how our technology works. They're obviously more advanced than we are and being coy is going to do more for us tactically than being open," Katherine countered.

"The hell they're more advanced," Williams said. "Chemical rockets, orbital shakedowns, slow approach burns? We could get from the surface to here in a few minutes. It's taking them the better part of three hours." Williams' voice rough and fast.

There wasn't time to think it through, just gut feelings. Grey started talking the second Williams stopped, "I'm inclined to agree with Williams. Everything we've seen so far says we have the technological edge."

Katherine walked over to the Captain's door controls, jostling Williams as she moved through the cramped cabin. She hit the switch to lock the cabin then hit the button to open the door, nothing happened, the door stayed closed and locked.

"That isn't supposed to happen," Katherine said. "No one's noticed because it makes sense: lock the door, and the door doesn't open. But what's the point of locking a door from the inside to stop yourself getting out? The specs call for the door to open from the inside, locked or not. The contractor installing it messed up, and so did a decade of quality control, inspections, and three years living with it. You know how much stuff in this ship doesn't work the way it should? They built a ship in a week. They unraveled our language in two weeks. Their pilot learned a new language from a few hours of videos, in the same week that she prepared for an unplanned intercept mission. I'm not saying we don't have a more powerful ship, we do. I'm saying we have absolutely no idea what these aliens are capable of. Maybe they just don't like spaceships but have all sorts of crazy technology on their planet we can't even imagine."

Grey looked to Williams, "maybe they don't like spaceships..."

Williams shrugged.

It was time for Grey to choose, "ok, anything they want to know except when it comes to the secret sauce and performance data on shields, engines, and Earth's position. I don't want anyone with Fermi knowledge on the same deck as our guest."

Major Williams pressed, "what about weapons."

"Isn't that what you'd want to know the most about if you were them?" Katherine asked.

"Exactly," Williams said.

"Our weapons aren't that technologically impressive," Katherine's voice sped up, excited, "lasers, rail guns, and some antimatter bombs. We do a good job making them have a big punch, but there is nothing special about them."

"Agreed," Grey looked to Williams, "so let's assume for a moment we say hello, it doesn't want to kill us all, and things are going ok. Where do we take it?"

Williams shrugged, and Katherine raised her right eyebrow in an expression that asked whether he was seriously asking her.

"I could always use a bite to eat after a long trip," Williams eventually suggested.

"Alright... If we survive this, I want some serious thought given to how we entertain alien visitors aboard this ship. For now, first stop's the mess hall. Katherine, get a dozen crewmen who don't have pressing duties, and aren't fools, and get them into the mess. Warn them to be on their best behavior."

"What if it comes in shooting?" Katherine asked.

Major Williams answered, "security teams on the deck above and below the whole time?"

"Do it," Grey said, "but tell them I expect that alien to be given a world of slack. That thing rips my head off and says oops nobody shoots unless it does it again. That isn't a joke major. For all we know they shake hands by eating a bit of each other's brains."

With the push of a button Grey addressed the ship, "a few minutes ago we were contacted by an alien ship on an intercept course for us. They said that their intentions are peaceful, but they wish to inspect our ship before allowing us to approach their planet. We have agreed and we expect them to dock in just over one hour. All personnel are to report to their duty stations. I want all equipment stowed, and all quarters in inspection condition. If the alien or aliens come into your section you are to extend every courtesy, answer every question they have unless it relates to our engines, shields, or Earth's location, in which case direct it to your superiors. If you believe the alien is about to take a hostile action, you are to give it the benefit of the doubt. And, assuming the alien is friendly, try not to monopolize it's time." Grey shut off the comm. "Now if you two will excuse me I need a shower."

Major Bakker cleared her throat, "Sir, we should discuss who actually meets it. If it's hostile, we can't lose the whole senior staff."

"That's the easy part, Major. I'm meeting it alone. Williams you're in command if anything happens. Bakker, I want you in engineering."

CHAPTER 9

UNIFORM IN A CRUMPLED MESS ON THE DECK, two dozen armored plates scattered beside it, Grey walked into his cabin's head. His cabin was cramped, the head was coffin-like. The mere existence of a private washroom must have been considered luxury enough by its resentful designers. There was a small toilet, a sink, and a shower stall.

Nothing happened as Grey walked into his shower. He was on the clock. He swore and waved a hand at the showerhead: nothing. He waved both hands. He assumed the motion sensor was embedded in the showerhead. It took ten seconds of naked dancing before the shower started and Grey cursed it again. In three years, over a thousand showers, he might have had a dozen that worked the way they should have.

He considered removing the day's stubble but doubted that their alien guest would care; or know to care.

"50/50 some kind of spider monster eats me? A spider monster with a sense of humor?" He spoke aloud as he showered.

The water abruptly shut off and required another minute of frantic, nude, dancing to coax back on. The action made Grey feel especially powerful and dignified moments before making first contact.

As always, the shower shut off without problem when he was done. The precision of its negative response always left Grey suspicious of its motives. Jets of hot air blasted him from all sides and quickly blew every drop of water from his now clean-ish body. Without a chemical scrub before the shower, the best the water could do was dissolve some grime. Every drip of oil and grease that had built up on him was still there.

He was now far over budget on water use. It had crossed the line from an indulgence to abusive. A fifty percent chance said he was going to end up as spider food, and he resolved to deal with his water problems if he survived.

Tsang was the obvious person to speak with. But, like every business, there were competitors and Grey would rather not deal with a crewman he worked directly with. He would rather not dabble in the ship's black market at all, but water reclamation had to be balanced, and he had to have showers. On the other hand, it could also be a chance to reach out to Tsang: something to consider, after first contact.

Armored, collected, and as fresh as he was going to get without a vacation, Grey got to the airlock with ten minutes to spare. He had barely stopped walking when his hands began to itch. His gloves, along with his helmet, were back in his cabin, and he rubbed the scarred flesh with his palms, alternating one hand to the other.

He could remember every detail, every smell, every ounce of pain, from the moment the emergency call had come in, until he was hauled out of the water five hours later, but as he thought back to his first command, the Gazer, he couldn't remember how that day had started. Had he felt different? Had he felt the hairs on the back of his neck stand up when he shaved that morning? Was this going to be a day like that day had been?

For all his training, all his education, deep down a part of him was sure that it could divine what would come through the airlock ahead of him based on how he felt.

Outside the Galileo, the alien ship used its thrusters liberally to match the Galileo's heading and speed. Each thrust was carefully monitored on the bridge for a hint of the aliens' technological abilities. Bringing a ship on an intersecting course with another was easy, having their speeds and headings match when they met was a function of sensor accuracy, the precision of thrusters, and the competence of the pilot.

Along the starboard side of the Galileo every window was filled with faces trying to get a look at the alien craft. Unlike Jennifer's Tear which had been adrift in interstellar space, inside the solar system the aliens' sun provided ample illumination and reflected off the small ship's skin. It was visible from hundreds of miles away for those with sharp enough eyes. Had Grey been wearing his helmet its internal displays could have shown a feed of the ship approaching. He could have seen its brushed aluminum skin, the cone shaped capsule so reminiscent of Earth's own Apollo missions. Instead the young man stood waiting, helmet in his quarters, with an airlock door separating him from fate and hard vacuum.

The alien ship slowed as its engines flared. When it had matched the Galileo's trajectory, and speed, a mere three kilometers separated the two ships. The alien ship was not just similar to the Apollo capsules, it could have been displayed in the Smithsonian and not one person in ten would have known something was amiss.

With exact thrusts the alien capsule gently closed the distance and rotated itself until a single flaw in its hull, a circular hatch, lined up with the Galileo's illuminated airlock. A dozen yards separated the two ships when the hatch opened. Relative to the planet below they were both traveling at thousands of kilometers an hour yet, to each other, it was as though they were frozen in amber.

A figure emerged from the alien ship and leapt through the vacuum towards the Galileo.

On the other side of the airlock door, Grey heard something land against the hull, then footsteps. The deck under Grey's feet rumbled slightly as the outer airlock doors closed. Air hissed into the airlock and when it stopped something shuffled on the other side.

A bright green button would be illuminated on the console inside the airlock. A simple push and the inner door would open. Of course Grey could order the door open, but he waited.

Three and a half minutes ticked by, four hundred beats of Grey's heart, before the inner airlock door's internal locks released, and metal parted open.

It took a shamefully large amount of mental effort not to take a step back as the doors opened.

The alien threw itself forward.

Captain Peter Grey had exactly enough time to process the thought 'girl' before it, she, embraced him. His body went rigid. She was soft and squeezed herself gently against him.

A moment later the alien released the embrace. She was short, her head barely reached the middle of Grey's neck. A quick glance revealed that she had, essentially, all the 'normal' parts: two arms, two legs, hair, a face with a mouth, a nose, and eyes, even a slight bulge in the chest where breasts would be.

Not only was she recognizably a woman, she was a beautiful one. A casual glance, Grey didn't want to stare, revealed only two immediate differences from a human woman. Her skin, while smooth and undeniably supple, was a deep bronze. Michelangelo might have picked this shade had he been hired to paint the Virgin Mary, after she'd spent a summer overdoing it on a beach.

The second difference was her legs. Her knees bent backwards, and it looked like she was wearing a pair of high heels in reverse. The shoes would have broken any human's ankle with the first step. A glance behind her revealed a black space suit and helmet crumpled on the deck of the airlock.

Grey had worked with officers and enlisted men from a hundred different countries. He'd seen uniforms designed for everything from combat to playing polo. He'd also seen all those men after hours, and the woman before him wore clothes that screamed civilian.

Her top was a white knit fabric, her pants a dark brown that flattered her skin and was shapely. Her boots looked artificial, shining, black, and decorated with pointless chrome and leather fastenings. She even wore jewelry, a necklace, and earrings.

"My name's Dorothy," her voice had the same rhythmic, easy, dance as it had over the radio.

"Mine is Peter Grey. I am the Captain of this ship, the Galileo." At least he got the basics correct.

"Thank you for inviting me…" her voice trailed off as she looked eagerly around the corridor like a child, her attention darted from Grey to the wall panels, to his uniform, and the airlock behind her.

"Would you like a tour of the ship?" Grey asked. There was a little speech somewhere in his cabin. Something about footsteps, and friendship, and bridging distances. Neil Armstrong had two lines, and he botched the first. If there was an afterlife, he and Grey would down a bottle of something and talk about how history and speeches shouldn't be mixed.

Dorothy smiled, her teeth were flatter than human's yet still teeth and still smiling as a human would. "Yes. Take me to your leaders!" she sang the words, bursting into laughter. "I'm sorry this is all overwhelming," a smile was still on her lips even as she apologized.

For a half a second Grey questioned whether she was entirely sober, pushed the thought aside, then wondered if this was some kind of prank, and pushed the thought aside again. He did a quarter bow, turned to his side, and waved his arm down the hall. He nearly fell when she took the unspoken offer up, and grabbed his free arm pulling him forward with her.

"You're not what I imagined..." was all he could choke out as he was led down the hall of his own ship by Dorothy. 'How could her name be Dorothy?' he asked himself but pushed that aside as well. He had a rapidly growing list of unanswered questions, and that made him cautious. On the other hand he wasn't spider shit yet, and that was a positive sign.

"That's the pot calling the kettle black," Dorothy said, "do you have any idea how much heartache you caused by showing up looking like we do? Joking like we do? Behaving like we do? Have you met any other aliens? You're our first. Are there more out there like us?" She slowed her pace and looked up into his eyes searching for answers.

"You're our first as well. To be perfectly honest I would have been happy to find a plant or insect, never mind a walking, talking, thinking person."

"Our thoughts exactly, that's why we never bothered looking. We thought that if we were lucky enough to find intelligent life we wouldn't be able to talk to it. A number of very eminent scientists had their status questioned because of your arrival. It feels great actually. We're not often wrong, and it's a fun experience."

Dorothy gave Grey's arm a squeeze, "so, tell me about this ship of yours. If anything it seems a bit smaller on the inside than it is on the outside."

The two walked arm and arm down the hallway, Grey silently guiding their path towards the mess hall. "What would you like to know? We have seventy-three people on board, men and women."

Dorothy interjected, "what does it mean? Galileo?"

After three years of recycled air, Grey could smell spring on his guest. Her clothes, hair, and skin were saturated with the smell of flowers, pollen, even sunlight. The smells were different from those of Earth, but his brain registered the life in it nonetheless.

"Galileo was the name of one of Earth's great scientists. When we were living in stone buildings, before electricity, Galileo figured out that the Earth rotated around our sun.

People had always thought that the sun rotated around our planet."

"It's good to hear that you venerate a man of science and not the warriors of your kind," she said.

"Warriors are celebrated in life, scientists in history. But scientists who really change the world are never loved in their own lives, too many people have too much to lose when the world changes. Galileo was persecuted by the religious fanatics running his country and was nearly executed."

Dorothy grimaced, "we went through our own periods of that. Terrible what people will do to one another when they think they are acting for a cause." She counterbalanced herself with Grey's arm and leaned in towards an exposed wall panel. Inside three dozen shielded optical cables connected with a micro-processing hub routing signals to engineering.

"How do your people disseminate scientific knowledge?" she asked.

The question took the Captain back to university, a psychology elective he had taken for fun in first year. "Scientific knowledge? When a scientist runs an experiment with interesting results they write a paper describing what they did and their results. They submit it to one of several journals, and the journal asks other scientists in that field to review the paper and comment on it. If they think it's important and well done the journal will publish it and other scientists and researchers in the field will read the journals regularly to keep up to date on the latest developments."

Dorothy laughed, "well that's something we'll be able to help you with at least."

The two arrived at an anonymous hatch along the hallway. "This is the mess hall. It's where the crew eats their meals. There're going to be a few crewmen inside eager to see you. Are you ok with a bit of a crowd?"

A grin was her only reply and she tapped the console beside the mess hatch. It slid open and she led the Captain in.

Imagine a doorknob. After a lifetime of seeing doorknobs, of expecting them on nearly every door, there's a part of the brain that recognizes what to do with a door lever: grab and twist, just like a knob, but different. Green buttons mean go, or safe, red buttons mean stop or danger. Dorothy had never seen the controls before, yet she worked them flawlessly. They were supposed to be intuitive, but intuitive to humans based on a lifetime living on Earth. Just how deeply had she assimilated the videos they sent.

The Galileo's mess was large enough to seat three dozen crewmen at a time. A dozen small square tables dotted the room and three large machines served as food dispensers.

The food dispensers were each the size of a refrigerator and contained images of food to select from along with a single slot at waist height that dispensed trays. A few crewmen sat at tables, their trays for show, more however stood by the mess windows, the planet below in view.

The mess might have been described as cold, impersonal, antiseptic, except for one wall. Just to the right of the mess' hatch, an internal wall had been adorned with a collection of items. The most prominent one was a pipe segment, two meters long, and four inches wide. In the center of the segment a charred, gaping, hole blew outwards. Just to the left of the pipe was a glass sample container with a handful worth of black rocks. A few drops of perspiration clung to the inner wall of the container. There were other items, a plastic ballpoint pen, an aluminum buckle with a frayed nylon cable running through it. There was no explanation needed to the Galileo's crew about the backstory of the items.

Every eye in the room was on Dorothy. She would likely have drawn less attention had she been a six-legged, lizard creature.

She released Grey's arm, walked into the room as though she were walking into a friend's party, and offered to shake the hand of the crewmen closest to the door: Corporal Taylor.

Grey didn't exactly see his life flash before his eyes; he did however see a significant portion of it leading to this encounter. He had met Corporal Taylor for the first time, 'in the field', while she was working in Antarctica. The Antarctic summers, in contrast to winters, were cool but survivable. Corporal Taylor, just Maggie at that point, was on a two-month expedition to the continent looking for some kind of rock. She was five foot six, five-five without heavy duty field boots, had auburn hair and freckled heavily in the sun. She was also one of the most-soft spoken people Grey had ever met, which suited her appearance.

Two months after launch, Maggie had come to him asking to cross train in security. It was common for the crew to cross train. Some were qualified in four different areas, which Grey thought was to be expected when intelligent, driven, people were cooped up with little else to do for years on end.

Maggie's request was a surprise. The soft spoken, gentle woman wanted to suck up a huge amount of P.T. and weapons training. More interestingly, as Williams taught the courses, it wasn't just about learning the skills. A person had to have a switch in their brain that would let them inflict horrendous violence on others and Williams had to see it turned on to pass them. Most didn't have it, and Grey didn't think Maggie, of all people, did. But there was no reason to stand in her way and he'd kept an interested eye on her ever-increasing combat aptitude reports.

Williams had created a monster. The diminutive Taylor not only could inflict sadistic injuries, she could shrug off the same in turn. The week before, Corporal Taylor had literally ripped a crewman's arm out of its socket when he'd surprised her from behind. A year before that Williams had snapped her forearm in training, and she was back at it as soon as the bone healed. And now Dorothy had picked a rose, with thorns of titanium, to smell.

Dorothy was adept at making friends, and a twinkle in her eye infected Maggie. A few seconds after the two had shaken hands Maggie laughed and the women traded their earrings. Grey's heart restarted.

Dorothy charmed her way through the rest of the room and what had been apprehension was replaced with smiles. When Dorothy's attention eventually turned to the food machines, Grey resumed his role as tour guide.

"Each crewman's activity is tracked, and the machine gives them two meals a day; lunch and dinner," Grey explained. "We do grow a small amount of food onboard, but it's rationed. The vast majority of our food is pre-packaged."

Dorothy gently ran her fingers over the images the machine displayed.

"You can pick your flavor, but really it's all just a paste made up of the needed chemicals."

Dorothy looked disappointed. It was the same look Grey had the first time he was briefed on the nutritional arrangements for the voyage. "You enjoy it?" she asked.

"No. But it's a sacrifice worth making."

"How long have you been traveling?" Dorothy asked, tapped a button with the image of corn, and bent down. Grey retrieved his ration card and tapped it to the machine. A globule of yellow paste extruded onto a tray in the dispenser as Dorothy watched, rapt.

"Three years," Grey replied, and then considered the absurdity of explaining anything using units. "Each year has three hundred and sixty-five days, each day has twenty-four hours, each hour has sixty minutes, and each minute has sixty seconds." He raised his arm turning the displayed time towards Dorothy as best he could, and tapped it to show the seconds, "that's a second. So..." he paused to do the math.

Dorothy cut in without a moment's hesitation, "ninety-four point six million of those." She dipped a finger into the globule of 'corn' and moved it to her mouth. Grey raised a hand, moving it towards the gap between her hand and mouth in warning, "you sure you want to be eating alien food?" Dorothy gently extracted her arm, shrugged, and licked her finger.

"Not bad, but ninety-four point six million that's, of this, is just depressing," she sucked her finger clean and grabbed Grey's arm. "So, what's the next stop on the tour?"

CHAPTER 10

"DON'T TOUCH ANYTHING," Major Katherine Bakker used a tone that would have brought any of the crew back to kindergarten. "I really can't stress enough how dangerous everything in engineering is. There're bare power wires, panels that are charged, pieces of equipment that are unbelievably hot, or coated with toxic chemicals."

Dorothy shifted her weight onto her right foot, and bent her left leg unnaturally forward, at the knee. The reverse articulation of her legs would have caused Katherine to shudder if she hadn't taken the stretch as an insult. Katherine straightened her back and expanded up to her full height.

"To be honest I don't really care about engines and conduits..." Dorothy glanced along the empty hallway. The two women stood outside a heavy double sliding door bearing foot high red lettering 'Engineering - Restricted Access'. Dorothy's features, perfect and color coordinated with what must have been make-up, were only drawn out more by Katherine's obviously bare face. Even their clothes spoke of a chasm in life experience; Katherine wore her armored uniform, helmet clasped in a titanium hand, and Dorothy was ready for a date.

"Well, what can I tell you about then?" Katherine's voice was neutral as she tried to work out whether to be relieved at not having to take the alien on a tour of her domain, or offended that the alien wasn't more interested in her life's work.

"What was it like growing up on Earth? Can you tell me a story about your family?"

The human face has dozens of muscles. Some move by conscious design, others will betray emotion unless well trained. Katherine wouldn't show anything unless she wanted to. Every one of her face's muscles registered its own tiny hint of displeasure at the question.

With a swing of the arm Katherine tapped the control panel next to Engineering's door. The heavy doors clicked and parted. "Let me show you what we have here," Katherine turned her back to the guest and walked into her lair.

Entering engineering was like being four inches tall and walking under the skin of a well-maintained airplane. It was pristinely clean but the space for human activity was dictated by what the room's equipment did not need. Everything in the massive room was odd in its scale. A screw was just as likely to be the size of a pinky finger as it was a forearm. A half a dozen engineers moved through the room expertly weaving past one another, and the outcroppings of equipment, as they worked.

By far the largest, and most focal, piece of equipment was a spherical tank in the center of the room. Machines the size and shape of refrigerators grew out of it like spikes on a porcupine.

The sight of it turned Dorothy's face blank and ashen. She came to a dead stop and simply stared a mile ahead. It was as though a switch had been thrown. She blinked, and it was over. Her eyes danced over the room. She shuffled forward and side to side with tiny steps as she maneuvered for views of various items, "my dear this isn't a fusion reactor, is it?" She gestured to a massive reaction vessel connected to the spherical tank by a meter wide pipe. "Where are the pumps and fluid exchangers?" She shuffled over to Katherine. "Is it antimatter?" Dorothy asked in a hushed whisper.

"I thought you weren't interested in this kind of thing," Katherine started, surprised.

"My life's work. My life's work. But this... I never thought I'd see it," Dorothy said.

Confused, Katherine began the introduction to the Galileo's engines she had given a hundred times on Earth before the journey started. "The Galileo is powered by antimatter..." no need to explain what that was, she moved on, "we use Gadolinium as the antimatter base element. That's what we call the element with 64 protons in its nucleus."

Dorothy cut her off, "because of its magnetic properties, high atomic weight, and ease of handling. Yes, yes, that makes sense. How much is in there?" Dorothy asked with a wave at the huge sphere.

Katherine considered a moment; units wouldn't be much help. She stretched out her arms as far as she could, "a sphere a little wider than this."

Dorothy blinked in surprise, "that is enough to power our planet for a lifetime."

"How did you work that out so quickly?" Katherine asked perplexed at the speed of that calculation. Converting the diameter of a sphere into its volume was easy enough, then the mass of Gadolinium inside was doable, if you were up to speed on your periodic table. But it was something that would take a minute to do in your head. The nuclear energy from that kind of mass was not something that you could just guesstimate, and the scales involved meant that missing a zero was the difference between ten years, a hundred years, or a thousand years. Dorothy had done it in her head, while talking.

"How did you stabilize the containment field? I haven't been able to construct a magnetic container without at least one sink hole," Dorothy asked, and raptly awaited the answer.

Katherine smiled as though the idea had been hers, "you sure you wanna know? You might be angry with yourself."

Dorothy grinned like an eight-year-old schoolboy asked if he wanted to peek at his Christmas presents and nodded emphatically.

"We didn't. We needed a way to draw antimatter out of the containment sphere anyways so we made one, big, draw point that can't be closed and run that into the magnetic piping to the reactor."

Dorothy's face paled, the smile gone, "you mean to tell me this thing can't be turned off?" Katherine smiled and shook her head no.

"We can vent the antimatter stream into space, and we can increase or decrease the flow rate," she didn't add 'if we're lucky,' and continued, "but we can't shut off the stream. This engine's been live since the moment it was fueled."

Dorothy's face dropped, "so I am no closer to something a reasonable person would use to power their own world. Is this how your people do things normally? No, you'd have blown yourselves up a long time ago if you did."

"I told you, everything in here is dangerous."

Dorothy's face went blank for a moment and then she blinked twice, hard, and frantically rubbed her head, ruining her hair's styling as she did so. Her words came rapid fire, "let's see the engines. And I am going to throw up if you tell me you got here in stasis or that you are the great, great, great, grandchildren of the original crew. Don't you dare tell me that!" she strutted, shoulders firing back and forth like locomotive pistons, pacing in front of the storage chamber, her eyes off it, interest lost.

"No. legitimately faster than light," Katherine said proudly but also caught off guard by the change in focus.

The two women exchanged looks, Katherine of confusion, and a half second later Dorothy exploded, "well? Let me see it already."

Katherine led the way through engineering towards the FTL drive. Ensign Waters was using a large piece of equipment a few yards away. The machine looked like some kind of steampunk incubator. A display showed a link of chain from a necklace.

"Do you need to be doing that now, Waters?" Katherine called over the mechanical pounding of the various systems that grew louder the closer she got to the FTL drive. Waters turned, looked at Dorothy slack jawed, and then, almost sheepishly, walked up to the Major. "I'm kind of out of mess credits... and I'm off duty."

Katherine nodded once in consent and exhaled sharply.

A small port in the wall, opposite the entrance to engineering, marked the FTL drive. The port was barely big enough for a person to fit through and unlike the smooth metal walls of the ship it was very slightly pitted and off silver. "Non-conductive," Katherine said, tapping the port with her helmet to a resulting dull thud.

Behind the port was a small room, the size of an infant's bedroom. In the middle of the room was a sphere the size of a soccer ball. Its surface was mirror perfect and it hovered absolutely motionless in mid-air. Katherine climbed through the port and grabbed a handhold on the opposite side, "no gravity in this room. Make sure you hold on and do not touch the sphere," she cautioned as Dorothy climbed in.

"How does it work?" Dorothy asked.

"It bends space-time. Inside its influence we stay sub-light, outside we are clipping along much, much, faster than light."

"But how?" Dorothy asked.

"We're going to keep that secret for the moment. I am sure you understand."

Dorothy stiffened, made a noise between a growl and a curse, then looked at Katherine with fury in her eyes before turning back to the sphere. "Fine, let's do this the hard way. More fun that way anyways. So…" she exhaled through her teeth, "it's floating." Dorothy moved her head closer to the sphere and drew a warning from Katherine to keep her distance. Close to its surface a slight screech was audible, like steel being torn, "that sound. That's air shear. It's spinning?"

Katherine made no reply.

"How fast is it spinning?" Dorothy asked.

"Fast."

Dorothy closed her eyes and her face contorted with effort, "alright, so it's spinning, fast, yet it looks like a perfect sphere.

It's floating and it warps space-time. I'm willing to bet it keeps its shape even though it's spinning because it doesn't have mass in the conventional sense. Which means this whole thing probably has something to do with the artificial gravity you create." Dorothy scrunched her face then it relaxed, "oh. I bet this is something we are going to have to merge quantum mechanics with macro mechanics to solve, isn't it?"

"You haven't figured that one out yet?" Katherine asked.

"We had bigger problems to deal with first. Hold on we're probably going to want one of our mathematicians to talk with you," Dorothy's face went blank for the third time and she gently drifted in zero gravity – almost – losing her grip on the door handle before the spark returned to her eyes, "so… that's the tour of engineering?" she asked and pulled herself back out the hatch and into the gravity of the main engineering chamber.

Footing unsure from the rapid change of gravity Dorothy wobbled and tried to calm a small tremble in her legs. Katherine followed her out, and as soon as she had closed the hatch behind them turned on Dorothy, "what the hell is going on with you? Why are you an expert in antimatter one second, then indifferent the next?"

***

THERE'S A POPULAR MISCONCEPTION that astronauts are fitness nuts. The original astronauts were womanizing, drunk-driving, chain-smoking, man's men for whom the primary mission requirement was being unbothered by the prospect of a closed-casket funeral.

John Glenn changed that. In the 1960's NASA was given more money than America had spent fighting WW2, and a board of doctors, with more time than real responsibility, recommended that astronauts be able to run two miles. Almost the entire astronaut corps rejected the idea flatly: 'will we be running in space?'

John Glenn, with nothing but venom and ambition in his heart, started running four miles: right past the flight director's office, and right past the astronaut barracks. The message couldn't have been clearer 'join me and I'm a leader; sit out and you aren't a team player. Heads I win, tails you lose.'

In reality physical fitness, beyond a certain level, is actually counter-productive to space travel. Exercise increases muscle mass, red blood cell counts, and lung capacity. Exercise turns a person into a calorie burning, oxygen guzzling, machine. The half-starved mangy dog that can track its next meal for a week is more efficient than the prize stallion that has to eat a banquet every six hours.

But every prison has a gym.

The Galileo's fell silent as the Captain entered. The room contained a variety of machines that would have made a professional gym's look like bargain equipment. There were a dozen treadmills that could clock more mileage in their operational lives than a good car. Asked to design an all-purpose weight machine for the Galileo mission, several fitness companies on Earth had pulled out all the stops. The result was a dozen machines that could be rigged up to work any muscle group worth working. Grey was sure for every one of the machines aboard the Galileo, there were ten million in homes on Earth acting as expensive clothes racks.

The clang of metal slapping metal slowed and then halted as Grey waited. Certainly the machines could have been made to be silent, but engines could be made not to growl like lions, and chocolate could be made to taste like wax.

Silent patience is often the best strategy and in a few seconds all eyes were on the Captain, "clear the room gentlemen."

Without objection the crewmen began grabbing towels, gloves, the debris of exercise, and returning their machines to their stowed positions. "Corporal Tsang," Grey said, and Tsang, who was a face at the back of the group, turned and looked. Grey nodded from the corporal to a bank of treadmills.

When the room was empty, but for the two men, the Captain set one of the machines to a brisk jog, placed a carefully folded towel down, and started to run.

Tsang had a rule: be prepared. He'd never seen the Captain in the gym before. He'd never heard of the Captain ordering a room, besides the bridge, cleared. And he'd never imagined the Captain would be requesting he join him.

Tsang had a decision to make. Stand and wait to be spoken to, or take the initiative and get on the machine beside Grey's. If Grey had been a gambling man he knew which way he would have bet: command authority or not, men competed with men for dominance.

After a few seconds waiting to see if the Captain would talk, Tsang set his machine to the same speed as the Captain's: no need to show the old man up, run the same pace, but do it easily; and he started to run.

"Do you know why I don't approve of you being the ship's king rat?" Grey asked.

The lay of the land came into view. Tsang had expected this conversation, but three years ago. That it had never come had become its own reality which was now broken. It was, however, a conversation that he prepared for, and that was a comfort. "King rat, sir? I help friends barter the occasional item to other friends. There's nothing in the regulations against it, sir." He would have liked to be more direct in the answer, but that was part of the game.

Grey enjoyed the feel of his simple cotton clothes. The contrast between a cotton shirt and shorts, and his uniform couldn't have been greater. The cotton was soft, airy, and absorbent.

"Why don't I approve of *you* doing it? Every ship has one, I don't object to the occupation itself."

Tsang's heart rate was higher than it ought to have been. This wasn't a good conversation to combine with exercise. He breathed rhythmically; the gym lights suddenly too bright.

"I didn't know you objected, sir." Neutral, deferential even. A safe answer as it was supposed to be.

"Please. If you're going to lie, make them believable. But... Rank comes with privileges. Some are given so they can be managed and used for the crew's benefit. Others are to establish position and respect from the crew," Grey said and sucked in a hard lungful of air. A fat bead of sweat rolled down his neck. As it reached his shirt, the cotton sopped it up and it was just gone. It felt like magic, he was so used to each drop completing the entire journey to fingers or feet.

"I've never used my rank improperly, sir."

Grey huffed a long breath, "and you'll never get the chance to. If I think you view the crew as a path to gain for yourself, I'll never give you power enough to abuse." With one sentence Grey had elevated the conversation.

"So, stop bartering or never get promoted?" Adrenaline was now fueling Tsang's run. He stopped breathing hard, he stopped feeling his body.

"It isn't a threat Tsang. You're smart, hard-working, and clever. No matter what, I'm going to make good use of you aboard. But," Grey breathed hard to catch up on missed oxygen, "you decide you're going to work for your benefit, that means one life. You decide you want to work for this crew's benefit, that means a different life."

Grey shut off his treadmill and stepped down from the machine. "I don't want an answer. This isn't something you tell me. You need to show me."

Tsang pushed forward on his machine another half minute before turning it off and dismounting.

"What's the going rate for shower credits?" Grey asked.

A question, an easy answer, and the lay of the land shifted again.

"Sir, they're essentially worthless. They can't be transferred like mess credits, the ship's computer recognizes biometrics of the person in the shower. I don't even know who has any."

"Sergeant Daniels has three hours of excess credits. She agrees to sell them, let me know and I'll manage the computers."

The gym had a massive air circulation system. Without a large group of grunting, sweating, red-faced crew, the room was quickly becoming frigid. The thin sheen of sweat absorbed into Grey and Tsang's clothes the perfect conduit for the temperature.

"If you control the computer, why not just create the credits?"

"Because everything on this ship is interrelated and dependent. We have the credits we have because that's what the ship's systems can handle. A few gallons here, a few gallons there, and suddenly nothing works the way it should. That's command Tsang."

He was exaggerating of course. Tsang knew enough about water reclamation to know a few gallons more or less made almost no difference. Grey's real question was whether Tsang would appreciate that was the very definition of honor; the right thing whether it mattered, or not.

"And I am sorry, sir, but why not ask Daniels yourself? You clearly want me to give this up, why feed the fire so to speak."

"How is a Commander, the ultimate authority over a person's life, supposed to negotiate a fair exchange with them? How can anything between an officer and subordinate truly be done with consent?"

And that was the other shoe. Command was trust, absolute implicit trust. You couldn't have that and bargain. You couldn't have that and date. The lives under you couldn't even fear a bias. Red hot guilt stabbed into Grey's gut like a knife.

"Yes sir. That just leaves the question of price," he would have done it for free, but he suspected the Captain intended to pay, and never leaving money on the table was another rule.

Grey picked up his towel and carefully opened it. Nestled in the folds of the cloth were three, one-ounce, miniature bottles of scotch. "I'm not going to negotiate price. I know what these are worth, and I know it's several times what I want. Let me know when it's done." He passed over the towel and walked out of the gym. At the hatch Grey stopped and turned back, "and Tsang. Who it's for stays between us, and us only."

CHAPTER 11

THE SMELL ALONE WOULD HAVE CAUSED A RIOT among the crew on any other day. The bursting flavor of fried fresh vegetables filled the Galileo's mess hall and the corridor beyond. The very air was edible. Though even that was mere garnish compared to the main dish: meat. Katherine had heard rumors that the Captain kept a stash of food, but she hadn't believed it, it seemed too petty for him. She would have been disappointed in him if she wasn't so busy being excited for dinner.

Two tables in the mess had been pulled together; a crisp, white, linen sheet draped over them. China place settings for four people were laid out, and a bottle of champagne swam in a bucket of ice beside the table. The galley's windows had nearly the same view of the planet, and its moon, that had greeted Katherine in the Captain's cabin so recently; though this time the planet was 'upside down' compared to how it had been. Dorothy had mentioned in passing that her people printed maps the other way 'up'.

Katherine had to swallow a mouth-full of saliva before the hatch had even closed. Dorothy, Major Williams, and Captain Grey stood admiring the view and talking. Dorothy pointed towards some feature of the planet below and all eyes followed her finger.

With Katherine's entrance everyone approached the table. The Captain pulled back a chair for Dorothy, Williams performing the same courtesy for Katherine. Dorothy looked at the offered seat, and then at the Captain with a half-smile. Grey looked perplexed for five long seconds and Katherine took the initiative, "perhaps turning the chair around Captain."

Dorothy smiled and looked down at her knees. Her legs wouldn't be able to fold down to sit on a conventional chair. Grey turned red and spun the chair around and Dorothy straddled the seat with the ease of a twenty-two-year-old rock star.

When everyone was seated Captain Grey took the champagne bottle, tore off the foil top, and unwound the wire safety on the cork. "This is a drink that comes from a small region of one country on Earth. It's only made in that one place and famous the world over for its taste... and opening." Grey thumbed the cork out of the bottle and a loud pop echoed through the room leaving Dorothy to laugh like a delighted child.

The Captain poured everyone a glass and Dorothy led them in toast. Katherine wondered how she'd had time to watch what must have been everything the Galileo sent in its opening message.

Each crewman had been allowed to bring a volume of personal goods with them for the journey. When it came to alcohol, a carbonated, low %, drink was a ludicrous choice. Hard liquor, while valuable, was obtainable onboard. Of beers, wine, or champagne, this was the only one consumed in three years.

A Yeoman, demonstrating an impressive degree of self-control, served the food. Katherine recognized the look on the Yeoman's face. It was one she had last seen on a teenaged boy in high school. Given half a chance the Yeoman would be squatting in the corner, eating with both hands ready to howl with satisfaction when finished.

Dorothy looked at her plate, concerned, "is this how the officers usually eat?" She tried to keep her voice neutral, but it vibrated with strange undercurrents, the cadence of the words losing their polish.

"This is so many credits, the three of us are going to be eating porridge for the next year," Williams helpfully offered and Dorothy visibly relaxed.

"Concerned for the crew?" Katherine asked as she speared a green bean with her fork and braced her tongue for the sweet, salty, fresh morsel of food.

"The duty of the powerful is the welfare of the powerless," Dorothy said.

Major Williams took a swig of champagne like it was beer, the Captain's look of caution prevented a second belt, and he stifled a belch.

"A man named Cicero once said that the welfare of the people was the greatest law," Grey said.

"I trust he came to a better end than the namesake of this ship?" Dorothy asked.

Captain Grey, seeing that the Majors had both taken rather large bites of spam, answered the question, "there's something about the human condition that resists change. But history tends towards justice. Cicero was killed by a tyrant of his day and had his tongue nailed to the main government's door as a message about defying power. That was thousands of years ago though."

"We were much the same. Tyrants, wars, millions of people married to millions of opinions that they had never really bothered to examine," Dorothy said, then took a small sip of champagne. "We overcame it. I think Major Bakker picked up on how when we were in engineering."

She reached up, as though to stretch, and gathered her hair into a single, long, bundle. Dorothy twisted away from the table and showed the three officers her exposed neck. At the base of Dorothy's neck running down under the fabric of her top was some kind of metal implant over her spine. The implant was black metal and plunged into the skin in a half a dozen places along her spine. It wasn't bulky, but rather delicate. Had it been cast in gold it might have passed as jewelry.

"We call it the Commons. It's a computer network that joins almost every one of us. We share news, scientific research, and information about our world. And we share memories and experiences. While I'm sitting here with you billions of people below are experiencing everything I do, every thought, taste, sound, sight. They ask questions, they make suggestions, they comment and debate with one another."

It clicked for Katherine, and she swallowed a mouthful of the best food she'd had in three years, "they take control of you?"

"Not normally. We've never done this before on any kind of large scale. This is the first event billions of people wanted to experience as it happened. This is the first time the Commons decided an expert might do a better job directly than having someone ask their questions for them."

Williams finished his glass and poured a second, "so what, this is always happening? Can you turn it off and have some privacy?"

Dorothy laughed gently, "privacy's just a mask that covers shame."

"Excuse me?" Williams asked, roughly taking another pull on his drink.

"You sent us hundreds of hours of film with your greeting to us. You know what none of that film showed?" She looked around the table to blank faces, "how your species extrudes wastes." Major Williams turned a quarter shade red. "Ah, so that is a taboo."

Dorothy went on, "fair to say when you extrude waste you wish for privacy?"

"You bet your ass," Williams shot back, his words well lubricated. After three dry years his tolerance for alcohol would have made an eight-year-old girl and her pet unicorn appropriate drinking partners.

"Why?" Dorothy asked. "Why do you want that to be private? You all do it, don't you? It isn't different from person to person. It isn't something you rationally should want privacy for. Yet we suspect you'd feel shame if you had to do it in front of many others."

"I would feel embarrassment. I am not sure that is the same thing as shame," Captain Grey interjected.

"If you know and accept everything about your fellow people why is it that this needs to be done in private, why should anything be done in private unless it makes you feel ashamed of yourself in some way."

"So, anyone can watch you use the bathroom?" Katherine blanched.

"Oh, a euphemism, using the bathroom?" Dorothy asked with a spark of amusement, "and yes anyone could. Most aren't interested, except for medical researchers. A few find it sexually stimulating, though that's rare. Sexual fetishes are mostly eliminated when the forbidden aspect of the fetish is removed." Dorothy closed her eyes for a moment, "prior to this conversation memories of me 'using the bathroom' had been accessed three thousand five hundred and two times, only once for non-research purposes."

"That's damn odd," Williams muttered into his plate.

"It seemed that way to us at first, but when you open yourself to the Commons, every memory is open to everyone. When you see that every shame you've have is misplaced, that you're truly accepted by all, then you're completely free."

"Your people have no judgments? Does that mean no rules, no laws?" Katherine asked.

"We have many rules and laws, and we almost universally follow them. Why break a rule but for personal gain, and why would one need a personal gain if it comes at the expense of another who you know completely and love? There are people we judge. Criminals who are excluded from the Commons because they lack empathy for their fellow people. But it's rare."

Grey finished his meal and let a mouthful of champagne clean his mouth, trying to keep the memory alive as long as he could. Williams hadn't been exaggerating. A few bites of real food and next: a year of porridge. "Some people have secrets that are hard to let others know," he said.

"Across the stars, between societies that have no reason to be the same, this is the exact conversation we had when the Commons was born. What decided things was actually experiencing it. As more and more people were connected everyone simply saw how everyone has secrets, shames, embarrassments. If you were to tell your husband or wife your deepest secrets, what couldn't they accept? If you could see the entire life that led to a regret, or feel just how genuinely and deeply those acts are regretted, how could you not accept? It would be very, very, rare to do something, feel something, believe something that was unforgivable in and of itself."

Dorothy's face slackened, the cadence of her voice changed moving up a half octave, "when I was a little child, six years old, there was a fire at my home. My younger brother died. I spent ten years hating myself for not saving him. I was his big sister and I felt like I had a duty to save him. When I joined the Commons, in the space of a day, I lived out thousands of years' worth of experiences of firefighters. I learned it was impossible for a six-year-old to save anyone other than herself from a fire. The world forgave me, billions of people said it was ok, and I believed it, finally. I miss him but I am freed from guilt, or shame, that he died." Dorothy's face shifted back and she gently wiped the edge of her eye, "it's a shame you can only hear the words and not feel the emotions that goes with that. Have you ever felt redemption as vivid in its remembrance as the moment it is first felt?"

Ben pushed his cleaned plate aside, "I can imagine that being very attractive to some people."

"Almost everyone wanted it," Dorothy replied.

"And those who don't?" Grey asked.

"Those who don't are free to make their own choice. It's, frustrating, but freedom has its own value.   It is a very uncommon, rare I mean, choice. The Commons offers so much. Anything you want to do with your life the Commons can make better.   Imagine being able to be a doctor one week, an amazing doctor with lifetimes, hundreds of lifetimes, of experience.   Then the week after be a janitor or engineer, or artist."

"Is that how you built your ship and learned English so quickly?" Katherine asked.   "We were looking at photos of the launch site and it seemed like you built the ship there in just a few days."

"The Commons is hugely efficient for completing projects. We'd never done anything on that scale before, but everyone who isn't busy can become an engineer, or contribute in other ways. And it's organized, and carried out, instantly."

Everyone's meal finished, Williams leaned back looking sleepy. Katherine had a leg tucked up under herself. Grey held his champagne flute at an angle, a few golden drops bubbling at the bottom of the glass. After three years of paste, real food filled quickly.

"So out of billions of people, why were you chosen to come here?" Katherine asked.

"There are some people it's easy to put yourself into. They react the way you expect, they feel like you expect, they think of the questions you expect. They're more comfortable to view events through. I'm someone like that. Imagine if you were trying to view events through someone who'd spent half their life focused on architecture. It could be interesting, but if you're not an architect it would probably be frustrating."

Grey took a small package from his uniform's breast pocket and set it in the center of the table, "one tradition on our world is, after a meal, to have dessert: a sweet dish that's just a small plate. It's also the most popular part of our food." He paused for effect, looking at Katherine. He'd planned on sharing this with her, but their dinner had been interrupted. She had reputedly paid a king's ransom to Tsang a year ago for a chocolate bar half this size.

"Of deserts, the most popular one is chocolate. It's made from a plant that's very hard to grow, and because the end product isn't very nutritional, we didn't bring any aboard the ship as part of the food rations."

Katherine eyed the bar like a viper eyeing a rat. Grey turned back to Dorothy and continued, "however some people love chocolate so much that they brought a small amount with them. I have some left and I'd like to share it with you Dorothy." Grey unwrapped the package. A slim piece of chocolate, wrapped in plastic and coated with almond slivers and caramel, sat on the table.

The reaction from Katherine was visceral. Grey watched with a half-smile as Katherine's eyes narrowed, her nostrils flared ever so slightly as the scent of the bar hit the air. Grey broke the bar into four pieces, each the weight of a person's pinky finger, and handed them out.

Katherine tried not to shake as she reached for hers. It had been a year since she had a bite of chocolate. She brought the morsel to her mouth and took a half a bite. The rich, silky thickness of the chocolate melted and coated her mouth. Her reaction was involuntary, as though she had special neural receptors just for chocolate, and tears began to roll down her face.

Dorothy was equally enthralled. A gentle moan of pleasure escaped her lips as she savored a second bite. Major Williams nodded from Grey towards Katherine and raised his greying eyebrows. Williams rapidly chewed the entirety of his piece but seemed to enjoy Katherine's reaction as much as his dessert.

Dorothy gently held her half eaten morsel, "would you mind if I took that packaging and saved the last of this?" She asked Grey. When he nodded, she took the wrapper and gingerly re-inserted the last of the chocolate.

"Full?" Major Williams asked.

She looked at the chocolate longingly. "No... But right now, five of our top research labs are getting ready to try synthesizing more of this, chocolate. If I don't bring the rest home, there could be riots."

She grinned easily, "chocolate has just become the three hundred and twentieth most experienced moment in our history, and it's rising fast. Twenty billion experiences so far and counting."

"Well, now we're internet famous," Major Williams quipped. Grey flashed his first officer a confused look and Williams grumbled something about that not being a 'thing' anymore.

"One thing about the Commons: when you impress it, it's very generous. We've decided to invite you to come down and let us host a meal for you. And," she raised her eyebrow, "to give you a gift." Dorothy extended her arm over the table and closed her eyes. Her bronze forearm was flawless. Before their eyes a small, dark, line barely an inch long formed and the skin split as though cut by a scalpel.

A drop of black blood fell and landed on the tablecloth with a bounce. The drop sat, without soaking into the fabric, more like a marble than a liquid. A dozen drops fell from the tiny wound on her arm. The flow stopped as suddenly as it had started, and she took her arm back. The black drops of blood on the table rolled on their own accord like a solid, except that as they bounced into one another they merged and settled idle. Six small equal black spheres, each the size of a pea stood still, waiting, all in a perfect line.

"These are nanites: microscopic robots that can live inside the body. They represent the pinnacle of our medical technology. Each sphere is enough for one person, no more, no less. They will do a survey of your natural bacteria, so inject them when you are healthy, and thereafter, for the rest of your lives, they will protect you from any other bacteria, virus, prion, or poison that invades. In return for chocolate, you can now explore without fear of illness."

And the Commons was pleased. More and more it seemed likely it would willingly get everything it wanted with time.

CHAPTER 12

ENSIGN MINDY ARNOLD had lost track of the time. There had
to be an error in her orbital calculations, and she had to find it.
Everything seemed correct. A half a dozen data-pads were
spread over her legs and workbench. The only sound in the
large weapon's bay was the squeaking of her chair as she slowly
swung back and forth from pad to pad.

At the distance the Galileo had been from the center of the
moon, and the mass of the moon, the speed for a stable circular
orbit was 25,000 km/hour – the exact amount of delta V she
had given her missile. She had fired the missile in the correct
direction. Her simulated missile should have cleared the other
side of the moon a few minutes after being launched, and then
acquired the satellite. She had been perilously close to the
surface of the moon, 2,000 meters, but there shouldn't have
been any surface features above 1,500 meters. Could there
have been a simulated range finder error? She pored over the
data looking for a tell-tale hiccup in distances that would
indicate a system error.

Everything looked right: again. She had an idea. If she had
been lower than she thought, the Galileo would have been
going faster than expected, with a shorter distance to travel
before coming out of the moon's shadow. She checked the
times. The satellite had come into view at the exact moment
expected. She checked the orbital path again and verified that
if she had been 500 meters lower she should have been almost
a full thirty seconds faster.

She would have given anything to smash every one of the
data-pads to pieces and start fresh. On Earth she had a bad
habit of destroying pads that frustrated her. It had gotten so
expensive she tended to do most of her work on paper so that

she could tear the pages to confetti if they refused to give her the result she wanted.

Dorothy watched silently. When it seemed that Mindy was on the verge of biting her data-pad in half, Dorothy tapped her foot on the deck lightly. Mindy nearly jumped through the armored overhead, and four pads scattered on the deck with metal twangs.

"Sorry Ma'am, you startled me," Mindy choked out, gathering up her data-pads, dropping one again in the process.

"What are you working on?" Dorothy asked and walked into the weapon's bay.

The room was one of the few on board the Galileo that actually looked like the inside of a proper spaceship. The walls were solid metal, no removable paneling in sight. There was a single large computer terminal with a central input panel mounted directly to the wall. The floor of the room was taken up with four ramps, each the size of a surgical table, that ran to meter-wide octagonal doors. Fire control was simple, uncluttered, and every surface in it solid.

Mindy gave Dorothy a long, examining, look. The alien woman was elegant and curious. She lightly touched almost every surface within arm's reach as she made her way forward.

"A test," Mindy answered.

Dorothy glanced over the data pads, "would it be cheating if I told you the answer?"

Lower lip squeezed between her teeth Mindy slowly shook her head, "it wouldn't... The Captain offered to tell me as well.

But the answer isn't going to help me. We only get three tries at this test and it's different each time. I've already failed twice so if I can't figure this out myself, I'll know I'm not ready for my third, and last, try."

Dorothy's face contorted with outrage at that, "what do you mean you get three tries? What happens if you fail the third time? What's this a test for?"

The young woman stood up and tried to shuffle the pads onto the control panel and out of sight, "it really isn't that big a deal," she stammered, trying to sooth Dorothy, "the test is to see if I can be a bridge officer. Right now I'm in charge of weapons but if I want a command position I need to pass this."

"And if you fail again you're forever prohibited from a real leadership role on this ship?" Dorothy raised her voice and shifted her hands to her hips.

A diplomatic answer to the question was not written on the chamber's bulkheads, but that didn't stop Ensign Arnold from looking them over quickly for help, "uh... yes?"

"Well, how does that make any sense?" Dorothy thundered, "if you pass the fiftieth time you know it as well as if you had passed the first time!"

"Preaching to the choir," Mindy chimed back and stopped Dorothy mid rant. "Things must really be different when you have the internet in your brain."

"Yes. But also no. People are people, technology just gives you options. But enough about me, you said you were the weapons officer."

Mindy tensed under her uniform. Orders were orders, but she didn't have to like them, "yes ma'am."

A sigh, "Mindy, honestly I don't care. The Commons has an absolutely juvenile obsession about big explosions. So how about you tell me about the biggest explosion you can make, and the Commons will be satisfied without knowing every little detail."

Mindy traced the tip of her left index finger along the corner of the control console. "Do you know what antimatter is?" she asked and tapped a sequence of buttons on the console. Before Dorothy could answer, a missile descended from the ceiling in mechanical arms that gently set it down on one of the room's four tracks. The titanium door at the track's end opened, waiting for the missile to be loaded.

"So, these are antimatter rockets? Very simple."

"That's the beauty of antimatter. You take an atom of antimatter and combine it with one atom of regular matter and the two completely annihilate each other giving you two atoms worth of energy. You don't need precision or even to worry about radiation. Only one rule: don't let a single atom get loose until you're ready."

"So do the rockets come preloaded, what's the biggest one you have?"

The ramp, though appearing solid, had an articulating edge on one side that Mindy raised. A foot long section of metal rose from the side of the ramp and clamped onto the side of the missile. "Part of my job is loading them with the correct amount of antimatter. With Gadolinium you can get a pretty big explosion, one megaton, with a volume the size of half of the tip of my finger" Mindy extended her pinky finger towards Dorothy to make the point.

"And the biggest?"

Mindy shrugged and then considered the question, "technically inside the missile is a magnetically charged hollow sphere of regular Gadolinium that weighs a kilogram. In theory we could perfectly convert 42 Megatons worth of energy: or the biggest fission bomb humanity has ever made. However, the magnetic field, and the RM Gadolinium sphere inside the missile, are about the size of my head. Theoretically, if you were lucky, you could get an explosion five hundred times bigger."

Dorothy's face slackened and she said nothing for nearly thirty seconds. "Do you have any idea what an explosion like that would do?"

"I know I don't want to be on the receiving end of it, ma'am."

"It is enough to destroy a planet."

"Yes ma'am, it is."

"Doesn't that bother you?"

"That's more of a question for a bridge officer, ma'am. I don't decide what gets shot at or with how much A.M. I just load em."

"And as an aspiring bridge officer, what is the official answer for using force like that?"

Mindy's eyes closed in thought, "this isn't a warship ma'am. We're explorers. Explorers who can defend themselves, but we aren't here to expand the influence of Earth or carry out Earth's foreign policy."

"And what if something went wrong with the loading process? Is it dangerous?"

"Moderately," Mindy unclamped the missile and, with a slow dozen cross checks, sent it back into the ceiling. "The main problem is making sure everything is a perfect vacuum. AM reacts with anything, not just its RM paired atom. Over the years if even a few atoms of air leak into one of the missile storage containers, or the lines that feed them, well that's a nuclear explosion right there. But we can mitigate it." Mindy pointed to a handful of flow rate controls. "My SOP is to inject a few dozen AM atoms through the system to test the seals. If we had a leak, we'd lose the room, not the ship."

"The room, and you," Dorothy corrected.

"And me. But I'm fine checking out that way. So long as it isn't my screw up I don't care if I die."

"A human trait?"

Mindy rubbed her uniform above her heart. Under the polymer fabric a golden cross hung tight to her chest, "no ma'am. Some people think their lives are all there is, all that matters. And some know that it's about how you live."

***

'EVERYONE HAS A VICE.' It was one of Tsang's rules, and today's job was to find the right vice before he spoke to

Daniels. 'Preparation' was another one of his rules. Together the faith that everyone had a vice, and that he could find it before negotiations by preparation, had served him well.

Buying shower credits would have been a trivial task had any of four dozen of his previous customers had three hours' worth of them — they didn't. Them he knew: a chocolate bar for Major Bakker, an ounce of alcohol for Ensign Carter, a week's fresh hydroponics for Corporal Marks, and two week's fresh hydroponics to Corporal Marks for Corporal Bailer. Everyone had their vice, and their price.

Grey hadn't been exaggerating that he was over-paying for the shower credits he wanted, and so Tsang had some slack to make an investment in researching a new customer.

Since time immemorial business and food have been interconnected. In Rome, Piazzas, small market squares, had been centers of commerce for thousands of years. To this day imported carpets and textiles could be bought steps away from cured pork sandwiches. Even in the world's financial centers, more real business was done in restaurants than boardrooms.

Which meant... "Please, allow me, Ensign." Tsang reached across the surprised young lady and tapped his mess card to the food dispenser.

Surprise turned to suspicion faster than water to steam in the ship's reactor as Ensign Vivian Lucia recognized her benefactor. The thirty-six-year-old quickly threw on a mask of gratitude she'd last used in a bar back home, smiled, said "thank you", performed a sharp 90 degree turn, and walked away. Rejection was so complicated.

Tsang followed as though she had invited him. ESP alerted the Ensign that Tsang was on her six and she scanned the room looking for a single empty seat that would block Tsang's advance. There were none: preparation.

A person's shoulders can tell you a great deal about them. Ensign Lucia's were raised, closer to her neck than they should have been as she sat down.

"I don't want anything Ensign," Tsang said as he sat down beside the woman. "You bunk with Daniels, right? I have a customer who wants to get her a gift. He just isn't sure what she likes. That's all I am trying to figure out."

And it was that simple. Vivian's shoulders relaxed and curiosity replaced apprehension. "So... She does have a secret boyfriend."

Now it was Tsang's turn to be surprised. Who was single and who was taken, was a matter of vital public knowledge. Why would her bunkmate suspect a secret relationship? Why would Daniels keep a relationship secret?

One of the virtues of a lie is that it can reveal more than the truth would have.

"I never asked why he wanted to get her a gift."

Give a person a secret, a potentially scandalous one - for what other reason could there be to hide a relationship - and it was like showing a child a toy they couldn't play with. She almost squirmed in her seat.

"I help you; you tell me who your customer is," Vivian said at last.

"Can you help me?"

Vivian, eyes gleaming, focused into the distance and thought. It didn't take long. A slight inhalation, a widening of the eyelids, a curl of the lips. Tsang would have robbed her blind at cards.

"Oh, I very much can," she said.

Exactly how much was loyalty worth?

"Tell you what. You can choose. A mess credit for one piece, small, fresh produce. Or you take one guess at who my client is, and I give you a yes or no."

There was no hesitation. He was losing his touch; a good offer left a person painfully conflicted. "Major Williams?"

He let the surprise show on his face, "no. Why did you guess Williams?"

Now she looked conflicted. Tsang wasn't going to lose the deal over idle curiosity however, "it's ok. You don't have to tell me why. I was just curious, he's an odd choice." Tsang retrieved a ripper from his left hip pocket and inserted his mess card transferring a small produce ration. "I don't want you walking away empty handed," he offered. Vivian didn't need to be encouraged and swiped her mess card.

"Ok, twist my rubber arm…" She glanced around them to make sure they were not going to be overheard. "She once told me he reminded her of her dad." That raised an eyebrow on Tsang. "I know!" Vivian replied, seeing his surprise.

"It was your idea," Tsang reminded her, and the young lady shrugged.

Five minutes later Tsang left the mess with the information he wanted. He hadn't needed to be generous, but the Ensign's initial hesitation bothered him. Why be nervous about talking to him? Besides, he was going to turn a substantial profit on this deal regardless, and now Vivian, who had been concerned about doing business with him, had a good impression. Who knew what future opportunities that could open.

Lieutenant Waters would be coming off duty in engineering any minute, and a half a dozen mess credits would secure the final piece of the puzzle.

CHAPTER 13

MAJOR WILLIAMS STOOD STATUE STILL and looked over his 'men'. The trick was looking with the eyes and keeping the neck fixed. Five crewmen faced him in a straight line, arm's width apart from one another, exactly as the drill manual depicted. Of the five, three were women, the other two barely needed to shave. None had ever fired a shot in anger. The Major looked them over slowly, taking his time. Each wore their full space suit – helmet and external armor included – just as the Major did. Each one also moved nervously waiting for the Major to begin. There was a difference between the itches, aches, and shifting of men at attention, and the quick, jerking motions of men who are afraid. They had heard he had a surprise in store, but no one had the balls to tell them what and risk the Major's wrath. They glanced at the person next to them in line, and they all sweated apprehension through the airtight fabric of their suits.

The room they occupied, the largest cargo bay on the Galileo, had been cleared for this class and the six occupants took up only a small fraction of the basketball court sized room. The ceiling towered thirty feet overhead, and aside from the six armored crewmen the room was totally empty.

Five sets of eyes watched the Major through the visor slits in their armored helmets. "Welcome to Low-G combat training," the Major's words transmitted over radio from his helmet to the recruits – and to the Galileo's computer. The Major watched them for a hint of eagerness, aggression. Lambs could be trained to be the best lambs they could be: wolves are born wolves.

"Your first, and only lesson today, is this," he took a slow breath, "adapt or die." A fraction of a second later the gravity in the room inverted – exactly as the Major had programmed it to. Instead of 100% Earth normal, gravity shifted to negative 30%, pushing everything in the room towards the ceiling.

There were two immediate effects of this. The first was almost beautiful. Every speck of dirt, dust, debris, and lint on the floor of the cargo bay lifted off the deck in unison. Some would drop like the tiny rocks they were, others would slowly drift "down", but for the first few inches of the journey they all traveled at the same speed. It gave the floor the impression of shuddering in the reversed gravity. It looked powerful. The Major always loved it.

The second effect was that people fell – fast.

Everyone on board the Galileo had been through zero gravity familiarization. Zero gravity, and negative gravity, are very different things to the human animal. In the case of zero gravity you're floating. Zero gravity, or ZG, is like swimming in a pool. Negative gravity means falling: upwards. It presents the human animal with an impossible, Escher, reality that literally hurts the brain.

For an added measure of malice, unrestrained negative gravity also tickles the ancient part of the brain that governs falling. It would be a week before any of the Major's students slept through the night.

The recruits, all seasoned crewmen, reacted as anyone would. They raised their hands over their heads, screamed into their helmets, and plummeted upwards, tumbling end over end as they did. One of the recruits – Major Williams had lost track of which flailing doll was which – managed to activate their suit's thrusters. They were rewarded for their quick reflexes by narrowly avoiding the roof as they rocketed forward. They slammed into the cargo bay wall, and Wile E.

Coyote'ed to the ceiling. The others collapsed on the ceiling in crumpled messes.

The first time Major Williams had taught this course, nearly twenty years before, he had programmed his suit to automatically compensate for gravity changes. When his pupils had fallen up, his suit had kept him pinned to the deck and he literally walked around, upside down. As the years had passed, he had improved his technique. Now his suit's thrusters were completely manual. He hung in mid-air, his feet a meter off the deck. To the recruits on the ceiling below he would have looked like St. Peter, crucified upside down. His arms were extended to allow fine controls from the small thrusters on the back of hands. The position required the same kind of coordination as an inverted iron cross on gymnastic rings.

His suit's jets provided counter thrust as Williams hung in the room. His head swelled slightly as blood rushed into it, and he maneuvered silently over the recruits - behind them. "Adapt or die!" he shouted over the radio and drew his sidearm, an MX-3.

The weapon was large for a handgun, wider as well. A regular handgun held a magazine of bullets in the handle. This weapon had a double thick magazine well forward of the pistol grip, near the end of a very short barrel.

The weapon, and its rounds, were completely custom creations. Only two hundred of the guns had ever been made. It was also the Major's favorite hand weapon, and standard issue aboard the Galileo.

The reason for its strange appearance, and the Major's favor, were the bullets it fired. An ordinary bullet contains an explosive charge and metal slug. The explosives are burned inside a gun's barrel, and the expanding exhaust propels a metal slug forward. The slugs reach maximum speed at the lip of the barrel and slows down thereafter. This is simple and efficient but has a very significant side effect: the force pushing the bullet forward is also pushing the gun backwards; action and reaction. In zero gravity each shot would send a man tumbling out of control. The more powerful the gun the bigger the problem.

The MX-3's rounds were small rockets. Their chemical charges burned the entire distance of travel accelerating the round to several times the speed of an ordinary bullet. The gun was more semi-automatic rocket launcher than handgun.

Williams loved everything about the MX-3. He loved that it didn't recoil. He loved that, with each pull of the trigger, there was a split-second where he could see the small bullets as they exited the barrel. He loved that the pop, pop, pop of a handgun was replaced by the viper-hiss of a rocket motor, and then a loud crack as the bullet broke the sound barrier. He loved that the rounds hit with several times the force of even a large caliber bullet. And he loved that, like all rockets, the MX-3's rounds were entirely made of a polymer plastic explosive that was rigid enough to provide the rockets with structural strength for their launch, and explosive enough that, when they hit a target, it would die.

As this was a training exercise Williams was merciful. He leveled the MX-3 on the worst of the recruits, giving the others more of a chance than they would have in combat. For the one recruit still struggling to figure out that standing on the ceiling was an option, Williams leveled his weapon and fired.

A firing pin leapt forward and impacted a primer on the rocket engine of the MX-3's first round. The initial explosion and exhaust pushed the round out of the MX-3's stubby barrel and for the smallest fraction of a second the round coasted through the air. Then its rocket motor caught, and it exploded forward. From the round's perspective the recruit was frozen in time. Tiny stabilizing fins kept the rocket straight and true as it smashed through the sound barrier, a sonic wave forming behind it. With a dozen meters between it and the recruit a war shot would have just been starting its acceleration. Instead, its rocket motor cut out, the training round's load of fuel exhausted.

These training rounds had been hand-made by Williams. He'd carefully reduced the fuel load in each round and disabled the rocket's explosive fuse. It was not the final touch of personalization to William's weapon. Most of the Galileo's MX-3's looked as though they had been sealed in plastic the last three years, but not Williams'. Every piece of his gun showed the subtle scratches and wear of a hundred cleanings. The stock polycarbonate handle had been replaced with chestnut wood that Williams had personally whittled. The wood gave the weapon a slightly back-heavy weighting that he preferred. Even the pull of the trigger had been customized down from the standard five-pound pull to four and a half, which William's found resulted in a smoother motion for his hand.

Williams had aimed at a heftier piece of armor and the rocket slammed into a shoulder plate. Had the round's explosive body been live, it would have blasted the recruit's head and arm from the remainder of his body, even with the armor. Ensign Tsang flipped sideways and skidded across the deck three feet from where he had been a moment before. Even the training rounds made a satisfying impact. Williams smiled.

For some people violence was abhorrent. Williams was prepared to admit that this was true now of almost everyone.

But for him it was part of his DNA. He had known as a teenager that he didn't want a pretty little condo and a collection of cufflinks and sunglasses. He wanted to fight.

And so, he did the only thing that had made any sense; he joined the Marines. He quickly realized he was different from his fellow enlisted men. He could plan, organize, and lead as well as follow. It had been decades since the realization that he should apply to officer's school. But all the dinner parties, planning meetings, and office politics a lifetime could give had never dulled the simple pleasure of reaching out and hurting someone.

Time is the most valuable commodity in combat and Williams had all of it he could want. The remaining recruits were drawing their weapons and looking back and forth where Williams ought to have been had he fallen with them. All of them knew their way around the MX-3 and had spent a dozen hours on the range back on Earth. One was smart enough to begin turning and Williams rewarded the intelligence with a shot to the back of his leg. The recruit somersaulted in the air twice before landing. The reduced gravity made what should have been a slip or a flip into a Hollywoodesque spectacle.

It took another recruit going down before the last two turned on Williams and began to raise their weapons for a clean shot. Williams considered simply shooting them both, it would have been simple. Instead, he thrust sideways and forwards and coaxed his suit into a powered orbit around the remaining two recruits. He pushed the acceleration up to three g's and whipped around the recruits like a tornado. They emptied their magazines at him – hitting nothing but the cargo bay wall. Hitting a moving target is hard, hitting an accelerating target is next to impossible except by luck or a huge degree of skill. Williams fired two quick rounds hitting both recruits in their chests before coming to a stop. All five were down, crumpled on the ceiling.

With the tap of his gauntlet, gravity reverted to positive 10% and everything in the cargo bay began to drift back to the deck. For two of the recruits it was too much. They wrenched off their helmets and vomited into the bay. The streams of vomit stretched out to a dozen meters long before they fell to the deck. Major Williams was, with experience, well out of the way.

Once everyone, and everything, had landed in neat little puddles, he restored full gravity and induced another recruit to empty her stomach.

"You will be taught to shoot. You will be taught dexterity of movement. You will be taught strategy. Because I am a good teacher you will learn these things. But you will not pass this course unless you show me that you have honor. We work as a team, we fight as a team, and when we pick up a weapon we're saying to the universe that there are things more important than our lives. If you can't show me that you value your teammate's lives more than your own, you have no business holding a weapon."

A lifetime in the military and its codes of honor were as inviolable as his DNA.

"Your next lesson is in 48 hours," Williams said, leaving his own helmet on to avoid the smell that filled the bay.

"Be ready. This was the only easy lesson," he looked at the five recruits, only one managing to rise to their knees. "Major Bakker is going to want her cargo bay clean before you go off duty."

He strode out of the cargo bay, holstered his weapon, and checked his suit's fuel status: 2%.

CHAPTER 14

"THE MORAL IS, when an alien with the mental power of an entire planet's population tells you that microscopic robots are the pinnacle of their technology, they aren't going to be simple," Katherine started to build a tower of a dozen data pads scattered over Grey's table.

"I was in Vietnam a few years ago for work," Williams didn't elaborate on the work and Grey knew well enough not to ask. "This liaison officer I'd been trading shit with for a few weeks asks me to have a drink with him. We go to this bar, a kind of watch out for your fillings place, and they take out a live cobra. Right there in front of me, on the bar, they cut its head off, slice open its body, and snip its heart out."

Williams held two fingers up, pinched together, and then opened them. "Plunk. Right into a shot of tequila. So, I had a choice. Either it was poison and they meant to kill me, or it was about showing I wasn't a pussy," he paused for effect, "tasted like a poisoned jolly rancher."

"So, it comes down to trust?" Grey asked.

"No. It comes down to method. If they wanted to kill us they could have sent up a nuke in their ship."

Katherine had her eyes downcast and bit the edge of her lip. Grey pressed ahead, "so, what if it's to gather intel. Read our minds and learn all our secrets."

"They never said one of the engineers or navigators had to be who we send down. Besides, based on Arnold's conversation they seem concerned about our retaliatory capacity," Williams responded.

Grey's stomach rumbled. Crème Brulé was all he had left on his budget this week and he couldn't bring himself to eat it.

"So, Williams, you're saying do it, but no one with classified information?" Grey asked, and Williams nodded his affirmation.

Both officers turned to Bakker and waited for her opinion. "I say no. We can just keep our suits on when we go down," she said, "no need to expose ourselves to their bacteria, and the risk is high."

There's a well-known bias in decision making. As people acquire an expertise and gain decades of experience their perception of the severity of problems drops. At the start of a lawyer, or military officer's, career everything appears to be an earth-shattering decision; at the end of a long career earth shattering decisions seem trivial.

Williams broke the silence, "you're downplaying the upside. We risk a few lives but maybe discover a cure for every illness. Let's say they offered to let one of us join their Commons. Imagine what we could learn, and the cost is a life. We lost Chetan for some rocks."

"We can't treat human life like poker chips," Katherine responded.

Williams looked at Grey and there was the answer. The horrible truth of command. The lives, the dreams, the futures, of men and women were resources that sometimes had to be gambled, or spent, in the name of the mission.

"I take the first dose," Grey said, "if it works on me we inject two others, both volunteers."

Williams' face broke into a grimace with wrinkles creasing it like old leather. "I'm not going to let you volunteer unless I do."

A scowl was all Katherine had in response to the two fools in front of her. "Who else?" She asked, "I suppose half the ship will want the last spot."

"I suggest we ask Arnold first," Williams said.

Grey was surprised by that, expecting one of Williams' star combat students to get his nomination. "She failed the command test twice... spectacularly failed it... But she's an excellent weapons officer and wants to feel like she's growing. We give her some excitement, show her she can stay where she is and still grow as a person, and maybe she gives up and accepts her station."

"She did handle first contact on the radio, figured out their joke. Katherine?"

She shrugged, indifferent, "everyone under me has Fermi or FTL knowledge."

***

DOROTHY LAUGHED AT THE INSIDE OF THE CHURCHILL. At first it was the exposed fuel lines that ran over the roof of the cabin. Then she noticed the hand held fire extinguishers. Then it was the manual wheel to dog the entrance hatch. Each elicited a fresh, incredulous, response.

One of the Galileo's two Orbital Thrust Vehicles or OTVs, the small ship had enough thrust to achieve a stable orbit around a planet but not enough for planet-to-planet travel. Shaped like the head of a spear the craft could seat a dozen fully armored crewmen: if everyone exhaled when the door was being closed. It could seat four comfortably with room for cargo.

The ship was Russian made, part of the international partnership that had contributed to the Galileo. For all the passage of time, countries had long memories and Russian engineers preferred simplicity and reliability over clever technological trickery. The Churchill's designers could have used automated fire extinguishers, or computer-controlled doors, just as had been used throughout the Galileo. For Grey it was a welcome change in philosophy. He only wished the Russians had been tapped for the shower systems as well.

Grey, Bakker, and the chief Russian designer had been on a test flight of the Churchill before the mission. Katherine had remarked, bluntly, that the ship was too heavy and that a bit of finesse in the design would have saved significant weight. The Russian designer had replied, "people who can't make rockets talk about finesse."

Captain Grey entered the OTV through the Churchill's only hatch, located on the craft's port side just aft of the cockpit. The Captain gave the ship's interior a quick scan. The presence of two foot-locker-sized cargo crates strapped down at the aft of the crew compartment, told him everything he needed to know.

Twelve hours ago there had not been a panel closed, or square inch unoccupied inside the craft. It had taken two dozen crewmen to run through the pre-flight checklists. To make the ship ready for actual use, dozens of seals, valves, and rubber hoses that wouldn't have survived three years of inactivity had to be installed.

Dorothy and Major Williams were in the crew compartment. The Major was seated opposite Dorothy, sitting on a bench along the port wall facing into the center of the compartment. He was strapped into his seat and could have been used as the demonstration for correct harness placement in the Churchill's manual. No fancy interlocking armor couplings on the Churchill, just five-point manual harnesses.

"Your legs really take some getting used to. How do you wash your feet?" Dorothy asked the Major as she lay down on the bench, crossing and folding her legs forward and taking her right foot casually in her left hand, propping her head up with her arm.

"You sit down and wash 'em," Williams glanced down at his knees, as though he had suddenly lost perspective on his own body.

Dorothy released her foot and reached out, tapping the topmost footlocker in the middle of the compartment. "When you eat and digest food there must be something left over that has to be expelled. How does it work? I know it's a taboo, but don't be shy. If you ate the whole footlocker how much waste would be left? A quarter, a half? How efficient is your system?"

Ben stiffened and blushed red, "well... maybe a half... never thought about volume."

"What are you doing? You changed colors?" Dorothy asked and leaned forward to look more closely.

Grey smiled through his suit, "explain it to the lady, Major," he ordered trying to keep his voice neutral.

Major Williams jaw clenched almost imperceptibly, his temples pulsed twice and then subsided, "it is a reaction to embarrassment."

Dorothy leaned forward to the brink of falling off the bench looking at the Major's face, "amazing, so you all change colors based on how you feel? What does it mean when you turn brown?" she clapped her hands and watched the Major intently, waiting for him to change color again.

Coming to his rescue Grey interjected, "that's a little more complicated. The Major will need some time to do it justice. To make sure he gets it all correct."

The cockpit was separated from the crew compartment by a bulkhead. Grey had to squeeze through a narrow opening to spot Ensign Mindy Arnold at the controls. The Churchill's cockpit had two seats. The starboard seat was for the pilot, the port seat for the commander. The rubberized grip of the cockpit's hand holds ground against his armored grip as Grey lifted himself, and his suit, off the Churchill's deck and swung himself over the commander's seat. Inch by inch he lowered himself as his feet banged their way into narrow slots in the forward instrument panel. It took thirty seconds but eventually he was seated. It took another minute to attach the five-point harness. In an armored suit he couldn't feel where the different arms of the harness were and had to locate them by sight.

"Nearly ready Ensign?"

"Yes sir. Dog the hatch," the Ensign shouted into the cargo bay by way of reply. An engineer appeared at the door a moment later, slammed it shut, and Grey watched as the inside wheel rotated locking the hatch down. Thirty seconds later and a klaxon warning sounded in the cargo bay; notice that its atmosphere would be pumped back into the Galileo. The progress of the vacuum was evident by the intensity of the klaxon warning. The less atmosphere to conduct the sound, the softer it got, until it was silent. Two doors, each ten square meters in size, opened beneath the Churchill with the slow force of hydraulic power.

One of the great ironies of space travel is that the slower one goes the faster it feels. It's a simple trick of perspective. A planet growing in size from a softball, to a basketball, to a beach ball over a few minutes looks like nothing, but requires almost unimaginable speeds.

In three years the Churchill had never been going slower than when it hit the planet's atmosphere. The friction was enormous. Flames of speed whipped its hull from the intense atmospheric friction and blasted past the window like a welding torch. Supersonic air buffeted and condensed just outside the cone of fire that engulfed the ship. Variations in the atmosphere, and transient aerodynamic effects created by the extreme heat, reverberated through the hull of the ship. Shaking clouds, roaring flames, and howling air battered the Churchill.

The Churchill plunged through the air and slowed to just below the speed of sound as it approached a thick layer of cloud. It was like plunging, as fast as the human mind can comprehend, straight at a wall. The logical part of the brain saying, "it's just cloud," and the animal part of the brain screaming obscenities.

Inside Grey's helmet the speakers activated with a chime. "Hey Peter…" Sergeant Rebecca Daniel's voice came over the airwaves, a private broadcast just for Grey.

"This isn't a good time," Grey replied inside his helmet.

"But I'm lonely..."

The Churchill ripped through the two-hundred-foot-thick cloud as though it were tissue paper. Ensign Arnold activated thrusters on the belly of the ship to further slow its descent. Grey didn't register the acceleration, though it pressed him hard into his seat. Now that the Churchill was through the cloud cover, the planet's surface was in sight and far more jarring than any thrust the Churchill could manage.

"I'll call you back," Grey said and cut off the transmission.

The planet's entire surface, that he could see, was covered by skyscrapers. Their designs seemed impossible. Entire buildings curved into the sky like leaves. Some were joined by spider silk thin bridges that glistened sunlight. Hundreds of the buildings seemed to be solid shards of red, pink, and light purple crystal that towered over other hundred story buildings.

"This is amazing," Grey said aloud. Major Williams strained in his seat for a view.

"We are very proud of it," Dorothy commented.

"How long did it take to build?"

"That depends on what you mean. Three thousand and eighty-seven years ago was the first construction but most of what you see was built in the last fifty years since the Commons."

"You know the year so exactly?" Grey asked, surprised but not taking his eyes off the city.

"It's an important city. After centuries of war one ruler invited a representative of every known country, tribe, and people, to meet her. She asked them, "what would end all war?" and they decided that the only way to end war was to know each other as we know ourselves."

"This City was founded on that spot with each country, tribe, even person, invited to add to it to show the height of their culture, their spirit. It was a turning point in our history."

The Churchill homed in on preset coordinates that moved it away from the crystal shards and skyscrapers. The ship flew towards a patch of undeveloped ground. "That's the oldest part of the city. The very ground we first met to consider our future as a people."

At five thousand feet above the surface the buildings that surrounded their landing site seemed to close in on the small craft, reaching up from the ground towards the ship like fingers. The city's sheer scale became more and more obvious the closer the Churchill got. What had looked to be a park the size of a football stadium was closer in size to Central Park.

The Churchill sank into the city; down into the hundreds of stories worth of skyscrapers that surrounded their landing site. At three thousand feet the ship shuddered. Grey had exactly enough time to look at the instrument panel before a metallic thud reverberated through the hull and the ship began to fall, uncontrolled.

Years of collected dust rose from every nook and cranny that Katherine's engineers had missed cleaning, and filled the cockpit with a thin haze. A single screw joined the dust and floated in mid-air between Grey and Arnold as the small ship plummeted.

Regardless of rank, a pilot is the master of their ship and Ensign Mindy Arnold was piloting. The Churchill had fallen barely two hundred feet before she started working the problem. "Master Power…" Mindy yelled even as her fingers found the switch and confirmed by touch it was up.

Captain Grey had one eye on the altimeter and his other found the master power gage, "reading 93%, cross check voltage 1-1-5."

Two thousand four hundred feet above the surface the Churchill reached its terminal velocity and began to rotate like a top as it fell.

"Nozzle clearance?" Mindy asked, her voice cooling as the pressure increased.

"Gauges are clear… Cross check," Captain Grey hit the emergency valve and dumped compressed hydrogen into the Churchill's exhaust nozzles. If they were obstructed they would hold a pressure charge. The gauges all read normal atmospheric pressure. "Clear!" Grey snapped back. The Churchill was fifty seconds away from auguring into the ground below.

"Intakes?" Ensign Arnold asked and activated a control thruster on the Churchill's nose. Thruster fired and pitched the craft down to expose the air intakes to the stream of air racing up past them. The change in orientation presented a smaller cross section to the onrushing air which accelerated the Churchill faster towards the ground. Everyone aboard felt themselves slide forward in the ship like going down a hill on a sled. Losing ten precious seconds of time to impact also exposed the problem.

"Negative flow!" Grey reported.

"Switch feed from atmospheric to reserve," Arnold ordered. The Churchill was a spaceship. That meant it had fuel and oxygen tanks. In a planet's oxygen atmosphere she automatically took in air through two large intakes to save the tanked oxygen for when in space. Some engineer back on Earth had worked out that this would save weight and give it a better range.

The problem was, intakes could, and apparently had, become clogged. With the feed switched to internally stored oxygen the problem was, technically, resolved but the engines still needed to be restarted and given enough time to arrest their fall, assuming that was the only thing wrong.

"Check valves one, two, three, five – open"

"Nozzle aperture set to one hundred," Grey replied as both officers worked the engine startup checklist with twenty seconds left to their names.

"Flow control to automatic," Arnold ordered, and Grey replied almost in tune, "ignition control to automatic."

Ensign Mindy Arnold rammed her hand forward into the control panel. It's rare for things that could be large red buttons to actually be large red buttons in military aircraft. The emergency engine restart button was the exception. It was large, red, and easy to hit, hard. Mindy punched it, and almost as a prayer after the fact said, "emergency restart."

The Churchill was ten seconds above the surface when its onboard computers received the signal to execute an emergency restart of its engines. In civilian vehicles, in anything civilians use, there's a degree of reasonableness built in. Pushing the gas pedal to the firewall of a car is no different from pressing it two inches. The good engineers at the car company know that their customers don't intend to blow out their engines, or stress the steel of their piston rods to the point that they would need to be replaced after ten minutes' use. Taking into account what a civilian will tolerate in terms of fuel economy, lifespan of parts, maintenance, and risk of catastrophic failure, civilian engineers give their customers a "reasonable" amount of control over their products.

Military ships do not share this philosophy when emergency procedures are invoked. The Churchill fully opened the valves to her hydrogen and oxygen storage tanks and began dumping 1% of the ship's fuel per second into the engine lines. When the fuel reached the thrust nozzle a dozen separate ignitors, which ordinarily took turns sparking for a quarter second each, all flared constantly. This would burn them all out after only a few seconds.

The fuel, fully ignited, and as much as the hoses from tank to nozzle could carry, burned so hot it threatened to melt the nozzles designed specifically for it. The thrust was tremendous and hit the Churchill so hard that her structural frame would need to be x-rayed to ensure it wasn't damaged. With a hundred and fifty feet to go, the height of a very tall tree, the Churchill arrested its fall. In the aft of the craft Williams "umpfed" as the fifth strap of his harness stopped him sliding off the bench to the floor.

Somewhere a Russian engineer was laughing, very pleased with himself.

The Churchill started to shoot up higher for a moment before Arnold cut thrust to a reasonable level and hovered. She gave herself a half second, and then began going through the landing checklist. Grey was impressed, most of his mind was still on the near crash. It's one thing to be cool under pressure. It's something else to shrug it off a moment later. His weapon's officer, on a visceral, instinctual level, really didn't care if she died.

A minute later, three landing wheels extended from the nose and tips of the arrow headed ship and, with Ensign Arnold's gentle touch, the Churchill came to a rest.

The landing site itself was small and surrounded by stone buildings. Each building had its own unique architecture, materials, style. A handful could have been Roman or Greek. Tall columns of marble stretched five stories into the air, so close to the Churchill that they almost obscured the towering skyscrapers behind them. Other buildings were made of simple stones and mortar while others were covered in faded paintings that obscured their materials. One was made entirely from copper, oxidized, and rotted with age.

Neil Armstrong's name is spoken along with Columbus, Newton, and Churchill as one of the most significant people to have ever lived. Few, outside of historians, know the name Buzz Aldrin. The difference between the two men was decided by an engineer at NASA whose name is lost to history. He placed the door to the lunar lander on Neil Armstrong's side by random chance and thus dictated that he be the first man on the moon. Buzz Aldrin followed seconds after Armstrong, but missed history's camera flash. In this tradition Major Williams was the first human to set foot on an alien world.

The human mind, and body, have various needs. When those needs are not met a weight is placed on the psyche. Gram by gram it builds until it's hard to think of anything else. Fresh air, the safety of ground under foot, the feeling of the sun on the face, they are as much needs as food, sex, companionship. As much as they had been anticipating setting foot on an alien world, simply being out of the confines of their ship was an equal reward.

Helmets tucked under their arms, Major Williams, Ensign Arnold, and Captain Grey exited the Churchill in turn following Dorothy. The three breathed deeply and looked up at the sun as sweet fresh air inflated them. A gust of wind caught Ensign's Arnold's hair. It was the first breath of wind she'd felt in three years, and she almost purred with pleasure. Even Major Williams' face was upturned towards the sun.

The closest building, tall Romanesque columns towering at its entrance, opened. Two huge metal doors, each a foot thick and two stories tall, swung on ancient hinges. Two figures walked out from the internal shadows of the building.

Sunlight cut through the doors casting a long patch of harsh light over tiny internal tiles. The two men, if a lack of breasts and pronounced hips indicated the male gender, walked out calmly. One of the men was tall, his copper skin set off against white aluminum teeth. His clothes were deep purples, reds, and whites. The nearest equivalent would be robes but these were tight enough that "dress" might have been accurate as well.

The other man was short. He looked heavier by far than either Dorothy or his companion. His copper skin was scarred and cracked with age. He was completely bald and his clothes were instantly recognizable as military in nature. Insignia dotted the closely fitted black uniform.

Dorothy greeted both men by presenting her open palms for a moment to each of them in turn. "I would like to introduce you to..." she stopped mid-sentence as though considering, "Doctor Stuart," she motioned to the tall man in colorful robes as she did. "And Admiral Lousinsorinsiri," she said, giving the Admiral a scowl.

"On behalf of the People of Earth, I would like to thank you for welcoming us to your world," Captain Grey began.

"Captain?" Dorothy asked, "perhaps we might be allowed to show you and your crew our world. Professor Stuart has been voted by the Commons as the best person to show Ensign Arnold around, and Admiral Lousinsorinsiri and Major Williams will have a great deal in common."

Captain Grey gave each of his officers a nod in turn, "and I assume you'll be giving me the tour?" She slipped her arm through his, and pulled cold titanium armor against her warm side.

CHAPTER 15

"YOU KNOW WHAT THE COMMONS IS LIKE? When some baby-faced officer walks into his first command – thinking he knows everything. Thinking he's a god and is going to make Admiral by the time he's half your age," Lousinsorinsiri slapped down an almost empty shot glass on the table, sending two glistening droplets of the spirit flying. "And imagine if he was right. If he did know everything. Every book, every rule, but he didn't know shit about actual soldiering." He took a nearly empty bottle like it was a mace and refilled his glass, almost chipping both in the process.

Ben Williams leaned forward in his seat, resting on a padded pole that rose vertically from its front, and drained his own shot glass. "So that shared memory shit isn't perfect?"

Lousinsorinsiri fired back another shot and clenched the glass in his fist. "I can relive a thousand different murders if I want. A father killing his daughter's rapist, a woman killing her husband because she thought he was going to leave her, or any of the men I killed. But living a memory in someone else's place doesn't mean you know how you'll react to it, or whether your hand will shake when the moment comes." He let the glass drop from his hand. It hit the table and tumbled to its side, rolling a half a foot. He half lurched, half stood, to retrieve a fresh bottle for the two men. "Are there many professional soldiers on Earth, Major?"

"Just call me Ben. And there are some but it's a dying profession. These days they want to put bad guys in jail and be all nice and civilized about it."

The Admiral scoffed and inspected the label on a new, sealed, bottle before pulling the stopper out of its end. "You have the nanites? Cause this one has just a little poison in it – for flavor." He poured both men a double measure of the scarlet contents. Ben nodded and took his glass.

"The Commons was pissed that I wouldn't pick one of your Earth names. But why don't you call me L," L drained his glass and Ben tipped his own into his mouth. It tasted like venom and he nearly spat it out; but fought the instinct, grunted, and swallowed going pale as the liquid burned his esophagus the whole way down.

"I was wondering about that. Didn't want to say anything but it's weird you folks all have English names."

"They're terrified of offending anyone. It's been so long since we have even bothered to make friends with someone who wasn't in the Commons we forgot how, and they are just desperate for you to like them."

Ben took up the bottle and blinked hard trying to force his eyes to focus on the hashes that made up a completely alien language. After a minute he gave up deciding he was too drunk.

"So why introduce me to you. I'm sure there're young ladies somewhere here eager to make friends with an earthling?"

L laughed, his head tilting back revealing that he had two rows of teeth. "One of our most prominent biologists lives close. She's been saying that she can be over in five minutes with her equipment to examine you if you would like." L's eyes drifted off for a half moment before snapping back, "she also says you can see hers, if she can see yours."

It took two hours for Major Williams and the Admiral to finish their second bottle. Without the nanites Williams would have been passed out and half dead.

"So there Downey is, just as happy as a kid, sitting in the sand and throwing this mortar shell into the air and catching it in his helmet. – Klang, Klang, Klang. And I'm running at him screaming bloody murder and wondering why I'm not just letting this asshole blow himself up."

L shook his head in disbelief then laughed. "So did you get to him in time?"

Ben nodded with a snort, "but it wouldn't have mattered. That kid was the dumbest person I ever knew but god loved him. He stepped on a landmine the next week and you know what – it was a dud. He wound up going home and winning a pile of money in the lottery."

L looked at Ben with silent alarm, his muscles tightening under his now half open jacket. It had taken hours, but the Common's patience had been rewarded, "you believe in a god?"

Ben's head swirled, "nah. You got any more about that lady you were telling me about before?"

L relaxed, slumped forward against the padded pole of his chair. One down, two to go. "She was a piece of work, Ben. Absolutely gorgeous but completely uninterested in sex. She had never had it, never wanted it, never even lived out any memories of it through the Commons. You see someone you like the look of, anyone, and you can relive a memory of someone who got them. But if they never had sex…" He rolled his empty shot glass under his hand grinding the glass against the table top. "That was... frustrating. You have this beautiful woman and you gotta wonder what it would be like with her, but no one knows, not even her. You want to know how to make yourself crave something? Don't let yourself have it."

L inspected the bottom of the bottle, disappointed, before continuing. "Anyways, so we're out doing a non-com patrol. That's stopping in and checking up on people who weren't joined to the Commons. Once you're joined up everyone knows everything about you so there is no lying, no surprise attacks, no organizing in secret, everything is out in the open and there's no need for men like me. But not everyone joins, and they could be up to anything, so we pay them a visit from time to time, make sure they have what they need, you know, a real eyes open kinda helpful."

"How many don't join?"

"One in a million thing back then. Now really it is just the Theists who refuse. So, we went to this one guy's house. Now, the Corporal, she had this theory: you want to know the state of a man's mind, put him in front of a beautiful woman; he gets too interested, there's something wrong; he pretends not to notice, there's something wrong; he treats her badly or rudely, there's something wrong. But all polite, a little flirty, well then you know he isn't too far off."

"You don't have guys who are more interested in guys than women?"

"Of course we do. We have everything. When it comes to sex if you can think up an interest or combination that no one in the Commons has ever tried they'll practically give you a medal. But it takes a certain kind of person to turn down the Commons. They're people who don't want to connect with society, don't want to feel like they're accepted or have to accept others. I am sure it happens, I just haven't met a non-com who was attracted to the same gender."

"Fair enough, I am certainly not trying to be the diversity police."

"You have diversity police?"

"That, my friend, is a completely different story I'll have to tell you. Finish yours."

"So, we're talking with this guy, and he is drooling over the Corporal. He is looking at her, big eyes, glancing up and down like he is thinking about which part to bite first. Eventually we leave and the Corporal, well her theory says that this guy isn't right. She decides she's going to check up on him. Now without him being in the Commons we have to go through everyone else's memories to see who's seen him, where, when, and try to piece together what he's been up to. All the information is there but you have to really work at putting it all together in a way that makes sense. It takes a few days, but she figures out he's been going to parties and at every-single-one, a beautiful young lady ends up passing out after having a few too many drinks – or so they all thought. She just had a sense about the guy from the way he was looking at her and she stopped a serial rapist."

"What's she doing now?"

"Dead," L stopped. "Theist's got her a few years ago."

"I'm sorry." The room was quiet. L looked at his hands on the tabletop while the seconds slowly ticked by.

"They also killed my daughter Ben."

Williams tried to focus, tried to force the fog in his head to clear, "who killed her – you had a kid?"

"I never said that aloud before. Everyone just knows. We don't have many fights left in us. But the Theists are religious fanatics and felt the Commons went against god. They started bombings, abductions."

Ben listened wishing he hadn't drunk so much but making a conscious effort to focus. "At first we just used the police. We arrested the violent ones, tried to get one of them to join the Commons so we could understand 'em. They refused. It's so hard to understand someone when you don't know the whole story, Ben. Not after generations of the Commons."

Ben nodded, "how did your daughter get caught up in it?"

L slumped forward, a man defeated by drink and time. "My fault. I eventually got sent after them. We took out a few camps and in revenge they started abducting and killing the kids of the military officers. Sivapathsandra, my girl, was the first. 15 years old, she hadn't even been connected to the Commons yet..." His voice trailed off and he rubbed his temples, grief written in a universal language across his face.

"You have to understand Ben, for us that is the worst thing that a person can do to another – killing someone before they join the Commons. Once we're connected, everything about us, our whole lives, who we are, is shared. My father's been dead twenty years and I can relive every moment we ever had together as though it were happening right now. I'll never know my daughter that way. I'll never really understand her.

Do you have any idea what that would be like – to not understand your own girl?"

Ben gave his friend a nod in support and couldn't help his thoughts turning to his own family and what he would give to understand his daughter. "Did you ever catch them?"

"Yes, and no… The thing about having everyone in your head is that they know when you can't do your job properly. They wouldn't let me close to the Theists after that. They sent the police in, lost a few of them as well, but eventually rounded up the last few dozen fanatics and put them in jail."

Williams nodded, "I hope they have long lives rotting in there."

L brightened and gave Ben a half smile, "actually some of them won't be."

Ben leaned back eyeing his friend suspiciously, "you have the death penalty?"

It was a calculated risk, though what in life wasn't. L knew the Commons had ulterior motives for what it was allowing, and the Commons knew that L couldn't have cared less.

"More, a… tradition. At the end of their life most people pour themselves into the Commons, living out other people's memories of luxury, sex, meals, whatever it is they want, and eventually their bodies fade away peacefully. But a few decide that they want to do something that's never been done before – bring a completely new memory into the Commons. I wish it translated better. We call it, 'The Impossible'. It is only a handful of people a year, and only with their consent. Some choose to fight wild animals barehanded, or climb a mountain without safety equipment. I invited the leader of the fanatics, the man who killed my girl, to a duel."

Ben shook his head, "don't do it."

L took a long, slow, breath, "Ben. Don't tell me what to do. The one thing that makes us who we are is that we're free to make our own choices. We debate in the Commons, we share a million different points of view and experiences, but it is for each of us to decide what we do and what we value. Sometimes life is about the mistakes we make."

L slid his hands over the table in front of him, and pushed aside small droplets of liquor as he did, "the Impossible... What a thing. See he had to agree to it as well, and the only way he would agree is if it's him and nineteen of his buddies vs. me."

Williams' face drained, "when?"

"Tomorrow. The bastards are looking forward to it I bet. But you know what? So am I."

L ran his hands over the tabletop, specks of liquor broke and absorbed into the surface. "They offered to let me have a second man with me. Damn well knew none of my old officers would want to go against those odds."

The truth, but not the whole truth. It was as far as L was willing to go for the Commons.

Williams nodded, "sounds like a very pretty suicide."

L let his face slacken, "it is. But I get the pleasure of killing a few more of them in the process. There're no more battles to fight Ben. These fanatics were the last bad guys."

"Good hunting my friend."

***

REBECCA DANIELS TRIED TO IMAGINE SOMETHING other than immersing her long brown hair into a bucket of sewage. She had tried pretending it was a mud bath. The muck's harsh chemical smell broke that illusion. The brown sludge in the bucket soaked through her hair and hit the back of her head, clumpy, thick, lukewarm. Her whole body shuddered.

The Galileo's water recyclers couldn't handle shampoo and conditioner. And so, the 'mud bath' had been created. L'Oréal wasn't going to be selling it back on Earth any time soon.

The industrial slurry was, of course, perfectly hygienic. It just looked, and smelled, and felt, awful. But it cleaned hair, and even better it did so without wetting it. Like water drops off Teflon, after a few seconds of immersion Daniels simply lifted her head out and her hair came out clean and dry.

"Still better than shaving it all off?" Vivian asked as she climbed into the bunk under Rebecca's. The thin sheets and mattress were still warm from their previous occupant.

"Another three years and we'll have to see."

"Don't be hasty. You want to be pretty for the cameras back on Earth when we get home. Movies, magazine covers, we're going to be famous," Vivian said as she pulled the sheets over herself, already half dreaming of cocktail dresses and beach parties.

Daniels strapped on her titanium armband, picked up a data pad, and exited the closet-sized cabin. And came face to face with Tsang.

"You need something Corporal?" a slight inflection on the last word to remind him of his place.

"No, Sergeant, just on my way to medical. I think I pulled something at the gym."

"And you just happened to find yourself outside my quarters on your way?" Rebecca set a quick pace that Tsang matched. He moved calmly, putting the lie to his excuse.

"Actually, I had a deal for you," he kept pace and dug into his right hip pocket.

"There's nothing I want Tsang..." her voice trailed off with her footsteps. In his right-hand Tsang dangled a necklace. The string was a simple heavy red thread, but at its bottom a crystal pendant. Technically it was Plexiglas with refractive properties matching crystal. What was important was Daniels' four seconds of silent incomprehension.

"How did you get that?" Daniels asked, her eyes on nothing but the pendant.

"I heard you broke one like it and have a friend in engineering. It wasn't easy but we printed a new one," he slowly twisted the string showing off the craftsmanship.

"It's identical..." Rebecca said to herself. Then, pulled her attention back to Tsang and asked exactly the question he was hoping for. With preparation everything comes easily.

"I understand you have three hours of unused shower credits. That's all I'm after."

Rebecca took the pendant lovingly, cupping it in her right hand a long moment and then slipping it over her neck. "Done. But transferring them is your problem. I have no idea how to do it," she turned and began to walk away.

Had Tsang not had his fill of brisk treatment, had he not felt the need to show how well connected he was, what magic he could accomplish, he would have said nothing. He would have taken his victory for what it was and walked away.

"Don't worry. I have a guy."

Rebecca rolled her eyes, "yeah. A guy with access to the computer control system... And who needs shower credits..." Saying it aloud she realized at once who Tsang meant. Her legs locked, planted on the deck. "That bastard!"

She turned on Tsang, face flush, "he told you about this breaking... How much it meant to me!" She pulled the necklace off, nearly tearing the cord from her neck. "He would rather tell you about this than even talk to me himself!?"

Tsang froze on the spot completely off guard. Rebecca boiled for six seconds and then ran down the corridor, footsteps echoed long after she was out of sight.

Tsang headed back, towards his quarters. Had he done his job, save some hiccups? Or had he done his job, plus learned something?

In confusion comes opportunity: another rule. Now he just had to figure out what he had learned.

CHAPTER 16

MINDY STOOD IN THE CENTER of a cavernous, circular, room. The lights were dim, and she could feel hundreds of eyes on her from the room's periphery. Dr. Stuart stood beside her, grinning like a schoolboy. He shifted from side to side as though his old legs couldn't bear his weight for long. Why had she allowed herself to be led into a room like this? Why had she just followed Dr. Stuart from the Churchill's landing site? "Every benefit of the doubt," was the order.

"Now... Don't worry, please we're all so eager to meet you, and we think we can help you as well!"

Mindy glanced over her shoulder and then back. Her body readied, her feet spread apart, her weight shifted down ever so slightly.

"My friends and I are very much interested in teaching styles and thought we would hold a class in orbital dynamics for you."

"I thought everyone learned through your internet implants," she said, wondering if she had misunderstood.

Doctor Stuart grinned excitedly at that, "oh we do, we do. But you know it's a very interesting problem how to teach people information without the benefit of that technology and me and my friends here have a very active community talking about different theories of learning and how they might be applied without the Commons."

The buzz of the room inverted. Mindy was reminded of the unbridled excitement her last boyfriend on Earth had when talking about antique wrist watches. She considered asking what practical use that would be, and remembered the look of hurt in her ex's eyes when she had asked him the same question. She could use a good orbital dynamics class. She hoped her broad smile wasn't over-doing things, "that's really interesting!"

Doctor Stuart glowed and waved to everyone as though to get their attention. The Commons, it seemed, could be willfully blind.

"Now Mindy, let's start by imagining the planet 'Cube'," the Doctor held up his hands and over their heads appeared a giant cube, easily the size of a car. It just hovered in the air overhead. Orbiting the giant cube was a small, crude, human doll.

"This is of course not to scale." The model doll orbited the cube planet quickly. The doll was oriented so that its stomach faced down towards the planet and flew around it like it was a superhero — head always pointed forward, stomach always towards the surface of Cube. The Cube stood stationary beneath it.

"As I'm sure you know, there are many ways you can orbit a planet. You can have a circular orbit, an elliptical orbit, or you can not be in orbit at all and go by so fast the gravity of the planet barely has a chance to change your path."

"The calculations for each of these are rudimentary. Plug in the numbers for the mass of the planet, your position, and velocity and you're done. Any computer can do that for you."

Rudimentary wouldn't have been her choice of words to describe solving the basic orbital dynamics equation: 'possible - with effort', or perhaps 'vexing.' That was the word. God designed the perfect challenge for her combining math and theory, in a counter-intuitive package to test her patience and resolve. It was vexing, until she overcame it. But she held her tongue.

"Now... Let's talk about frames of reference. Right now we're actually thinking about things from the point of view of the planet. You're orbiting the planet, the planet not moving under you. The planet is the frame of reference. But there's no reason why it should be this way and, at times, it can make things harder to understand. For example, when you're orbiting the planet like this, are you spinning?"

Biting her lower lip, "I am staying stationary. If I was spinning the planet would be going around and around under me."

Professor Stuart smiled and motioned upwards. The model had changed. Instead of Mindy's doll flying around the planet like superman it was now always pointing in the same direction. It seemed to be tumbling as it did so. And Mindy saw it. The doll had to spin around to keep its belly towards the surface of the planet.

"If you were not spinning when you had your belly towards one side of the planet you would have your back to it when you orbited to the other side. It is only by spinning you stay facing the planet as you move around it."

Professor Stuart gave her a minute and let the lesson sink in. "Why does this matter, you might ask. Because it is very easy to forget about what frame of reference you are thinking of and make a simple mistake. Let's say you calculate the speed for a circular orbit is 100 meters per second. You're orbiting Cube in one direction at 100 meters per second and want to fire a rocket in the opposite direction."

The model changed. Mindy was again orbiting the planet and this time was holding a small rocket launcher that she had pointed towards her feet in the opposite direction of her travel.

"This was my last command test. I never did figure out why it didn't work."

"Because of frames of reference," Professor Stuart smiled. The little model fired its rocket. The rocket stopped dead in space and then fell to the planet. The speed, 100 meters per second, had simply cancelled out the speed of the ship it had been fired from and so, relative to the planet, its speed was zero. It was like driving down the highway at 60 miles per hour and throwing a fastball backwards. If you could throw at 60 miles per hour the ball would simply stop dead and fall to the road. You would have to be able to throw at 120 miles per hour for the ball to go backwards at 60 miles per hour.

Mindy felt her face flush with embarrassment, "my god. It's so simple."

Professor Stuart smiled, "mistakes are the best teachers."

The Professor shifted more slowly, and rested his weight on his left leg, "as a side note... That expression 'my god' was it. That's a religious reference?"

Mindy nodded, her eyes glued to the model above. The Common's task over, Professor Stuart lightened and followed Mindy's eyes back up. "Now... Would you like to know why, if you throw a hammer away from you in orbit it will fly around you and hit you in the back of the head?"

CHAPTER 17

THE STADIUM WAS SMALL. Its main floor slightly bigger than a tennis court's, and only four rows of seats surrounded it. The ceiling, which on Earth would have towered hundreds of feet overhead, was no higher than that of a large warehouse or industrial plant. It was also nearly silent, yet hundreds of people sat in their seats, breathing slowly. Only four seats were empty, but no one spoke, no one ate, no one waved flags or signs.

Grey, Williams, Mindy, and Dorothy walked easily through the rows of seated spectators. There was a tremendous variation among the audience members. Grey had enough trouble keeping up with human fashion trends when he had been on Earth, but he could recognize that there was no uniform color, fabric, or style that tied together any large group of the audience. Hair was likewise worn in dozens of different styles, colors, and with various degrees of attention and ornamentation. That said, the human eye does pay attention to certain things: race being one of them. Had half the aliens all had a mole on the same spot on their left hand, and the others not, Grey never would have noticed. But there were two tones of skin color, and that was noted.

A little more than half the aliens were the copper-bronze of Dorothy, L, and Professor Stuart. The rest were lighter. He tried not to be too obvious in his observation but looked nonetheless. The ones with lighter skin tone were still bronze, but they looked almost dusty, sickly. Sickly. The word struck him as correct even as he thought it. Grey examined the aliens with the sickly skin more carefully. They were thinner on average than their darker compatriots. What flesh they exposed looked less muscular than the others. Their clothes seemed newer, less worn. He tried not to smile as he imagined the French aristocracy and their powered skin and impractical outfits.

Despite the bulk of their armor, there was no jostling. The seated crowd silently made way for them to reach their seats, front and center. They were great seats, the only thing between them and the arena was a glass barrier that spanned from the floor to the roof of the arena. Each panel of glass as wide as a horse.

"Why is it so small?" Mindy asked Dorothy softly.

"Why would it be any larger?"

"Don't more people want to see this?" Mindy asked.

"The people here each have a different perspective, and everyone else can watch through their eyes to get a full perspective." Dorothy stretched back on her seat, grasped the padded support pole in front of her with one hand, and her ankle in another pulling her leg forward until the sole of her boot almost touched her stomach.

"What do you mean, a different perspective?"

"Different people react differently to the same thing. We try to make sure every different kind of person is here; so we can experience what they see from every point of view."

The floor of the arena was a painted heavy metal. There were no jumbotrons, no scoreboards, no advertisements, not even painted lines on the floor. Without the perfume of hot dogs, popcorn, or beer, to dilute the stale acidic smell of old sweat the stadium was decidedly uncomfortable.

After nothing but silence for a solid minute Grey leaned towards Dorothy, and following social cues that ought not to have applied to an alien, whispered, "some of your people here look different from the others. Their skin is... ashen? Less dark than the others?"

The audience smiled in unison at that, eavesdropping through the Commons on their guests even as they watched the arena.

"Some people spend a great deal of time inside the Commons," Dorothy whispered back, "they don't get as much exercise or sunlight as others."

"How many hours a day do they stay connected?" Grey asked, and the audience's smiles turned into a gentle laugh that vibrated through the stadium before fading away a moment later.

"Think years not hours. Some people are consumers, others producers."

Grey inhaled for a follow up question when he caught motion in the corner of his eye. There was no fanfare. A young man, cheeks drawn and hollow, stepped up and into the arena from a sunken tunnel.

The crowd was totally silent as the young man walked forward. His steps were hesitant, his gait odd, even considering the exaggerated sway that was natural to Dorothy's people. The young man was wearing heavy material from head to toe. It could have been leather from the way it bent and bunched as he moved. In his right hand he carried a simple, short, sword. The sword's blade was a perfect triangle. It had no hilt, was six inches wide at the base, and tapered down to a fine point over its two-foot length.

Dorothy's whisper was the only sound in the arena, "that is Magedastrarika. There was an accident at his work, and he was irradiated. He won't be getting better, despite our best efforts." When Magedastrarika reached the center of the stadium he stopped and turned in a slow circle, looking at the crowd almost as though he were just seeing them for the first time. "And that is a Lextrum."

Grey almost didn't see it at first. The animal was the size of a full-grown black bear, but no one would have made happy children's stories about it. Its skin was bare, grey, and thick like an elephant, yet huge muscles rippled beneath the surface as it moved. Its head was elongated halfway between a bear and a crocodile. Two large fangs, tinted red and green, pushed its lips aside as they extended from its mouth. The fangs grew from a few inches to nearly a foot long. Despite its size the creature's motions were smooth. It didn't so much walk as shift its shoulders and hips. When it saw the man in front of it, the creature opened its mouth. Its lower jaw was split down the middle each half moved independently as it howled in rage.

"Wait," Mindy said standing. Captain Grey took her arm and sharply pulled her down into her seat.

"Stand fast Ensign!"

The creature sniffed the stadium air and paced in front of the door that had let it in. Its movements were cat like – graceful yet restrained. It paced back and forth thirty yards from Magedastrarika but did not advance, instead turning its back on him to inspect the crowd.

Magedastrarika crouched low, frozen in the center of the stadium watching the animal but not advancing on it. "Why doesn't Magedatraka attack it? That's what this is right?" Grey asked.

Dorothy took her eyes off the court and looked at Grey as though he were a naughty child, "the lextrum gets to decide if it wants a fight too. It would be unethical to simply attack it."

Mindy looked mutinous as she huffed in her seat at the reply.

The creature in the arena seemed to make up its mind. It turned towards the man, then hissed a challenge. "No one has ever fought one of those before?" Williams asked their host. The animal lowered itself close to the ground, thirty yards separating the two. It widened its stance, flattened its body, and despite the light-years between their worlds, looked very much like a cheetah coiled to strike.

"Not since the Commons," Dorothy answered, then reconsidered, "actually in the Common's early days one person once climbed into a lextrum pen at a zoo. He was too foolish to check what the pen was for and thought it would be funny. But that doesn't count."

Magedastrarika's hand tightened on the grip of his sword and he fixed a look of determined fear on his face. It was a look Grey recognized. The creature bound forward. Its strides were long, too long, it almost flew across the ground. Ten yards from the man it threw itself at him. A half a ton of death dove at Magedastrarika like a linebacker sacking a quarterback. The creature came down on the spot Magedastrarika had been standing a heartbeat before, with two clawed paws that would have eviscerated him – if he had still been there. With speed unfitting his appearance, Megedastrarika dove forward at the last second, rolled under the lextrum and struck at its hind legs with his sword.

The animal howled in rage and pain, blood ran down its right leg and it turned on the man. He plunged his sword forward stabbing at the animal's flank, but the thrust was not straight and sliced along the Lextrum's side instead of penetrating.

The beast shrugged off the pain and, as Magedastrarika's thrust ran out of steam, it lunged forward with its fangs. The man raised his left arm just in time and the lextrum bit down on it instead of his head. Magedastrarika screamed in pain as fangs sunk deep into his flesh, but he was not incoherent, and rammed his sword up and into the beast's throat, burying the blade a foot into the animal.

The lextrum released Magedastrarika's arm. Blood issued from its mouth. For a split second it looked like the man had won but, mortally wounded, the lextrum still had strength, and slashed Magedastrarika's chest with its left arm. Brutal claws cut through clothes, flesh, and bone, and he collapsed onto the ground silently. The lextrum had only a few seconds to savor its revenge before it too fell.

"Well. That was fun," Mindy said and crossed her arms in front of her. The metal of her suit's armor ground against itself as she did.

"It isn't about fun," Dorothy said, adjusting her own bright clothes. "It's about someone who didn't want to live anymore giving the Commons a new experience, teaching us something along the way even if we don't always know what it is at first."

Grey flashed Mindy a sharp look.

Workers swarmed in. A handful retrieved the bodies of both man and lextrum and carried them carefully from the field. More dragged heavy barriers in, working to assemble them in seemingly random spots on the court. The barriers were flat, metal, each two meters high and wide. The workers quickly assembled the barriers into random patterns creating obstacles, dead ends, and pathways: a giant maze.

"Admiral Lousinsorinsiri is about to start," Dorothy informed them.

"No announcers?" Williams asked, squeezing the words out through grinding teeth.

"No. The Commons gives each observer exactly the information they need when they need it. Most know why the Admiral is here, through his own memories, or the recollection of others. Some have no idea what is about to happen or why. This way the Commons observes the event from all perspectives. The whole story."

Ben closed his eyes for a moment, "bastards."

Ensign Arnold, sat straighter, "wait. That's the Admiral we met earlier. He isn't going in there is he?"

Dorothy nodded, "the Commons solved most of our social and political problems. When everyone shares thoughts and opinions every opinion can be tested and accepted, disproven, or referred for further study. However there were some people who chose not to join the Commons. They claim that a being controls the very fabric of reality and our purpose in life is to worship this being. It is of course patently false, but these people didn't want to know whether or not it was true."

"We call that religion," Mindy added.

"We still don't understand them, not really," Dorothy went on. "Who would choose not to know the truth?" She shrugged, "but if they didn't want to know, we're under no obligation to force them. We decided to simply leave them to do as they wished. But they surprised us again. It wasn't enough for them to be left alone, they insisted that we worship this being as well and saw the Commons as what prevented that."

Grey put a hand on Mindy's shoulder, a warning, a comfort.

"After several violent attacks on engineers who maintain the Commons, we had no choice. We had to use the military to act and protect ourselves."

Mindy breathed in to interject and Grey cut her off, "we've had many situations on Earth where we had to use the military to settle disputes. *Many*," he emphasized the last word looking into Mindy's eyes.

"You have to understand that none of this made any sense to us. This is the greatest mystery we have. Why couldn't they accept just being left alone? Why wouldn't they want to know the truth about the world? Why wouldn't they want their views challenged, weighed, fairly and fully debated if they were so passionate they were right?"

"And why wouldn't they fight honorably when you sent the military after them? Why would they attack the families of the officers?" Williams asked.

Mindy trembled in her seat as Dorothy answered, "that we understand. Vengeance. Rage. We didn't expect it, but we understand it."

"How did it happen? – the Admiral's daughter," Williams asked.

Dorothy's face slackened, her eyes drifted forward, then clicked over to Williams, "Lealseantra, that's Lousinsorinsiri's daughter, me, and a few other kids were playing squares. These two men came up to us, asked if she was Lealeantra, and as soon as she said yes, they grabbed her arms and started pulling her away. I ran to get help, I was only 8 and couldn't fight them, but by the time I got an adult they were gone."

Dorothy's face slackened again and when she came back she looked at Grey, "we went after them immediately, and it only took an hour to find them but by that time Lealseantra had been killed, mutilated. She was ten.'

Williams' voice vibrated like a stressed steel cable, "you didn't think that you'd need to protect military families?"

Dorothy narrowed her eyes at Williams, "you probably get away with questions like that a lot, don't you? Try turning your keen eye for hindsight towards the future and we'll talk."

The sound of the arena doors opening put an end to the conversation.

Major Williams expected L to enter the arena first, but when the doors opposite them opened, twenty men in clean, thin, black clothes entered. Each carried a large black rifle. Bulbous sights were mounted on the top of the weapons and the butt and barrel grips were wood. A few of the men pointed their weapons at the crowd threateningly. Others raised their rifles over their heads, two-handed, and shouted in triumph and challenge. They were excited, they wanted this.

One of the men leveled his rifle at the crowd, and fired. The laser beam was visible, yet only lasted a fraction of a second. Looking at it was like catching a glimpse of lightning; you know you saw it but not quite how long it had lasted. The beam hit the glass barrier and terminated there, harmlessly. "Don't worry," Dorothy said, "this glass disperses the laser frequencies those fire."

One of the rebels stood a head taller than the others. He wore his hair shaved in two long strips that ran from temple to the back of his head. Dorothy pointed towards him, "that's Razek, their leader. He is the one the Admiral blames for his daughter's death."

Razek shouted something the three crewmen couldn't understand but made Dorothy sit up straighter with indignation. He had years to think of an insult and apparently had put the time to good use. Razek began signaling towards his men to move, and they spread out following orders about as well as civilians could be expected to – forming pairs or triplets and finding positions they thought would provide some cover and the opportunity to fire.

"You're going to let Lousinsorinsiri walk into an ambush like this?" Major Williams squeezed his gauntleted hands into fists at his sides, metal popped and clicked as it skidded and caught against itself.

Dorothy shrugged, "it was the deal he made with them. People can make their own choices. He feels it is disappointing none of his comrades were willing to join him though."

The small doorway opposite them opened again, the only announcement of L's presence there would be. It was enough. The rebels raised their weapons, ready, aiming carefully, waiting.

One of the rebels had chosen to stand behind the first barrier outside the door. His head and rifle, exposed above its protective edge, faced into the unlit entranceway. Stupid. In war if you can't see your enemy, you can't let him see you. The purest Darwinian process began as a lance of laser sizzled the air between the entrance doorway and the rebel's face.

The rebels hadn't mentally prepared themselves for the reality of combat and all turned to look at their comrade's ruined face. L exploited the opportunity and exploded into the arena, throwing himself against the nearest barricade with the force of a cannonball.

Grey doubted any human Olympian could have reached the speed L ran at, and a dozen laser beams hit the door in his wake. The weapons fired at the speed of light, but their operators' reflexes had a delay. Surprise, a moving target, and a lack of training cost them their best single shot.

L cowered against the bottom of his barrier, the smoldering corpse of the rebel he killed draped across its top. He let the rebels' fire hit the ground around him, the body of their comrade, and the barricade. None had a clear shot. He let their frustration grow and after a moment he hefted his own rifle, raised it tight against his shoulder and began hunting.

Three rebels, well concealed behind cover, elected to charge the Admiral, shouting in foolish rage as they did so. Street thugs would have had more sense, and the Admiral, with the benefit of cover, forewarned by their shouts, and with a lifetime of practice, picked them off easily as they charged.

With the dumbest fifth of rebels dead the Admiral began to move. The obvious strategy was to try and flank the obstacle course and, had his foes been thinking like career military officers, they would have made their flanks their strongest points.

Evolution teaches certain lessons regardless of the solar system, and without training the rebels had only instinct to rely on. They concentrated their forces in the center of the labyrinth like a pack of animals seeking protection from predators. This would have been the correct course of action for millions of years; no longer.

The Admiral managed to make it to the far wall of the arena safely and began circling around the maze of barricades. He moved slowly, methodically, stalking. There were however simply too many rebels. As he moved down a corridor of barricades a rebel rounded the other end of the tunnel not two meters away from the admiral.

It came down to who could pull the trigger faster and the Admiral won, by a hair. L was better than any of them, one on one he could have beaten them all. But one man against twenty, now fifteen, was an impossible task.

Major Williams sat, muscles tensing and shifting with adrenaline fueled outrage as he scanned the maze. He looked for Razek's distinctive haircut. If the Admiral could find Razek before getting hit he would at least have a fair chance at his revenge.

L caught two more rebels from behind before they started to get smart. One of the rebels climbed the barricades directly in front of the Galileo's crew. The top of the barricade was barely wide enough for him to stand, but he had a clear view over the entire arena. The Admiral was facing away, preparing to make his way around another corner in the maze. The rebel raised his rifle, aimed, took his time, and fired. A lance of laser light flashed across the stadium and struck the Admiral in the back, hitting his shoulder.

There was no physical force to the blast, it didn't send the Admiral tumbling forward or send blood spraying in all directions in the way a physical shot would have. L might have grabbed his shoulder in pain and froze – every nerve in his body was shocked by the laser's heat - but a lifetime of training paid dividends. Before the sniper could fire again L collapsed to the side and pressed himself tightly against the wall of a barricade.

Ben Williams shifted in his seat. Every soldier has a visceral hatred for snipers. From basic training you were taught to despise and fear them. No matter how skilled, no matter how alert, no matter how strong or fast or disciplined, a sniper hiding in a pile of rubble a half a mile away could end you with the motion of his finger. In combat they were far worse than training taught.

Thirty years later Williams could still taste dirt, blood, and fear in his mouth. He remembered watching a friend bleed out in agony while they waited for armored support to arrive. The man had been a dozen yards away, but the sniper made that an ocean. He had spent an hour watching, helpless, and burned with a rage he'd never known he had. Had the tank not killed the sniper Williams knew there was nothing, nothing, he would have considered evil to have done to the man.

L couldn't wait for help like Williams had. He couldn't wait for a tank to roll up, or air support to give him cover. He had to kill the sniper himself and the sniper was just waiting for him to stick his head up and try. All the sniper had to do was be patient.

Williams found himself on his feet. His body stood of its own accord, but once he was up, he knew what he had to do. His suit's thruster package fired off a quick set of test thrusts, a pound of force from each thruster, just enough to ensure everything was working. The back of his throat was coated in bitter bile. Every muscle urged him forward, pulsing with the desire to kill. He wanted to rip the sniper's head off and drink his blood. He turned on Dorothy. "That glass stop bullets?"

"Small ones," she replied.

In a smooth, practiced, ice cold motion, Williams gripped the chestnut handle of his MX-3, leveled it with the glass pane in front of him, and applied 4.5 pounds of force to the trigger. One round rocketed forward at the pane of glass separating Williams from the rebel sniper. The rocket round accelerated out of the gun, smashed through the sound barrier with a thunderous clap, and slammed into the glass with the kinetic energy of a jack hammer. And then it exploded. It was a war shot, fully powered, fully explosive.

The glass panel cracked; spider's web patterns snapped along its surface from floor to roof. The rocket's explosion blasted a hole the size of a melon from the pane, but it did not shatter. Williams, bare faced, arms tucked against his chest, jumped forward.

Grey had exactly enough time to shout, "Williams!" before the Major was clear of his seat.

As Williams pushed off with his legs, his suit's thrusters engaged, and flung him forward. He slammed into the glass. Weakened from the fractures running its length, and the hole from his round, the pane shattered into a billion pieces.

The rebel sniper had managed to turn his head in time, but turning on the thin divider put him off balance. His eyes and mouth were wide with surprise as the Major tackled him. Humanity making its first hostile contact with alien life.

The two men went down, hard, the rebel's bones broke under the force of the fall and the weight of Williams and his armor. Arms, legs, fists, and feet flailed and then the wet snap of breaking bones echoed through the stadium as the major twisted the rebel's head around 360 degrees.

There was no way to know how much force it took to snap an alien's neck, or what range of motion the alien's spine had. So Williams kept twisting until a lifetime of experience with violence registered the sound of tendons snapping, muscles ripping, and the sucking sound of flesh shearing apart. The sniper went limp. The medical term for the kill was 'internal decapitation'.

Grey was up and took a fast step towards the barrier before Dorothy caught his arm. "The Admiral was allowed a second. The rebels never agreed to face three. You can't go in."

With the immediate threat removed Williams rose and ran towards the nearest barrier. His boots dug into the painted floor, sending flecks of chipped paint into the air. Four steps away from the barrier he leapt, and his suit's thrusters flared, blasting him forward. He hit dead center, so hard he sent the barrier, and two Rebels crouching behind it, flying forward like twigs.

"Our suits can do that?" Mindy asked, wide eyes staring at the Major.

Grey pulled his arm free of Dorothy, "apparently."

The Captain had seen Major Williams shoot in training on Earth, in training on the Galileo, and as an instructor teaching zero gravity combat. He had never seen the man fire in anger. Williams slow, deliberate, movements in training morphed into oiled precision.

In the blink of an eye he fired twice, hit twice, and was sprinting again using his suit to accelerate his dash to superhuman speeds. The damage caused by an MX-3 hit was exactly as horrific as its manufacturer had promised.

Williams' feet no longer ran on the floor so much as jumped with each stride, applying enough upward force to spare his thrusters the task without dragging and slowing him down.

When Williams reached corners he didn't slow. He blasted through intersections sideways slamming into the opposite wall, sending it flying. It was effective but had a steep cost. Armor, and this is true of all armors from Major Williams' to a medieval knight's, works by spreading force over a wider area of the body. It does not reduce that force by a single ounce. With each barricade, with each hit, with each superhuman feat, Williams hurt himself under the armor. Bruises, cracked ribs, sprained tendons, torn muscles. Each impact had a toll.

It took mere seconds for him to reach the barrier L had been concealed behind. Two rebels, clad in black, and hefting rifles were about to encircle it from either side. They both had their flanks to Williams and attention firmly fixed on the Admiral's position. Williams fired on the further of the two rebels and missed, his weapon locked open, out of ammo.

He didn't have time to curse himself for losing track of his rounds, or at his hands for trembling from the accumulated trauma of multiple crashes. He didn't have time to weigh his situation or consider his actions. He had time to do one of two things: react, or die.

Williams thrust his suit towards the nearest rebel with everything it had. There was a reason Williams didn't train the Galileo's crew to use their suit's like this. A reason the suit's manufacturer normally locked out thrust in full atmosphere and normal gravity. For all the wonders of technology, physics cannot be ignored. As Williams accelerated the air resistance on his suit built up quickly and made him inherently unstable. Even with a lifetime of experience, he almost didn't make it. He almost spun out of control, almost lost his balance to the turbulent air, almost. He reached the rebel and slammed into him like a train.

The rebel had been quick. He'd managed to bring his rifle around, nearly got off a point-blank shot. Instead, Williams hit the rifle as he crashed into the rebel. The impact slammed the rifle back like a spear to the face, and crushed the rebel's head. It also broke three of Williams' ribs.

A half a second later and Williams turned on the second rebel, and the second rebel raised his rifle on Williams. Only three yards away, he fired. It was a wild, point-blank shot, and went straight for the Major's chest.

Several things happened in the tenth of a second that followed. The laser beam flashed through the air at the speed of light and hit the Major's left breast plate. As the laser superheated the breast plate's titanium surface the alloy melted to liquid, then boiled to gas, and as a gas, it absorbed even more laser energy super-heating into a plasma. The laser was so powerful the titanium armor's molecules broke up into their individual atoms which were then heated to such a temperature that their electrons separated from the nuclei.

Applied correctly the laser had enough energy to have melted through two inches of steel armor and the flesh of the person behind it. But that isn't what happened. Instead of heating the armor efficiently it superheated a small portion of it impossibly beyond the point of being necessary, or useful. The process is called ablation, the shedding of a portion of armor to waste most of the laser's energy. Instead of penetrating at low but otherwise lethal temperatures, the laser wasted its energy super heating metal.

After five-one-hundredths of a second, less time than a flap of a fly's wing, the laser beam ended. It had penetrated a centimeter into the plate armor. A centimeter was enough. The Major's breast plate was not a solid piece of armor, but a hollow tank filled with hydrogen fuel for his thrusters. Seven one hundredths of a second after the laser hit, the armored tank ruptured from the pressure. High pressure hydrogen vented forward. Nine one hundredths of a second after the rebel pulled the trigger the venting hydrogen hit the cloud of superheated plasma in front of the Major's beast plate.

The Major was thrown backwards, hit by a sledge-hammer explosion. The rebel who fired the shot was engulfed in a cloud of burning hydrogen and superheated titanium plasma and fell screaming to the arena floor.

It took a herculean effort for Williams to raise himself off the deck. He coughed, hard, his lungs attempted to exit through his mouth, and he spat a wad of foul metallic saliva onto the ground. He had never felt so physically abused in his life. Almost every inch of his body under the suit screamed of bruises and strained muscles. Getting to his feet was an accomplishment in and of itself. He holstered his MX-3, it's chestnut handle flecked black from titanium char.

"You still alive you stupid bastard?" Williams asked the barricade before looking around the corner.

L was laying on his side, his clothes soaked with blood, left arm folded over his wounded shoulder. In one hand he held his rifle like a pistol – trained on William's. For a moment L refused to believe what his eyes were telling him but, when it did his face transformed.

Williams had seen the look before. Men who had fought through the panic and fear of facing certain death had a resolve that was unbreakable by exhaustion, or danger, but would shatter at the slightest touch of hope. Over a lifetime in the military, it was an expression he had only seen a handful of times from fellow soldiers.

Unlike Williams, Admiral Lousinsorinsiri had never known the feeling was even possible. Never before in his career had he been without the Commons. He always knew where his men were, that they were coming for him, or that they weren't. It was a feeling no one in the Commons had ever experienced because they could never be alone, abandoned. So, they could never be redeemed.

Williams scanned the arena and gave L a private moment. A stray laser rifle, that would never be missed by its charred owner, found its way into his hands.

"Ben, thank you," L rose, wiping his face and resting the barrel of his own rifle on the barricade beside Williams.

The arena looked as though a tornado had cut a path through its center. Barricades were scattered, some stacked on top of others, some lay on their sides or were simply knocked about randomly. The left half of the maze had been cleared by the Admiral before he was hit and that left a sizable group of rebels left in the right half.

L glanced at the destruction, "you did that?"

"Don't get your hopes up. I'm basically out of fuel – maybe enough for one more good thrust."

L nodded "how many rebels left then?"

"Six."

Both men surveyed the remaining barricades in front of them. It might as well have been a bunker at Normandy. Two injured men against six fresh ones who were dug in, smart enough to survive this long, uninjured, and with all the time in the world.

"This isn't going to work," Williams crouched behind the barricade and shifted his grip on the laser rifle, holding the stock of the gun in his right hand. "On Earth every animal is afraid of fire. That true with you people?"

Williams set his left hand flat on the ground, palm down. His suit was dotted with thrusters of one size or another; the one on the back of his right hand was smaller than the others by far but still obviously a nozzle to direct and capture the thrust of the hydrogen/oxygen mixture the suit burned.

"Yes. If I could pick any weapon to attack a bunker like this, it would be a fire rifle. Burn them out or smoke them out," L replied looking at Williams curiously. The Major slammed the back of his hand with the butt of the rifle, deforming and warping the precision milled nozzle.

"The nozzle controls how the suit burns its fuel. Part oxygen, part hydrogen, you mix and ignite them and then control the burn, turning it into thrust. Fuck up the nozzle... and it just burns. All heat and no thrust."

He raised his hand and triggered the thruster. A seven-foot blast of flame raced forward and died after an instant.

Williams and L exchanged a smile. Left arm ahead of him, laser rifle in his right hand, Williams moved. He sprinted forward to the maze's left flank and, as he arrived at the first corridor, flames erupted from his suit.

L rested the barrel of his rifle on the edge of the barricade. In a war most shots taken aren't aimed. They are not meant to hit anything, but to force the enemy to keep their heads down so you are free to maneuver. L laid down cover fire on the labyrinth in front of them.

Flames began to penetrate gaps in the barricades as Williams moved through the structure.

It only took a few seconds before the first of the rebels fled into the no-man's land of destruction the Major had created. His clothes were aflame, his rifle abandoned, he fell to the ground rolling, trying to smother the fire. L fired once.

The rebel's rolling ended, the fire he was trying to escape was freed to burn, slowly, charring his flesh, burning away his hair and skin, engulfing him. Fire is the cruelest weapon.

Inside the structure screams began to fill the air with equal parts black smoke. The stink of burning flesh reached the Admiral and he inhaled the bouquet.

The barricades, while well designed to separate men from each other and block laser fire, had gaps more than large enough for flames to blast through. The Oxygen/Hydrogen reaction of the Major's suit had been chosen for rocket fuel specifically because of its violence, and it burned hot enough to set steel aflame. As Williams worked his way deeper into the structure the painted floor behind him bubbled, burned, and filled the air with toxic ash.

Somewhere inside the barricades a laser rifle's power cell overheated and exploded with the force of a grenade. Debris, fire, flesh, blood, and sinew flew in every direction.

What was left of the labyrinth was hell. Some of the rebels, whether felled by laser fire, overcome by the smoke, or simply burned to death, were still inside the structure, their bodies aflame. Yet the sound of laser rifle fire somehow persisted longer than seemed possible.

Men can find fighting exciting. They can have an appetite for testing themselves against other men and proving their dominance. For that the other man must have a chance. War is different. The job of professional soldiers is to make their enemy as helpless as pigs in a pen, and then methodically slaughter them. There is no excitement there, no honor. There can be hatred; a butcher can hate the pig; but the better the soldier the less excitement.

Razak was the last out. Flames engulfed him. He was mad with pain and panic and sprinted out of the ruins, as though his burning clothes and flesh could be outrun. He made it a dozen yards before he stumbled and fell. While the Commons lived the experience through L, he could not hear it, it would have polluted the experience and so for the first time since he was a teenager, L was alone with his thoughts. L watched Razak writhe on the arena floor, slowly roasting to death, paint bubbled around him from the heat of the flames that consumed him. L knew what the Commons would have wanted. It took four seconds before he listened and pulled the trigger.

A moment after the final shot was fired, Williams limped out of the maze. He coughed, his face covered in blood, soot, and exhaustion. The arena was filled with toxic black smoke and, squinting, Williams looked out at the audience for a sign of concern, a sign of what was to come next.

Every face in the audience had the vacant look Williams had come to associate with connecting to the Commons, almost every face: Captain Grey was distinctly angry, and Mindy's mouth was open. He'd tried to tell her, being excellent at your job was a worthy path in life.

CHAPTER 18

"Now this's more like it!" Ben Williams raised a cup in toast and a thousand cups joined him.   Libations, and medications, gave the Major a high interest loan on a few hours freedom from pain. Had Grey sat down and thought about how to put his executive officer in the best possible mood this would have been the answer: victory, alcohol, adulation, fresh food, and open space. Mindy Arnold raised her own mug and took a long drink of her first wine in three years.

Unlike the stadium, which had all the personality of an industrial park, the hall the crew stood in glowed. The walls were made of solid blue crystal. A mile above the floor the walls slowly converged on themselves at a knife's edge. Mindy would have believed the entire building was made of a single piece of crystal had it not all been semi-transparent. Just behind the ocean blue walls, black obelisks rose supporting the structure.

In the center of the hall a table, two meters wide, two hundred meters long, and made of a single piece of wood, was loaded with thousands of plates of food. Steam, smell, and smoking meats filled the air for twenty meters above the table with a cloud of flavor that was almost as intoxicating to Arnold as her drink. Her own plate was loaded down like a greedy child's.

The crowd was like nothing she had ever experienced before. She was constantly the center of a circle of people, two dozen large, who would smile, look at her with adoration, ask a question, then walk away as soon as it was answered. No one asked the same thing twice despite hundreds of people talking to her. It would have been a struggle to find the time to eat the hot, fresh, delicious food, between questions; but she had realized the real choice was between eating a little with dignity, or a lot with abandon: her face was full.

"When was the last time you had alcohol?" someone had asked. "The night before we left Earth," she had answered with a rose glow on her cheeks. "What activities outside of work do you enjoy?" she was asked, not even seeing the person who had said the words, her eyes occupied guiding a wedge of cheese into her mouth. "I love murder mysteries," she said and, fueled by the energy of the crowd surrounding her, she launched into a recitation of *The Midnight Axe's* plot.

"Can you fly like Major Williams?" This was asked by a boulder of a man. She barely missed a row of people with an uncontrolled thruster burst in reply. No one minded at all, and it was forgiven even as it happened.

Mindy had a new plate seconds later and her stomach was threatening to burst when a girl stepped up to take her turn to ask a question. The girl was tall, a head taller than Mindy, yet she moved hesitantly, her eyes on the floor.

Her hair was thin and tired as though it had been washed recently but for the first time in ages. Her skin was greying not from age but a lack of sunlight. Her clothes were bright but accentuated thin, weak, limbs.

There was no way to predict what she would ask. The crowd's questions had ranged from the absurd to the minutiae of life on Earth and the Galileo. But no matter the question the crowd was rapt at the answers. The lady's voice was raspy, unused, almost washed out. "What religion was Earth?"

"Earth has many religions. I don't know enough to talk about most of them. But my religion is called Catholicism." The volume in the room wavered.

"I believe that God, a supreme being, created the universe and gave us guidance on how to live in order to have a good life. After I die, I believe there is another life that goes on forever and if I live a good life now, and embrace God into my heart, I'll live forever in his glory and presence."

The girl who asked the question was silent: profoundly so. It took Mindy a moment to realize her silence seemed so deep because everyone had stopped talking. Even the steaming meats on the table seemed to stop crackling. The entire hall had been struck dumb. Then, like a wave had crested, the crowd began to withdraw. A thousand people turned and left in unison.

Mindy was about to ask what was happening when Dorothy found her. Nearly a third of the hall had emptied and more were rapidly making their way out, while Dorothy pulled the young officer to her side along with Captain Grey and Major Williams to usher them together.

"What's going on?" Mindy pressed.

Most of the crowd was out of the hall. Two dozen meters separated the Galileo's crew from the nearest tide. Dorothy straightened her clothes and looked from Captain Grey to Major Williams, "if we ask you to, regardless of the reason, will you leave us peacefully?"

"You have my word on that," Grey replied, and glanced at his officers for a hint of comprehension.

"Then we would like you to leave."

Grey had been dumped when he was sixteen. The feeling was the same. "Very well, that is your choice. Would you tell us why?"

Dorothy's face slackened as she consulted with the Commons. "Ensign Arnold is a religious fanatic, just like the Theists. She is also in control of an arsenal capable of destroying worlds. We have no idea what she is going to do, but it's a risk we won't take."

Major Williams actually stepped forward putting himself between Mindy and Dorothy, "that's ridiculous. Sure, she's a bit doe-eyed about god but she isn't a fanatic. We don't have the same religious rules as the Theists, Ensign Arnold is completely trustworthy... What can I do to prove it?"

Dorothy's face turned away from them, and she said, "you couldn't give us anything more than words."

The hall got quieter with each passing second as even the sound of the crowd's breathing and steps receded. It was Ensign Arnold who broke the silence. She placed a delicate hand on Major William's armored shoulder, her fingers pressed into the deep gouges that covered its surface, and pushed him to step aside, "what if you hooked me up to the Commons?"

Her face a slackened mask, Dorothy answered at once, "agreed."

"No," Captain Grey countered and took a handful of titanium plate at the back of Mindy's neck. With a sharp tug he pulled her back a step and behind him, "no one is getting alien implants in their brains."

"Sir! Please. I'm not going to be the one to ruin this. I screwed up; I have to be the one to fix it. Please!" Mindy tugged at her Captain's grip.

"The mission takes priority, doesn't it?" Williams asked.

"And she is consenting of her own will," the Commons added through Dorothy.

Grey pulled his ensign around to face him, "you look at her," he waved towards Dorothy without looking. "You prepared for that? You have no idea if you can even be disconnected."

The Commons answered that question, "we will be able to disconnect her, if she wants, after she has shown us she is not a threat, and after we have satisfied ourselves about the nature and value of correcting wrong religious beliefs."

"What do you mean, corrected?" Mindy asked.

"You have a belief about the objective nature of the universe. You are either right, or you are wrong, and if you are wrong, and can be convinced of your error, then the Theists likely can as well."

"You want to try and convince me not to believe in God?" Mindy's voice quivered.

"Yes, and allow you the chance to convince us to believe in god in return," the Commons answered.

"I'm not getting talked out of God. You can scan my brain or whatever and see I am not going to hurt you, but I'm not going to have some debate about my beliefs with you in my head."

"You don't have that choice. If you're connected to the Commons you're connected. You can't pick and choose what the Commons discusses with you," what Dorothy didn't add was that the Commons was more interested in this question than anything else the humans could teach them. They had suspected there was something like theism among the Galileo's crew from their first broadcast. Humanity's technology could be invented or replicated, its history was interesting but only on an esoteric level. That they could teach about themselves, that was the prize and what the Commons had wanted from the first.

"My belief is who I am. You can't take that away from me with some debate!"

"Then that will tell us something else if we can't. Either way the choice is yours to join or not. But the risk is your faith," Dorothy said flatly.

Grey cleared his throat, "No. The choice is mine."

Dorothy blinked the Commons away and looked at Grey, her eyes cutting, "your attempts to dictate what others do is repellent. Why don't you have any respect for her free will? And why do they just blindly follow your orders?"

"I think we've been more than tolerant of your culture's quirks as well. Men fighting each other to the death, fighting animals to the death. And for what? A good memory?" His hold on Mindy forgotten, Grey centered himself with Dorothy. She was inches from thumping her diminutive chest against his titanium plates. Dorothy shook her head hard, as if to tell the Commons to back off, that she had this one, and she inhaled to reply.

Mindy looked at Williams, her hands clasped against her stomach "Sir... I can't agree to gamble my faith. It's who I am. I'm sorry."

Dorothy and Captain Grey were inches apart when Williams spoke up, "I'll volunteer."

CHAPTER 19

"THAT, IS THE SINGLE DUMBEST THING I HAVE EVER HEARD! Not to mention paternalistic and sexist," Katherine said inside her helmet.

"I'm not sure I can disagree with you about it being stupid, but you're damn right that the difference between how I treat an Ensign and a Major has some paternalism in it. But this is happening. I am not reporting back to Earth that we can't get along with aliens," Grey replied. His signal, transmitted from the planet, played only in Katherine's helmet.

"Captain, I know you want to learn about these aliens, but haven't we figured out the big question already? We're not alone. Isn't that enough of a win?" Katherine gripped the command chair's arms with both hands.

"This is about the mission, Major. If this were about my personal preferences we wouldn't be doing it. And Williams volunteered; he has no Fermi Protocol knowledge; or anything about the engines."

The bridge's display was set to a custom program of Katherine's. With thousands of systems, hundreds of thousands of sensors, and millions of ways the data could be displayed, Katherine's program showed any reading that changed outside normal bounds. One small corner of the screen switched from the ship's main water flow rate - presumably an unusual number of crewmen had chosen that moment to turn on their showers - to a figure Katherine had never seen change before, solar output. It was a very small digit on a very large display. It would have been easy to miss. Anyone else would have.

"I need to go, do whatever you want," with a finger's push Major Bakker cut off the call and switched to communicating with her bridge staff. "Corporal give me a graph of SO - primary for the last day."

A few keystrokes later and the bridge's screen blinked and a simple plot appeared. For the last twenty-four hours solar output had been relatively stable but in the last minute it had dropped and then shot up. It was a wiggle, a six percent swing down and then ten percent swing up, but it was abnormal. "Astrometrics – Bridge: Why is TR-583 winking at us?"

Like a bank vault, the Galileo's bridge seemed to have its own gravity, a beat, its meter thick walls pulsing on the psyche. It took twenty seconds for Astrometrics to reply, "CME. Time to impact seven minutes, thirty-six seconds."

"Ship wide Corporal Tsang," she said as ice poured down her spine, "now hear this. Coronal Mass Ejection, Solar flare, detected. All compartments ready for magnetic impact in seven minutes. EM Safety officer of the watch contact the bridge."

Without being asked, communications flipped the bridge's display to the Magnetic Impact status board. The Galileo had seventy-six critical systems which were sensitive to major magnetic disruptions. From quantum communications to antimatter storage nearly every system that mattered was on the list and had to be made ready. Of the seventy-six only twelve were normally in a safe state, but most of the others would take only a few seconds to safety.

Systems were quickly being flipped over to green – safe – and Katherine watched the progress for a half a minute before starting to consider what was outstanding and why. One indicator struck her as odd, antimatter containment.

"Tsang, who is EM Safety this shift?" Katherine asked, eyes drilling into the AM containment indicator. Tsang pulled up a duty roster. "Chetan Gonzales, sir."

"Crap. No one revised that yet?" Katherine activated the com system, "Engineering – Bridge. Why is antimatter containment red?"

"Umm. One second, sir. We are going to set that manually."

The tone of her reply would have been gentler had they said they were vivisecting her parents. "Why are you setting it manually Lieutenant?"

"Ah... We have the tertiary vent down for some work at the moment. It is no big deal. All other vents should be working just fine. I don't know why the system isn't registering that."

Katherine nearly ripped a plate off her suit as she pulled herself out of the Captain's seat, "get tertiary back online right now! Right fucking Now!" Corporal Tsang and one of the other bridge officers raised a hand to the side of their helmets, as though the gesture would shield their ears.

As the bridge doors opened, Major Bakker twisted between them and then sprinted towards engineering. One of the benefits of built-in radio transmitters was that she could be in more places than one and Corporal Tsang's voice cut through her breaths as she ran through the ship.

"Sir. Should we raise shields?"

"No! Do nothing unless I tell you. I don't have time for stupid questions."

Even though Katherine's suit was made of titanium and an order of magnitude lighter than steel, even though it was tailored to fit her, even though she had years of practice wearing it, she would never ordinarily run around in it let alone jump over pipes, conduits, and wires in engineering as she ran. It was simply too heavy for acrobatics. Adrenaline pushed her body beyond its normal limits, and run, jump, and duck was exactly what she did.

There's a reason emergency systems and ordinary ones are separate. As adrenaline flooded her body, the human emergency system kicked in, she became stronger, she thought faster, her reflexes sharpened, and her brain did what the human mind does best; look for patterns.

It had been almost twenty years, but her brain remembered the last time it had been fed pure adrenaline. It remembered the last time she had run like the wind without discomfort or exertion. One of her brother's 'good' ideas. It was the local bank a few miles from her house. How could he have thought it was a good idea? She had been crying as she ran. Frustration, anger, impotence, had all boiled inside her until it forced its way out as tears.

Katherine rounded the AM containment tank in engineering and almost skidded as she tried to stop. Her three most junior engineers looked back at her, "what the hell are you people doing to my ship?"

Ten of the Galileo's crew were full-time engineers. Major Katherine Bakker was always either on duty or on call, a ship's chief engineer didn't have the luxury of being able to pass off that responsibility, even for an hour. The other nine crewmen rotated through eight hour shifts and were on-call the rest of the time if an emergency arose. Katherine kept her most junior officers on duty while she was awake and reserved her highest ranking, and most trustworthy officers, for the shift she tried to sleep through. Taking over command duties had meant that her least experienced engineers were left alone during their shift.

Lieutenant Waters manned the main engineering control panel and Lieutenants Roth and Lao lay on their backs under the tertiary antimatter shunt. Beside them, in pieces on the deck, was an access hatch and a small collection of parts.

Lao looked to Lieutenant Roth, then to the Major, and then back to the Lieutenant. Though everyone wore helmets and the radio signals that passed between them could only be heard by each other, Katherine felt the radio waves passing between them.

Her parents had given each other that look when she asked why they couldn't fix her brother.

"Waters! What is happening to my ship!"

Waters stood at attention, "Sir! Lieutenant Lao wanted to surprise you. He made some improvements to the tertiary antimatter vent... with my approval."

Her body felt impossibly slow as her mind raced and stomach plummeted. The collection of parts the two Lieutenants had strewn on the deck seemed to float into place in her mind, and she knew the answer before she asked, "is this," she pointed to the parts littered on the deck, "the tertiary vent?"

Ensign Lao's voice only waivered a bit, "Yes sir. We just need to swap out one part. We have it machined already. It'll only take a few hours and will improve reliability by twelve percent."

***

'HEY CATTY. I GOT A GOOD IDEA. You'll like this one!' Katherine's brother said in a voice she hadn't heard in 17 years.

***

"WATERS!" SHE EMPTIED HER LUNGS with the word and drew in a breath to finish the thought, "lockout all bridge controls now, and set shields, FTL, and weapons to manual engineering approval! You two," she pointed a furious finger at the two engineers laying on the deck, "get out from there NOW!" They didn't hesitate.

Engineering had been designed to accommodate the equipment it housed. The people who serviced that equipment were just that, servants, and the space for them restricted; intruded into by the equipment whenever it was necessary, desirable, or simply easier.

Katherine knew the chamber and dodged its pipes, outcroppings, and wiring, as she ran around the antimatter containment chamber. Lieutenant Loa's voice came through the radio, "Yes sir! But I don't understand. We have the primary vent and two other back up vents in case that fails even with this one offline."

Katherine reached the secondary vent control panel and pulled it off. "If you'd bothered to review the maintenance reports you would have seen I'd ordered third shift to do some work on the secondary vent." The secondary vent was in pieces inside its housing, exactly as the maintenance log said it would be.

"What about the fourth vent?" Loa asked as Katherine rounded the containment chamber, approaching him. Katherine grabbed a square meter panel and ripped it off the wall, letting its momentum swing it around in front of her before she flung it, two handed, to the deck. "You mean the one that didn't get installed at the shipyard?" Inside the compartment there was nothing. Five connectors stood ready to receive a piece of equipment that only existed in engineering schematics.

It was Lieutenant Waters that asked the question someone should have asked before doing anything to Katherine's engines, "if the solar flare hits, will the primary be able to vent enough antimatter?"

Two titanium gauntlets clattered onto the deck and Katherine dropped her helmet, letting it join her gloves, "no, it will not. I get that tertiary vent online or we lose the ship."

***

"But... What do you want?" she'd asked her brother. She couldn't remember what he was in jail for. Something stupid. As always. She did remember him looking down to the laminate table, deep gouges covering its surface, as he considered the question and then shrugged. "Tell me! If I know what, we can get it, and you can stay with me!"

***

TITANIUM SCREECHED OVER STEEL as Katherine lay down on the deck, then pulled herself up to the tertiary vent console. A toolbox was to her right, the components for the vent to her left, and somewhere there'd be a checklist that took an hour to run through and instructed on how to safely reassemble the vent.

***

"HERE'S TWO HUNDRED DOLLARS. I walked a lot of dogs for that… Just… now that you're home just… stay home a few weeks, ok?" her brother was so tall, she had to hold the money almost straight up to him. She didn't think it would work. But she had to try.

***

A SURGEON WOULD HAVE BEEN PROUD to have hands like Katherine. Small, accurate, and without tremble, she grabbed components from memory, positioned them, and connected their leads. The compartment was a mess of wires and there wasn't time to look at a schematic. Ordinarily work on any antimatter related system was as delicate as brain surgery. A single atom of antimatter had the energy of a hand grenade and so not a single chance could be taken. Not only would a single atom be more than enough to kill her, at this spot it would be enough to damage the antimatter storage unit and that would take out the ship, and every satellite and piece of space junk within ten thousand miles.

Katherine omitted checking the force of seals she made. When she felt a lug should be tight, she tightened it with a wrench. When she felt it should be fastened gently, she used her fingers. Lieutenant Waters watched pale-faced. The antimatter system was delicate. A bit too much torque and a connector could bend and break, too little force and there could be a leak. It had been a year before Major Bakker had let anyone but herself touch the system, and another year after that before she allowed independent work on it.

With ninety seconds left, and half of the components for the vent still on the deck, Captain Grey's voice filled the Compartment. "Major. What is going on? Corporal Tsang tells me we have a problem and shields are down?"

Katherine spat a small tension spanner that had been in her mouth onto the deck beside her. The delicate part would need to be x-rayed after that fall. "I'm working it. I'll let you know in two and a half minutes."

"Raise shields Major. That's an order."

"Belay that Waters or you kill us all!"

A drop of blood fell onto her face as she sliced a finger tightening a small nut by hand, "Waters explain to the Captain what you idiots did."

The final component, a device looking like a rib cage with a dozen connectors feeding into a central chamber, sat on the deck. The manual called for it to be lifted and positioned with a hoist. Katherine took it two handed and pushed it into place like she was bench pressing iron.

"Umm. Captain. We're down to a single antimatter vent. The shields won't protect us from a magnetic impact, we need to be moving at relativistic speeds for them to work properly on magnetic distortions."

"Time to impact Lieutenant?" the Captain asked.

"Just under forty seconds, sir."

Bile filled Katherine's mouth. The titanium wrench she clasped between her lips was corroding from her saliva, filling her mouth with the byproducts of the reaction. Titanium is a remarkable material, but it has to be cared for just so and bare titanium tools, as the wrench was, had to be handled exactly according to protocol or they would be useless. Katherine removed the wrench, spat, and started making the final dozen connections.

The hum of the ship changed. Regular cycling noises began to build up, but not spool down, the leading edge of the solar flare was entering the magnetic influence of the ship.

"Waters... Go prepare to activate the tertiary vent. On my order, not a second before you understand?"

***

WHEN SHE GOT CLOSE TO THE BANK SHE KNEW. There were too many police cars. There were two ambulances, and three fire trucks. It was too much for a robbery. She ran faster, angling towards an officer putting up hazard tape. 'I can fix this' she thought the words again and again and ran harder.

***

THE MAIN ENGINEERING BOARD showed all systems green for the magnetic impact except antimatter containment. Waters brought up the tertiary vent's initiation procedure with trembling fingers. The computer prompted him to execute.

"Five seconds Major."

Katherine looked over the connections for a half second trying to spot any obvious loose connectors. One chance.

***

A FIGURE WAS LYING FACE DOWN on the pavement in the bank's parking lot. He was the right size. The right shape. Paramedics stood to the side and a photographer took pictures.

***

"HIT IT WATERS!"

If there was a leak, if there was a missed connection or a misassembled part she'd be dead before she realized her mistake.

Outside the Galileo a massive solar flare dwarfed the ship, it dwarfed the planet the ship orbited. Auroras erupted across the planet's sky and the flare arched around the world deflected by its magnetic field. The Galileo was also protected from the physical impact by the planet's magnetic field. Its magnetic impact was another matter. Throughout the ship the intense magnetic fields induced currents in every conductor.

The antimatter tank was little more than a magnetic bubble. As the solar flare's magnetic field interacted with it, the bubble deformed and belched a week's worth of antimatter. The primary vent did its job. More than sixty percent of the excess antimatter was dumped into space harmlessly. It would make a hell of a lightshow in the planet's upper atmosphere when it eventually hit, but it would do so harmlessly.

The remaining flow was shunted past the out-of-order secondary vent and hit the tertiary vent. On a perfect day, when the vent had been tested, serviced, and fine-tuned, it had a ninety five percent chance of working. Odds only go so far however. Regardless of the chances either it would work, or it wouldn't, and a one in twenty chance of dying was still dying if it hit bad.

The vent opened.

"Yes!" Katherine raised her arms over her head, and lay, breathing hard, on the deck.

'And if you had trained your people right, this never would have happened,' the imagined voice of Williams poisoned the success.

CHAPTER 20

DOROTHY SPENT ALMOST AS MUCH TIME watching Grey as she did the monitor, "don't worry," her voice as reassuring as a doctor's.

"That's what all the aliens who want to implant their technology in our brains say," Grey kept his eyes locked on the monitor in front of him, arms crossed over his chest, metal slowly ground on metal.

"And I thought we were your first," Dorothy dead panned.

"How about I just say I don't like this and am seriously considering stopping it."

"Explain to me again how it's any of your business what Ben chooses, voluntarily, to do," Dorothy's voice lost most of its kindness.

"First, I'm not going to justify command authority to you. Second, how much choice did he really have in the matter: join your commons or let Ensign Arnold's religion ruin our relations," Grey sucked a breath of air through his teeth.

Dorothy didn't bother to reply. Major Benjamin Williams was front and center on the monitor: naked, pale, wrinkled, exposed, and lying flat on his stomach on a large white obelisk. He looked like a human sacrifice. Though perhaps Dorothy's people never did that, or did it differently, Earth's cultural history would have demanded this procedure be done differently.

Williams was in a small room, painted entirely white, with virtually no distinguishing features: its white walls curved back on each other in a circle without corners or seams. Even the obelisk, or table, the Major lay on was featureless, simply rising a meter out of the floor without handles, footholds, or covering. The ceiling was flat, white, and seamless, but illuminated the room with a soft glow. Aside from the table the only thing in the room was an old, dirty, ball. It was slightly larger than a soccer ball but very much looked like what it was: a used child's toy. It sat, inanimate, on the floor near Williams' head.

With each breath Williams took, his bruised back flexed, rose, and then sunk; again, and again, and again, as minutes passed without any other activity, and apprehension turned to boredom.

When it did happen, it happened silently. A mechanical arm began to descend from the ceiling. What had been seamless had a foot wide gap that the mechanical arm extended through. The arm was articulated in six places and moved like a snake. Each of its joints moving in unison to bring the end of the arm towards the base of the Major's neck. The arm didn't have what could be called a hand at its end, instead a series of small needles extended from it like a spiked fist.

It didn't exactly slow as it reached the major's spine; it swayed. The arm matched William's breathing, coiled back like a snake, and struck forward.

Williams felt the business end of the arm hit, but the sensation wasn't pain. A cup of cold water had been poured over his back and ran upwards from ass to head. Just as abruptly the sensation changed to a warm pressure from the metal on the base of his neck. That feeling too quickly faded, along with the room.

It was like a movie where one scene had faded out and another was a moment away. In the dark Williams' legs began to tingle. More out of surprise than concern he flexed them and felt nothing: no pain, nor any sensation of them responding. A part of him knew to be concerned by this and for the first time in his life he felt a disconnect between what he thought of as himself and his brain as an organ. His brain simply refused to respond with alarm, fear, or even anxiety to the information 'he' was providing to it.

The pain from his tired muscles and bruised flesh faded all over his body. Being paralyzed isn't the same as being free of pain. Every moment nerves send signals to the brain reporting what they feel. If not reporting pain they report the feel of the air on skin, the touch of cloth, the pressure of a person's weight against a bed, chair, or bottoms of feet. Paralyzed is dead silence.

Williams couldn't have said if he stayed that way for a minute or an hour but slowly he started to feel the weight of his body again, and then the pain of his muscles and bruises. Just as his brain was prepared to start listening to his commands to panic, the need for panic was gone. Finally the room began to come back into view.

There was nothing; no flood of voices, no feeling of being watched, just an old man laying naked on a table in an empty room. He shifted over and sat up. His body responded just as it had before. He felt heavy but that was from the arena not any implant. He would have felt relief if he'd been able to feel concerned.

He was just about to ask if it had worked when he spotted the ball along the wall. It was a ball, but also wasn't: it was a mystery, an invitation, a wrapped present with his name on it. He'd not so much formed a question about the ball, as formed curiosity about it, when it hit him: he suddenly knew what he could know about the ball. He knew it in the same way that he knew what books he owned.

In a flash he was looking at the ball in the hands of a laughing child: his child, but not. The sunlight was bright, but his eyes were adjusted already, and it warmed his face. The boy laughed and threw the ball to him and he caught it, throwing it back just over his son's head. A wave of pride struck as the toddler jumped for the ball, missed, and then ran after it. Chubby feet plowing through grass. He was so proud of him.

And he was back in the room, the ball sitting idle on the floor. Williams looked hard at the ball, blinked, and his gaze caught on its seams and the stitching that joined the ball's four panels. A stitch was out of place, crooked.

It only took the hint of the question to form in his mind and he was standing on an assembly line stitching the ball and awash in emotion. The emotion was a crushing change from the pride he had felt a moment before; anger, frustration, annoyance confronted him. He looked over at the worker beside him, a young man moving painfully slowly as he shouted a curse across the large assembly room. The curse caused William's hand to slip from surprise and anger, and he examined the crooked stitch he had just made.

CHAPTER 21

"WHY IS HE JUST SITTING THERE? It's been over an hour," Grey asked.

Dorothy smiled and tilted her head slightly as though watching a child learning to climb stairs. "He's learning about the ball. It's important he learns how to control the Commons, or it will be overwhelming."

"How much is there to learn from staring at an old ball?"

Dorothy looped her arm through Grey's, "your space suit. Do you know the men who designed it? Do you know where its metal is from, what the land looked like before it was mined, do you know the story of how it was selected to be yours?"

"And you know that for what you wear?"

"Everything has a story to tell Peter. I chose the things I have because I love the story they tell, because every part of them is beautiful and loved," she drew a hand across the knitted fabric of her top, "my grandmother made this for me before she died. She was a singer when she was younger, and this was her final performance and a present to me of her love. I don't see clothing when I see this, I hear the music she sang as she made it."

It took two hours before Williams stood up and walked, awkwardly with naked feet, to the room's exit. The wall yielded, parting without a sound. Grey and Dorothy waited on the other side.

"This is amazing," the words fell out of William's mouth more reflex than considered choice.

"Are you alright Major?"

"Fine, sir. But I really can't describe this. It's like I can know everything about... everything... and it's just a question of what I want to know."

"And that's just the start Ben," Dorothy said, music in her voice. "There are a thousand other things the Commons can do," Dorothy narrowed her eyes, grinned, and very much looked like she had a secret, "ever wonder what it's like inside a woman's head?"

"oh..." Williams muttered softly as his face went blank looking past Dorothy.

Grey cleared his throat and Dorothy turned slowly towards him, "he's going on a date with a young man I met a few years ago. One of my more highly rated experiences on the Commons."

"There's a rating system?" Grey asked.

"Of course. How else would we know which memories were worth living and which were ones of waiting in lines, or sleeping?" Grey filed that piece of information away, "so he'll be like this for hours?"

"No. Reliving memories in the Commons takes far less time than living them out. A second can mean an hour depending on the memory. Some are meant to evoke a physiological response and so take a little time." Dorothy grinned and glanced down to the Major's growing physiological response. "Others are meant to teach a piece of information and take almost no time."

"Holy hell!" Williams' face tightened and he jolted back, eyes wide. "Is that what it feels like for you?" Ben looked over his body, ran his hands over his chest, and his skin flooded with blood turning red but for old, faded, scars. He turned away from Grey and Dorothy.

"I'm... sensitive." Dorothy replied with a knowing grin.

It took four hours to get the Major dressed and underway. Grey spent the time alternating between concern, and wonder, as his executive officer zoned out for minutes at random triggers. Seeing himself in the mirror, putting on boxers, noticing something on, or about, Dorothy.

When Williams was finally dressed and had stopped pausing to relive the process of mining, manufacturing, and installing every light, nail, and wall panel in sight, Dorothy led the two men into a small room with ancient chairs. Williams mimicked Dorothy's motion in mounting a chair, leaning forward to rest his weight on the padded pole at its front.

"I hope you won't object to getting down to business. The Commons is eager to hear what you know about religion."

Grey and Williams both nodded their approvals. "Now Captain, for your benefit we're going to do our best to narrate this and slow things down as much as possible. This will also help Ben as this part of the Commons can be challenging. To get started Ben, can you tell us what you think about religion? Try to be as specific as you can."

Instead of looking like a vacuum cleaner had been attached to his anus the Major's expression remained thoughtful and sharp. He sat in silence for nearly a minute considering his reply.

"I never had much time for it. I've seen enough happen that if there was a god, and he was all knowing and powerful, then when I got to heaven I'd have some very serious questions for him. Faith, just blind belief, was never my way. To me religion, and it doesn't matter which one, provides answers to people who worry about what the meaning of their lives are, and I never did worry about that."

"So, you're not religious?" Dorothy asked.

"No. I was raised a Christian but lost my faith when I was young. The thing is, I don't need to be Christian to know that Ensign Arnold's trustworthy."

"How?" Dorothy asked.

"What you need to understand is that religion... there're different ways to see it. Arnold believes that when she dies she'll be judged on how much she improved the universe, and that bettering herself is the way to do that. That's why she works hard and doesn't try to convert others."

"You have to ignore a lot of the bible to get to a belief like that. But she's comfortable with it. She likes it. She found her answers. I think after thousands of years of violence, and editing, people just kind of found their way to a solid core in the Bible."

Dorothy's eyes narrowed and she pursed her lips tentatively for the next question, "and why would a religious person inflict violence against non-believers?"

Williams was silent, concentrating on an answer. It was Dorothy who spoke, after a dozen minutes, "the Commons is going over his life and religious experiences. We are building the answer to this question together, but it takes time."

Grey waited but, eventually, the Major spoke. "If God says what is good or bad, and only God, then anything is ok if it's God's will. Earth went through thousands of years of religious violence but eventually every religion decided that living by example is more convincing than blowing yourself up on a public bus shouting God's name."

Major Williams fell into the familiar expression of accessing the Commons and Dorothy turned to the Captain, "we are reviewing Ben's other memories but the debate over whether Mindy is dangerous is over. Ben trusts her, respects her, and so we do too."

Grey's chest relaxed without him even realizing he was tensing it. "Good. Now the Major can be unplugged," he said.

Dorothy drifted off and her lyrical voice shifted to a monotone, "we are an imperfect people. A thousand people are imprisoned because they believe differently than we do. Their distinctiveness, their perspectives, their uniqueness are not part of our common knowledge, and we are less because of that.

"We need to know whether their position is rational, logical, worthy of inclusion into ours. If they are wrong, we need to know if the Commons can convince them of that. They would be able to pursue their lives freed of their mistaken beliefs."

"You're considering forcing them to join the Commons?" Grey asked.

Dorothy blinked and her voice shifted back to normal, "considering it. It's the most active debate we've had for the last decade. Before now no one who joined the Commons had understood religion and we didn't know whether they might be right. We simply didn't understand. But there are many other options we are considering. If Ben shows us that they may be right we are open to changing our views as well, and they might welcome joining the Commons if we sought an understanding of God."

"Up until now you have been so vocal about individual freedom... I find it hard to believe you would want to force someone to join the Commons against their will," Grey said.

"I'm personally against it. But I acknowledge Ben brings important information to the debate, and I am open to changing my mind. I consider keeping people imprisoned an evil in and of itself, so there is no perfect solution. Our choice is a wrong against the body or a wrong against the mind."

"And Williams? Once you're done downloading your information about religion, you'll disconnect him?"

"If he wants. But why not let him learn from us as well. Hours connected to the Commons can give years of knowledge. Take him to your ship if you like, but why give up the chance to learn so much about us so quickly?"

"It's a bit like being pregnant, sir," Williams said, "now that I'm connected, we might as well make use of it – and I can attest that they think this is completely safe," he added before returning to his laconic state.

CHAPTER 22

THREE DAYS AFTER THE CHURCHILL left, it returned with its crew, and a shipment of fresh food. Any concerns over the safety of the food were met with the same disregard that lottery winners have that the wealth might change them.

The Galileo's mess hall was filled to capacity. An overflow line stretching into the corridor. Even with all those people, not a word was spoken. The only sound was that of cutlery scraping against trays and the sticky, sucking, noises from dozens of jaws chewing dozens of mouthfuls of food. The men and women who filled the room devoured tray, after heaping tray, of fresh produce. That the flavors were different from the food of Earth didn't matter. For most of the crew it had been so long since they had eaten an apple that, had they been given one, it would have tasted more like manna from heaven.

There are a few simple and well-known ways of improving the morale of a crew. Accomplishing a difficult mission is one. Coming through the unknown together is another. But the most ancient is giving them a great meal after deprivation.

In Captain Grey's quarters even Major Bakker seemed pleased with herself, sitting more rigidly upright. Grey was threatening to wear down the tips of his titanium gauntlets drumming them on his table when he realized he was making the gesture and cut it off. "Well, if Major Williams is going to ignore two reminders, and twenty minutes, I imagine it's for good reason and we should start without him." In three years Major Williams had never before missed a staff meeting, nor been even one second late.

"Would you like me to page the guards, sir?"

"I'd rather not remind him that we have him under observation," Grey said. "Where do we stand mechanically?"

Bakker tapped her gauntlet and brought up a large list of items, "now that we're out of FTL there're hundreds of maintenance items that should be done. We've already completed most of the must do's and I'd say in another week we'll be onto the would-be-nice-if's. I've had almost the whole crew diverted to help with the work."

"Very good... Shore-leave. I raised the topic of ferrying a dozen crewmen at a time down to the planet and Dorothy was receptive but cautious. I would be too in her shoes. Just the question of germs vs. inoculating the whole crew with those nanites – which I still don't really trust."

Katherine grinned, pleased with herself, "I do have something of a confession to make on that front. I enlisted Ensign Arnold's help and managed to access the memory of one of the nanites in her bloodstream. They're remarkable little devices and one of the things they do is record immune responses that require intervention."

"They don't seem to activate every time any stray bug makes it into your system. They're selective, letting your immune system take the lead normally and stepping in if they're unhappy with the response: not fast enough, not strong enough, etc. From her time on the planet the nanites did nothing. My theory is that while there may be dozens, hundreds, thousands of bugs down there that are deadly to humans the vast, vast, majority of germs are either easily dealt with by our own immune system, or simply not compatible with human biology. So long as the crew minimizes contact with potential pathogens, I would think it's relatively safe for them to go down untreated. Certainly, just cracking open a hatch on a shuttle isn't going to be dangerous."

Grey looked out the cabin window at the planet below, "that's good work."

He let his gaze linger on the planet a moment before turning back to his chief engineer. "I want you to slow the repairs down a little, give people some extra time off, especially the ones doing the most work. Say you'll clear it with me but make them think it's you being generous. If the repairs take a few extra days, I don't think there'd be any objection."

Katherine gave her Captain a look of frustration but acknowledged the order.

"A part of command – maybe the biggest part – is cultivating the right relationship with the people under you Katherine. There's a fine line between having subordinates ready to march over a cliff at your order; having ones who see you as just a person and your orders as questionable; and ones who are intimidated and act out of fear."

"Is this your subtle way of telling me I talk back too much? I'm still not exactly happy about how you handled things after Chetan died. Or ignoring my advice with Williams. I should have a say on decisions like that. Do you think that was the best kind of leadership?"

"A Captain doesn't get to apologize to his officers. But… sometimes… he can explain himself."

Katherine crossed her arms over her chest.

"Back on Earth I was promoted early and given command of an experimental tugboat: the USS Gazer. She was prototyping the Galileo's gravity shields. I was too young for the post but had done well up to that point in my career, the Gazer was just a tug, and I'd done an undergraduate degree focused on the theory of gravity shielding. So, the brass thought they would take a risk. Hell, maybe they were even thinking ahead, that the Galileo would end up with a young crew. We were trying, and failing, to find a way to make a shield that protects from all directions."

"As far as I can tell that's impossible," Katherine added.

Grey looked down at his hands and rubbed the scar tissue covering them gently.

"My best friend from the naval academy was my XO – Sam Rowatt. We were both overachievers and he wasn't happy about me being promoted over him through the luck of my degree, but he was a good XO to me all the same." Grey turned away and looked out the cabin's window. "Did you hear about the Boston Harbor incident?"

When Katherine made no reply, he carried on. "Boston gets liquefied natural gas shipped in about once a month. The tanker's bigger than an aircraft carrier, the biggest boat you've ever seen, and filled with highly compressed explosive gas," Grey paused and sighed. "It's just so stupid. I can't even think about it without feeling sick. You have a city that needs natural gas, and their solution was the laziest, sloppiest, easiest option. Just get it shipped in. They don't think about it from a systemic perspective. Why go through the trouble of changing to a safer fuel? Why bother building a pipeline?"

"Anyways, there was an accident. You'd appreciate it. A rubber O-ring sealing a maintenance hatch on one of the ship's tanks was getting old. It got swapped out as part of regular maintenance. The original O-ring's serial number was fifteen digits long and ending with an A, the replaced O-ring's serial number was exactly the same, except it ended with a B. Other than that, A vs. B, they were identical in every way. I've seen them both. They look the same, they feel the same, they weigh the same. What the mechanic who swapped them out didn't know, and what it took six months for the investigators to realize, is that the serial number was different because the B rings were made for maintenance hatches to the bunker fuel tanks and were made of a rubber that could be dissolved by natural gas."

"The ring leaked, the leak was ignited, and the whole ship was going to explode five miles away from Boston. The Gazer was the nearest ship by miles."

Katherine closed her eyes thoughtfully, considering the situation with the calm of an academic, "you can't use gravity shields in a situation like that. Even if the tanker's hull could take the gravitational stress, shifting the liquefied natural gas could set it off."

"Exactly Admiral Kaker's analysis. Add to that the fact that the shields were still in prototype and things didn't work properly yet. He ordered me to stand-down and sent in a fast response team for helicopter deployment. But the Gazer was a tug, and the ship looked like it could explode at any second, so I disobeyed the order. I took the Gazer in, left the shields off and started towing the tanker out to sea and away from the city the old-fashioned way."

"As soon as we got close, I could see the fast deploy team wasn't going to work. The hatch that leaked was facing the con tower of the ship and was geysering flames into it. The bridge was slag and most of the deck was glowing red hot. The outer hull was so hot the magnetic grapples kept slipping off." Grey held up his hands, "I got these trying to get the grapples to stick."

"We towed her for an hour and a half. My engineer," Grey looked away, unable to face his officer. "I lost my last chief engineer trying to keep my engines cool enough so they wouldn't seize up. He was pouring salt water directly onto them by the end. The steam..." the Captain stopped again and closed his eyes.

"The steam from that water was everywhere. I'd rather fire and brimstone than steam. When the fast response team arrived, we cut our towing cables, put a mile between us and the tanker, and turned on our shields just in time."

"The fast response team vaporized. We'd pulled the tanker far enough away that the city was safe. The shield bubble even mostly worked. A perfect sphere of protection except for a half degree sliver... just off center from the explosion," he raised a hand as if to point slightly to the right.

"That half degree let in enough energy to cut the Gazer in half. Sam must have been thrown clear by the blast and knocked out because when they found his body he'd drowned. My engineer survived... for a day before the burns killed him."

"So that's why you got this assignment. You were a hero. The Navy must have loved you after that," Katherine said.

Grey scowled then composed himself. "No. The Navy told me in no uncertain terms my career was over. I'd disobeyed a direct order and though the result was good, we follow orders, even bad ones. Admiral Kaker was demoted and given a desk job. But we still follow orders."

"Then how did you..."

"How did I end up here as Captain? The international selection committee thought it was a great story and lacked the Navy's rigidity. Since I had some experience with gravity shields I got shortlisted. The US Navy couldn't object too much, after all I was one of theirs, and the politicians all thought I'd done a wonderful job."

"You did do the right thing," Katherine leaned forward and put a hand on his. Soft flesh pressed against rough scars.

"What I did Katherine, was make a conscious decision to kill my best friend, and my crew. I knew we weren't all going to make it out of there, and I did it anyways. Hell, I didn't think any of us would make it out of there."

Grey winced as the young woman squeezed his hand. "That is the point I was trying to make before. When you act, you take responsibility for what follows. Half the time when I sleep, I am back there, steam and flames all around me. And when I wake up, I find I survived, the only one responsible for putting us there, and I survived. I know Chetan was an accident, but I swore... I swore I would never do it again."

"And now you think you've done that to Williams?" Katherine asked.

Grey took his hand from her, "give your people some time off. You don't want to be asking yourself if working them too hard got someone killed."

CHAPTER 23

IF A LIFETIME OF EXPERIENCES could be harvested, and the dull, common, or mundane discarded like chaff from wheat, what would be left? The most extraordinary experiences of an average life would take less than a week to run through. If, of those memories, ones common to most people were discarded: the first-time having sex, the best meal of a lifetime, holding your first child. Then each person might have two days of unique and incredible memories. And if those two days' worth of memories, from twelve billion people, were taken, ranked and only the best one in a million kept, you would still have sixty-five years' worth of memories.

Put another way, any single person would be more likely to win a million-dollar lottery than to have a single experience worthy of being on this sixty-five-year long list.

Major Williams was through the first weeks' worth, and working his way up, when the Commons reminded him that he should eat something. He sat up, every muscle in his body screamed promises of retribution. Some of his muscles were weak from a day of inactivity, others were still sore and bruised from the fight. Combined they conspired to make it a struggle to get out of bed.

He finally understood what Dorothy had been talking about on the planet. There was no end to breathtaking, must-experience memories inside the Commons. He'd just traded an hour of his life that he would have spent attending a tedious, routine, meeting, to spend an hour in the memory of winning round 13 of the world indy-jet racing championship. The race had been spectacular, one of the best he had ever flown, the city course itself a thing of unspeakable beauty and danger. And to win, to stand on the podium, to have the feeling of absolute victory on tap. If giving up one hour of life to experience one of someone else's was worth the trade, why not do that with every hour?

His cabin alarm chimed. He had a low gravity combat class to teach in ten minutes.

The thought of a meal, that on any objective measure, would be utterly unremarkable was unappetizing. Yet he knew he had to eat, and get to his class, so he got up and began to dress. Williams was about to open his cabin hatch when he remembered his letter to Julia.

So far Williams had been a spectator – taking from the Commons or having memories downloaded without his direct control. However, that was not the only way the Commons worked, and actively seeking the input of the Commons was, common. A brief inquiry showed that hundreds of thousands of people were interested in the family problems of the Common's only alien and Williams turned to his note, getting a world of advice on what to say.

Dear Julia,

I am sorry I wasn't a better father. You needed my love, attention, encouragement and guidance. Instead I treated you like a junior-soldier. It was all I knew. When I realized I was failing you, I pulled away hoping I would stop hurting you if I wasn't there. That was the biggest mistake of my life. I was afraid, I ran away, and I am ashamed of myself for it.

I have put everything I have into a trust for you. Please use it. I joined the navy because of my father; I stayed at first because I needed a job; then because it was all I knew; and finally it was all that I had. Please use the money to avoid that mistake. Live the life you want.

I have always been proud of you, love you, and wish I had been better to you. I'll be here for you, if you ever want me.

All my love,

Ben

There were no perfect words that would repair their relationship. But he could finally be honest, he could finally be open, and if she wasn't willing to give his true self another chance then that was all there was to it. He'd known that all along, but the Commons let him admit it. It let him make peace with taking his last chance.

Major Williams was about to have the letter sent when he realized the Commons had a list of top thousand father-daughter memories and he lay back down on his cot.

CHAPTER 24

THERE ARE SOME SKILLS THAT ARE LEARNED: writing contracts, playing the piano, performing heart surgery. But there are also innate talents. Beethoven was composing symphonies when he was barely out of diapers. Walter Cronkite discovered, in high school, that his principal was having an affair, and decided not to publish in the school paper for moral reasons. Dorothy had a nose for news unlike anyone else's. She could smell when there was more to a story and had the uncanny ability to know exactly where to root around for it.

In the Commons nothing was truly a secret, yet very little of what was available was ever reviewed and considered. Every single day twelve billion people's days were added to the collective memory. The spectacular memories were usually discovered and shared, yet when there was a story if only it could be uncovered, the connections made, it took talent to know where to look and what to look for.

Her audience was, generally, something of a non-conformist lot. Who else would rather avoid the incredible (yet often lived) experiences in favor of discovering how significant a hairdresser's life might be.

Yet among billions, if even a few percent were non-conformists there were still hundreds of millions to form an audience. Dorothy, along with many others, made it their mission in life to find stories, make connections. It was one reason she had been sent to the Galileo. Her audience generally did her the courtesy of avoiding spoilers and waited for her to present what she had, in her own time, and in her own way.

She sat on the floor of a vacant warehouse. Unlike the buildings the Galileo's crew had seen this one had no aesthetic, technological, or social importance. The doors to enter and exit the building were manual and swung on hinges, held in place with screws, in exactly the way they would have on Earth. The walls were brick, layered in an interlocking pattern with mortar and would have passed for an Earth cinderblock to anyone who had not worked much with cinder blocks. The roof was flat, steel support beams running under it, with pillars every fifty meters.

The floor was cement, and saturated in a chalky, heavy, industrial dust that covered Dorothy's pants. Spotlights were cast by large overhead emitters that, when the eyes had adjusted, provided just enough illumination to work.

She sat motionless for an age. She had been in the warehouse so long that her eyes had become accustomed to the gloom and could clearly see every detail of the structure. That wouldn't do, and she looked directly up into the light she sat beneath, her pupils contracting. When she looked away she could see nothing outside of the circle of light she sat in.

Dorothy turned her attention to her wrist and started the 'episode' the same way she had started every other. Her wrist was small, gentle, delicate, and adorned with a bracelet. Three strands twisting, tied, and looping through one another around the wrist to a well-worn clasp. One strand was leather, black, and saturated by the oils of a lifetime of daily wear. One strand was steel, flecked with white as it slowly oxidized. The final strand, a golden chain. The Commons had no memory of when the bracelet was made, it had been in Dorothy's family since before the Commons existed. It had been her grandmothers, and when she had died it had become her mothers, and now it was hers.

Anyone in the Commons watching her could choose to see any and every memory of that bracelet, the building she was in, anything she knew, experienced, or could observe or experience. Yet that was considered poor form, like reading a plot synopsis of a movie while watching it for the first time. The Commons watched Dorothy, and experienced as she experienced, felt what she felt, and it was her choice what memories to experience and show them.

She took the Commons to the day she had been given the bracelet. She was thirteen, close to adulthood, close to joining the Commons. Her mother was sick, dying. For as long as she could remember her mother had been sickly, becoming weaker with every year as Dorothy became stronger. By the time Dorothy was eight her mother couldn't keep up with her energetic daughter. By the time she was eleven her mother rarely left bed. Yet she always had a warm smile and hug for her daughter. She was never too tired, too sick, to talk about her little girl's day, her friends, her life, her dreams, and adventures.

When she had given Dorothy the bracelet, her mother had explained that it had been passed through their family for generations. The gold band symbolized importance, the steel strength and intelligence, and the leather mastery of lands and the responsibility that came with them. She told Dorothy that these were old values, old lessons, but they could still be important today if treated with care.

The show began. She stood, stepped out of the bright spot cast by the warehouse's industrial lighting, and found herself in front of a full-length mirror, carefully set up in advance. She looked into her own eyes and began to talk, the precision of words occasionally superior to the brevity yet disjointed nature of thought.

"We are on the cusp of a decision that is not about logic or knowledge, but values. One thousand people are imprisoned because they believe in imposing their beliefs on us through violence. With good reason we have judged their beliefs to be incorrect and given them every opportunity possible to convince us otherwise. They have not. So, do we as a people decide that we can impose our understanding, our knowledge, and yes even our beliefs, onto them? Or is imprisonment the better choice? Do we punish bodies, or do we punish souls?"

"I believe that if we choose now, for these people, that we are right and they are wrong, we cross a line that cannot be uncrossed. The Commons is about sharing, collaborating, coming together and working collectively, and yet it can also be used as a weapon on the minds of dissidents. In that it could be the most powerful weapon ever conceived. Many say that this is the power of knowledge, not the Commons, and the Commons simply strips away inhibitions, arrogance, vested interests, and leaves the mind open to being convinced of what is obviously true. I say that this goes to the heart of what it means to be an individual."

Turning to her right, Dorothy walked away from the mirror and towards another circle of light on the old warehouse floor. In the center of the circle an easel stood with a framed portrait. The work was instantly recognizable, and Dorothy allowed her mind to access the reviews, the praise, the awards that had been heaped on the work named 'Sex'.

The portrait was of a golden woman. She was old, with none of whatever beauty she had in her youth. There was something deeply lonely in her expression yet her golden eyes glittered, and her lips gave the hint of a hidden smile. As Dorothy got closer the finer details of the work revealed themselves. The portrait was a mosaic made of tiny fragments of gold that had been cut, and then etched, polished, sanded, and textured. Each shard of gold had come from a failed marriage's wedding necklace. Every shard spoke of infidelity, impatience, failing passions, guilt, and the entire story of the ill-fated couples they came from.

Yet nearly all the people who had owned these fragments of failed love went on to happiness later – freed of their failing relationships.

The message of the work, as interpreted by critics and audiences alike, was that artificial bonds, morals without necessity, were paths to nothing but pain and that embracing who we are is the path to happiness. It was a subtle work, a beautiful work, one of the best and most convincing works of art in recent memory.

Yet no one had bothered to ask about the artist. The work itself required so much attention and had such depth of memory as to be overwhelming. And since the artist had chosen not to be connected to the Commons, his was not an easy view to obtain, so none had bothered trying.

Dorothy had been interested when she first heard he had not been connected to the Commons – that someone would choose not to be was in itself an interesting story. Yet that the same man had made a work designed specifically for the Commons was a massive contradiction that she had to investigate.

She took her audience through her own memories. The artist, Esquremestique, had been scrupulous about avoiding commentary on his work. The only way to learn about him was through the people around him, and they were part of the Commons; his parents, what romantic interests he had, his friends, his neighbors, and relatives. While he could hide within the borders of his own mind, the people who interacted with him revealed a disturbed man. His mother had always suspected that as a teen he elected not to join the Commons to conceal sexual oddities and phobias. As he had grown his relationships with women and others had become more and more strained by privacy surrounding issues of sexuality.

Hundreds of interactions from large to small flew through Dorothy's mind as she connected disparate threads for the Commons laying out her case. Far from being a tolerant man trying to preach sexual liberty, this man was a puritan who, when he made the art, had attempted to find items with emotions associated with his cause. He hadn't realized that divorce was as much about rebirth as it was about destruction.

The art had transcended the artist.

Dorothy returned to the mirror and spread her hands to her audience. "Sometimes the best evidence and proof of a truth comes from passionate opposition. Had this man been forced into the Commons, while it would have done him a world of good, it would have deprived us of one of our best works of art. Had we changed this man's mind we would now be lacking one of the most evocative truths that we have."

She closed her eyes and dropped her voice to a whisper, "what art will we have when we all think there is only one truth?"

And she fell silent, tried to clear her mind, and waited for the Common's reply.

CHAPTER 25

"ARE YOU SURE YOU WANT TO DO THIS?" Captain Grey asked Ensign Arnold even as he climbed out of the bridge's command chair.

Heavy footsteps echoed dully through the bridge as Mindy simply took the offered command.

"Very well Ensign – good luck," Grey walked behind the chair and allowed himself a moment to silently hope she had heard sincerity in his voice. "Mr. Tsang, please set us up for simulated combat, bridge officer's test, attempt three." With the tap of a console the bridge display blacked out and large red lettering appeared over the main view screen 'SIMULATION'.

"Alright Ensign," Grey began, "once the simulation begins it cannot be stopped, however within the confines of what the simulation provides you there are no time limits. You can command the simulation to begin as soon as you..." Grey was cut off by the tiny clicks of the bridge door unlocking.

Major Williams fumbled to lock his helmet into place as he entered the bridge. His elbows nearly slapped into the sides of the opening door as he did so. The Captain turned his head slowly towards the Major and held it there. Williams couldn't see the Captain's eyes through the helmet but the silent, long, look got its message across. The reply did not however please the Captain. The Major shrugged and looked towards the main display. Grey was about to order Williams off the bridge when Arnold took the initiative.

"Begin simulation," she ordered.

Each of the three possible attempts to become a bridge officer tested for slightly different skills. The first test was the easiest because its potential problems revolved around intuitive orbital dynamic and combat qualities. The second test was harder because it required math skills. Candidates received the second scenario in advance so they could run the math, by hand, in preparation. The third test combined the most challenging aspects of both but denied any preparation time.

Corporal Tsang began reading off the test introduction. "Now entering the system the ESS Osprey was last in, sir," Corporal Tsang read without any of the passion or edge a real mission would elicit. "Their last transmission said that they were under attack by an enemy ship."

Mindy arched her head to the left, and a split second later began to issue rapid fire orders. "Corporal Tsang give me a system display together with geosynchronous orbital speeds for each of the planets you detect. Corporal Simao deploy EMF antenna and tell me if anything is radiating, fast scan, I want the big stuff, not low power transmissions. Bridge to Weapons – arm a two-megaton missile and ready tube 1, expedite! Bridge to Weapons – arm a twenty-megaton missile and ready tube 2!"

As she finished speaking, a map of the system came up, "small system, Sir," Corporal Tsang reported lazily. "Barely three light minutes across, four planets."

Arnold considered the chart. Grey was silently impressed. She was taking in the information nearly as fast as he was.

"Show me the third planet's visible field Corporal!" Ensign Arnold snapped. A few taps of the console and the display clicked over even as Mindy was shouting another command, "Bridge to Engineering, prepare to go to flank speed." Grey made a mental note of that – shouted commands were rarely needed, though a perfectly understandable reaction. Arnold had not yelled in the Churchill as it plunged towards the ground. Could the stress of a test be worse for her than that?

The new display map showed the Galileo sitting, visible to every planet in the system except the third. The fourth planet shielded the ship from the third planet's view. That situation would not last long. The size of the solar system dictated that all four planets were moving quickly about their sun. Imagine an ant and two turtles inside a baseball stadium. One of the turtles is "running" the bases, the other turtle is an outfielder meandering along the perimeter of the field. And then there was the Galileo, the ant, in the bleachers. For the briefest of moments, the ant and the two turtles were all in a perfect line. That was about to change.

In real life any one of the four planets, or more than one of them, could be inhabited and the base of the hostile ship. Had it been any but the third planet the Galileo would already have been spotted and there would be almost no chance of 'winning' the simulated engagement. The test was giving itself away by its nature.

Ensign Arnold had deduced, correctly, that to be given a chance of success meant that the third planet was the target and staying out of sight as long as possible was the key to success. Had he been in command Grey would have determined a course and speed to put the Galileo on the longest period orbit of the fourth planet that would keep it out of sight of the third planet, a computational nightmare. Math aside though, the ant had better haul ass.

The captain's console contained a small navigational pad with a dozen buttons. Arnold didn't bother calling out commands. She let her fingers dance over the console and, in a second and a half, had entered a rough course towards the fourth planet. A stroke of the execute key engaged the ship's engines at full power.

Captain Grey tried to keep the disappointment from showing in his posture, but he crossed his arms subconsciously. Orbital dynamics couldn't be eyeballed. Plus or minus a tenth of a thousandth of a degree can mean the difference between a stable orbit and crashing into a star. There was no way Ensign Arnold had done the math, and absent that her plan was doomed.

"Anything on the EM receivers Mr. Simao?" Arnold asked as she scrutinized the solar map.

"Yes sir, transient EM emissions from 3rd planet detected," Simao said, and Tsang followed a heartbeat later, "weapons reports missiles ready."

"Mr. Tsang, give me a plot of our current course. Set the third planet as the frame of reference."

Corporal Tsang brought up a display, the wrong display, discarded it, and then brought up the correct one. Grey had been right, the Galileo was not on an orbital trajectory with the fourth planet: it was going too fast for that. Instead, it would slingshot around the planet and hurtle roughly towards the third planet.

"Reduce engines to 80% Corporal," the display paths changed, the Galileo would still overshoot an orbit of the fourth planet, but now miss the third planet by a wide margin.

"Corporal Tsang, on my mark, cut engines, come to 0 by 0 by 3-3-0, fire missile 1, and then return to current course and give me 85% on the engines... Let me know when you are ready Corporal, I want it all to happen quickly."

Tsang tapped furiously, setting up the programmed maneuver, "ready, sir."

"Simulate it first Corporal let's make sure we do it right. Show the simulated path the missile will take on the display."

The display showed the Galileo slingshot around the fourth planet, and then passing roughly towards the third, yet still much too far away to enter orbit without further significant thrust. The missile would pass by the far side of the fourth planet and, though slightly pulled by its gravity, would miss everything of note and head deep into space, harmlessly.

"Set missile one to detonate one million kilometers after launch Corporal."

Corporal Tsang made a show of entering in the command and simultaneously asked, "sir, that's the two-megaton charge, correct?" Tsang was shrewd — questioning the order by reminding the Ensign she was firing a small missile at an empty point in space, and phrasing it as a confirmation.

"Correct, Corporal. And as soon as you are ready — Execute!" Arnold had taken it as condescension: her loss. Corporal Tsang shrugged with a calm he never would have had at a senseless order in real combat and triggered the pre-programed maneuver. The Galileo cut her engines so as not to disturb her flight path, turned left, fired a missile, then returned to her original course and fired engines a bit harder to make up for lost thrust.

The Galileo rocketed around the fourth planet; gravity bent its path like a soccer ball around a goalie. As the Galileo reached the apogee of its path Ensign Arnold cut the engines, reducing the Galileo's visibility to any ships or satellites in the area by two orders of magnitude.

Moments later and they were clear of the fourth planet and hurtling through space in roughly the direction of the third. The entire maneuver was rough, uncoordinated, but, in the most general of terms, achieved the correct result. "I want to know the second we pick something up on the EMF antenna, no active scanners," Arnold spoke much more softly now.

Space combat is a bit like a gunfight, in a completely black warehouse. Imagine having a gun and a flashlight and knowing your enemy is similarly armed. If you stand perfectly still making no noise and keeping your flashlight off you could wait, and the first to make a mistake loses. The problem with that analogy is that you can't stand perfectly still and make no sound. The Galileo had a living crew and mechanical systems that used energy. Thermodynamics demanded it be warmer than its surroundings: thus detectable to thermal imaging. The Galileo's skin would catch the light of the system's star, reflecting it at all angles: making her visible to optical scanners. The electrical systems onboard produced an electromagnetic field: visible on electromagnetic detectors. She would be seen, and in short order, and so using the flashlight, active scanners, became more and more tempting.

Missile One neared its point of detonation. Its nuclear charge was exactly two megatons.

When nuclear weapons were invented the sheer scale of the power they contained was almost impossible to express to generals and decision makers. The standard munitions in World War 2 were five-hundred-pound bombs. Between their initial explosions, and the fires that followed, those bombs could each demolish a city block of wooden houses.

The typical WW2 bomber carried three tons of TNT. A three kiloton, nuclear bomb was the equivalent of a bombing raid using a thousand bombers, none of which were shot down, missed, or suffered mechanical difficulty. A two-megaton bomb was six hundred and seventy thousand bombers worth of explosives. The explosion produced was so hot that black fertile soil would burn like kindling, steel wouldn't melt, it would ignite, brick would melt and turn to lava and boil away.

This was the "small" bomb that detonated in the vastness of interplanetary space. It hit nothing, destroyed nothing. Its only effect was to draw attention to itself, and thus attention away from the rest of observable space. If it hadn't been simulated it would have been the largest distraction in recorded history.

It worked. A ship, halfway between the third and fourth planets, that had been laying silently in wait, turned on its active scanners and began looking at the region of space the explosion had come from. Had it been a distant supernova? Had it been an antimatter asteroid exploding? Had it been something else?

"EMF emissions at 2-1-7 by 0-2-8 by 3-2-9, sir," Corporal Tsang reported.

"Come to that heading and fire Missile two – Expedite!" Arnold slapped her hand on the command chair. The Galileo turned, and fired. Its missile streaked through space.

"Go active on scanners! I want a firing solution uploaded to that Missile now!" She had launched her missile in the correct direction but without an exact target. The Galileo could correct the missile's path on route once it determined the exact coordinates to aim for. Radar, laser, and optical sensors flashed on and began bathing the target area in radiation looking for a return signal to pinpoint a location.

Of course the alien ship would detect this, but detecting it, and reacting properly to it, were two very different matters. Radar waves blasted out of the Galileo at the speed of light, reached across the vastness of space and reflected from the enemy ship. Aboard the Galileo the signals were interpreted by computer, exact coordinates calculated at trillions of calculations a second, and another speed of light radio transmission was sent to Missile Two, already well on its way to the target.

Whatever the simulated reaction time of the alien ship, Ensign Arnold was inside of it when Missile Two detonated. A small sun formed in the middle of a solar system as a huge nuclear explosion ripped the simulated alien ship apart.

CHAPTER 26

THE FIGURINE REFLECTED and refracted the infirmary's lights. Rainbows of color exploded inside it as it gently twisted on its string, sending cascading flashes of color through the room. If Rebecca waited long enough, she could even spot the same pinkish red as the day she'd gotten it.

It was a turtle. The glass, Plexiglas, Rebecca corrected herself, was crystal clear and clean, etched with the patterns needed to give form to turtular intent. It had always used to look green to her, not now.

The infirmary was immaculate. Every one of a thousand drawers was stocked, inventoried, and locked down. Every piece of medical equipment had been cleaned, sterilized, and vacuum sealed. The ventilation system for the infirmary was triple filtered and not even a speck of dust circulated through the two hundred and twenty-seven cubic meters of space.

Even the room's four cots were fresh, made, waiting, and ready. Or they had been. Sgt. Rebecca Daniels lay on the furthest one from the hatch. Her knees bunched close to her chest, her arm limply extended over the side of the cot, holding her necklace two feet in front of her face. The cot's sheets were rumpled under her weight, the carefully folded hospital corners untucked by the pull of her body on the bed's surface.

The necklace's string was looped through her fingers, which was all that kept it from falling. Her grip on the string was almost non-existent. She wasn't worried about dropping it: Plexiglas far more rugged than the memory it trapped.

Hawaii had been paradise. Her last night on Earth, and Rebecca was standing barefoot on the beach. The sun was sinking under the waves of the Pacific. A warm breeze from the tropical island blew through her, her dress, her hair, her fingers, depositing droplets of scents, pollens, decay, fruit, the vibrant bounty of life's cycle. The endless sky glowed red and pink like the embers of a dying fire.

"To remember home," the man at her side had said as he gifted her the necklace. He hadn't asked why she volunteered for the Galileo. He hadn't asked how she could have left him for that life. He was a good man. He was probably making someone a good husband by now.

The papers had called them the best of the best. Everyone who was going knew to add the phrase, 'willing to go', to that sentence. The world's best medic probably had a family, a few kids who screamed "Mom's Home!" to punctuate the end of the day. The world's best medic was probably happily satisfied with her life, her house, her place.

Rebecca was the world's best medic who hadn't had a family, hadn't wanted one to give her life meaning. She was the world's best medic who didn't want professional praise. She was the world's best medic who was willing to give up Earth and spend the rest of her life in a titanium box.

After three years she had started to wonder whether a person needed those things to truly be the best. Whether a person who was missing such huge pieces of life could be "the best" at their job, regardless of what it was. Somehow she'd thought that she'd started to build those pieces. She'd started to let herself think the future might yet hold a family for her.

Most of the jobs aboard the Galileo demanded constant attention. Engineers had an endless list of repairs, maintenance, or just system review. Communications had enough alien radio signals to keep them busy for a decade. Medics waited. If no one was hurt, there was nothing to do. But they had to be ready at a moment's notice. Which meant she was alone, with her thoughts, every day, all day.

At twenty-one years of age, she'd made a decision about the rest of her life, based on what she then believed about herself. But who was the same person at twenty-four they had been at twenty-one? And now the hope of something more than waiting inside a two hundred and twenty-seven cubic meter box, was snuffed out.

It came as a relief when she made up her mind. The end of bad food, dull work, and emptiness. More than anything though it was the end of loneliness and longing.

The brain and body responded to her decision with all indicators pointing towards it being correct. It was a perverse response. The question became how. Every compartment on the ship contained dangers of one kind or another. If a slow, painful death was your objective the options were almost limitless. For several minutes she considered the supplies in the medical bay: but that would be selfish. Morphine was a limited resource, and she wouldn't put someone else through agony for want of the drug.

She considered electricity. The electric chair had been invented after a newspaper article claimed that a stockbroker who'd thrown himself from a window died instantly when he landed on electrical lines. For passers-by the result would have been horrific. But the article got people, who had not seen the actual event or its aftermath, to think about using electricity as a humane method of execution.

It was a very short walk from the medical bay to a rarely used corridor with an electrical relay box. Had she been back home in San Francisco and started walking to a bridge, it might have taken the better part of an hour and given her time to reflect. Had she been on Earth she might have tried to buy the drugs needed to do the job and been delayed hours by the process. As it was, five minutes after the idea first entered her head, she was removing a piece of paneling from the corridor's wall and looking over the hub of power couplings inside. Doing this right shouldn't hurt — much. Screwing up would be very, very, painful.

The trick with electricity is its flow. Positive to negative and you have a current. Rebecca was fairly certain that the lower leftmost cable feeding the coupling was a negative pole. It disconnected with a reverse twist. The trick now was to find the positive.

Disconnecting the first cable caused a small indicator light to flash on a very large display in engineering. It was almost unnoticeable.

She was so engrossed in the task that Major William's metronomic footsteps didn't register. It wasn't until his shadow crossed over the panel that his presence hit, and she jumped hard, caught.

Rebecca, the medic, had no business touching any of Galileo's electrical systems. The system she was working on, as a matter of procedure, required two engineers to even examine, and every member of the crew had received specific safety briefings not to touch exactly the components she was handling.

Williams passed her, but a moment later his steps faltered. He took a half step, his foot stuck to the deck, then turned, "I'm heading to the mess. Would you like to join me?" Williams looked like he could use a meal, or ten. His skin was ashen and slack, what little weight he had in fat, had been drained away.

When Rebecca made no reply Williams leaned back against the corridor panel beside her and slid to the floor, "you know, it's ok to feel overwhelmed. We all do at times." His voice was slower, softer, than Rebecca had ever heard it.

"Yes... sir."

A small grin spread over his face and with his left hand he reached forward and patted her knee. "Don't bother with the sirs for now. How are you feeling?" He asked with utter sincerity.

"No sir," she began refastening the coupling she had disconnected.

"I'm not here to stop you. The positive charge is the top right cable by the way," Williams stopped, then resumed a second later, "it's your choice what you do. I just want to talk, or see if you want to talk."

"No... I mean..." Rebecca began. One cable in her left hand she looked at the top right one, the one that would complete the circuit and end it all, her right hand waivered reaching towards it.

Soaking wet Major Katherine Bakker weighed 120 lbs. She dove through the air. Any football coach in the world would have been proud of the tackle that sent Rebecca tumbling two yards down the corridor.

Bakker rolled off Rebecca, panted hard, and rubbed the shoulder she had connected with. It had been a sprint the entire distance from engineering. "What the hell do you think you were doing?" she breathed out when she could. Rebecca, winded from the impact, crouched trying to get a good lungful of air.

"And what the hell were you doing?" Bakker shouted at Williams.

CHAPTER 27

"WE SHOULD PROMOTE HER. But we can't promote her. Ship needs Ensign Arnold where she is. We have to look at this in terms of the whole, not Arnold as an individual," Williams said as though it were the most obvious thing in the world. He leaned back in his seat, the front two legs hovering off the ground like he was in high school experimenting with adult legs and balance.

Captain Grey gave Katherine a look that invited comment and she surprised him – pleasantly, "she's the best weapons officer we have, but she isn't the only one we have. If she wants to shift her duty assignment, we'll make-do without her. The crew's morale is going to be hurt if they think there is no chance for growth on-board."

After a few days in open air Grey could taste his cabin's recycled version. There was a hint of industrial lubricant, the salty acidity of other people, the limp, tepid taste of stagnation. The air filters he had become used to over the years were now just barely enough to keep the air breathable.

Williams rolled his eyes, "and what happens when everyone's earned a promotion, and no one wants to do the simple things? People volunteered for this mission knowing that these would be their jobs."

"You're both right, but we can always raise standards for promotion and make sure only people truly dedicated to moving up get to. It does need to be possible though, and no one can doubt Arnold's put her heart into this."

Katherine cleared her throat and Grey shifted his attention to a data pad sitting on his desk.

"Major Williams… I have a report here from Major Bakker about an incident at the forward electrical junction between yourself and Sergeant Daniels. Have you read this report?"

"I've had meetings like this myself, you know. Let's jump ahead shall we? Yes, it is accurate, and yes, I have something to add. If Sgt. Daniels is unhappy and wants to end her life, that's her business," Williams said, his chair teetering back to the verge of tipping.

"Of all people Ben," Grey started, his hands prickled and burned as he spoke, "you're the last person I would have thought needed to be reminded that our jobs are the lives of this crew. This says you were even helping Daniels."

"As I said. Her life, her choice," Williams replied with a shrug as though that were full explanation.

It was Katherine who was the first to shout, "what the hell! How do you justify denying a promotion to Arnold and then helping Daniels try to kill herself? How do you justify not trying to talk her down, show her that things will get better! That she should think about what she was about to do. This fucking Commons has screwed you up Williams, this isn't who you are!"

"People get to make their own choices, but we have to consider the greater good of the group…" Williams' voice faded as he spoke, animation draining from his face.

"Can he hear us when he is like that?" Katherine asked, and Grey shrugged.

"Well, screw this, even if he can, he has always been a miserable bastard and I doubt he is going to mind hearing it again. I don't like these changes in him. He's unreliable, distracted, and I am not the only one who has noticed. This business with Daniels is appalling..."

"Ben?" Grey asked his unresponsive executive officer.

"The cultural exchange is still worth it," Grey said, "but when the time comes for us to move on and leave the system, I'll be grateful to have my XO back."

His face a mask, eyes unseeing, Benjamin Williams stood, and without a word walked out of the cabin. Grey and Bakker, jumped up, and followed him. Williams walked back to his cabin, his steps were slow, mechanical, as though he were a marionette. He ignored shouts, obstacles, and orders to stop. When he reached his quarters he simply lay on his cot, on top of unmade sheets, and closed his eyes.

"Call Dorothy?" Bakker asked. Grey answered by marching to the bridge.

The Galileo's signals were ignored for nearly an hour. Grey got reports every five minutes about William's condition. The man had not so much as opened his eyes, his breathing slow but regular, a heartbeat watches could be set to.

When their hails were answered Dorothy's face was a surprise. She filled the view screen, face slack, eyes lifeless, and voice monotone as she spoke, "Captain Grey. We apologize for any confusion. Several important issues have required the full attention of the Commons. These issues have now been successfully resolved and there will be no further delays." On Grey's console a comms light illuminated, he ignored it.

"Very well. Does that have something to do with Major Williams? He's unresponsive."

Dorothy ignored the statement, "we have decided that further contact with your people is not currently desirable. If you wish to provide instructions for how we could contact you in the future we would consider re-establishing contact when we are ready. We now request you permit Benjamin Williams to come to the surface, and you depart."

Disengaging himself from his seat Captain Grey stood, and took two steps closer to the view screen, "What is going on? Why the change?"

Dorothy answered immediately, almost the instant Grey had finished speaking, "you have caused no offense. Your visit has been beneficial. We do not however wish further contact at this time."

Grey closed his eyes and took a slow breath before responding, "it is of course your people's decision whether to have further contact with us and we will leave in peace." A breath and a rush of adrenaline, "Major Williams is a member of this crew and will be staying with us."

The bridge's large door opened with slow mechanical precision and Major Williams walked onto the bridge. He moved smoothly, the slackness and rigidity of earlier gone, replaced by a cougar's grace.

Again Dorothy was speaking as the final syllable left Grey's lips, "Major Williams does not desire to remain with you. He would not be happy remaining on-board. His place is with us."

Grey almost didn't hear the words, his attention on William's appearance. "I'd like to hear that from Major Williams."

"I would like to stay Captain," Williams said, mimicking Dorothy's trick of speaking the instant Grey had finished.

"Without the commons telling him what to say," Grey said to the screen, face tightening.

A rhythmic hiss came from Williams' armor, Grey was too focused on the view screen to hear it. Having completed their opening sequence, the bridge doors began to slowly slide closed, their weight making the process a long affair.

Dorothy's face filled the screen, the muscles around her eyes contracted very slightly. "If you knew he was speaking freely, would you give him to us?" She asked.

Grey hesitated. To the Commons he might as well have glanced down at his cards and grinned.

It was as though someone had fired a starting pistol. The screen cut to black, the signal it had been displaying gone, and Williams dove at the set of closing bridge doors. Titanium shrieked as the exotic alloys of his suit sheared against those of the door's teeth, but in a half a second he was through.

"The OTV's!" Katherine said it before Grey even had time to think it, and she moved to lock down their computer controls.

"Who is security in the launch bay?" Grey asked. Williams needed to be stopped before he left the ship. If he hit space Grey's options would then all involve nuclear missiles, lasers, or railguns.

"Ensign Arnold has the watch, sir," Tsang answered, having smartly retrieved the duty roster.

"Page her and inform her that Williams could be on the way to commandeer an OTV. She is ordered to stop him."

Katherine turned from her console, "he's going to be able to override this if he gets into the launch bay. Can Arnold actually stop him?"

"No. Can we cut power to the bay? He can't open the outer doors without power," Grey asked as if in answer.

"Not in thirty seconds," Katherine replied. "The bay's air pumps are on the same power circuit and take a few minutes to discharge."

Grey considered the answer for three long seconds.

"Arnold would have a better chance trying to stop a volcano. Tsang, order her to get out of there, right now."

***

ENSIGN MINDY ARNOLD SAT at the far end of the Launch Bay. The room was cramped. One of the OTV's was half disassembled and laid out on the floor in front of her, the other, freshly serviced, and ready for use, sat in its docking clamps. She was three hours into a five-hour guard shift and was reading the technical specifications for an engine piece from the disassembled OTV. As she read she spun a glistening, symmetrical, copper piece between her fingers.

If there was one thing that government contracts did reliably it was produce paperwork. Every piece, every system, every tube, and bolt had its own documentation and guides. The engineers who had been forced to write them had resented the process, but Arnold found them fascinating. Every component represented a significant chunk of someone's life and the Russian sense of humor and pride permeated the documents. "If this breaks, it is because you did something terribly, terribly, wrong," was one of her favorite lines for the engine exhaust cowl documentation she was reading.

Her gauntlet chimed. "Bridge to Arnold. Be advised, Major Williams may be on route to the launch bay intending to commandeer an OTV. You are ordered to detain him."

She dropped the cowl, it reverberated with the impact of hitting the metal deck. Her helmet was within arm's reach and she pulled it on. The seven seconds that task took gave her time to come to grips with her situation. What had he said to her, "a monkey against a tank?"

She considered moving to the side of the large bay doors, perhaps take him by surprise as he entered. She considered hunkering down behind cover and simply waiting for the door to open. Williams was stronger, smarter, faster, and far more talented at the art of dispensing death. She wondered if the people he had killed were as impressed with his prowess as she had been watching. Her sidearm was in her hand without having consciously drawn it.

***

"WHAT WOULD IT TAKE TO CUT the Common's connection?" Grey asked Katherine.

She considered, "we don't know exactly how it works but presumably the further the distance between Williams and the Commons the less bandwidth is available to it."

"Corporal Tsang. Give me any heading out of the system, 80% power. Major Bakker please ready the ship for FTL and execute when ready. I'll be in the Launch Bay," Grey had barely finished talking before the bridge door was open wide enough for him to exit.

***

THE COMMONS WAS RAPT. Williams moved his body in ways they had never experienced before as he skimmed over the Galileo's deck plating. An Olympic sprinter on steroids would have been left in his wake. A flick of shadow ahead and the Commons told him to dodge, and he did, moving to the left just as a crewman rounded the corner into his path - unaware a bullet train had been coming his way. Williams could feel the Commons going through his memories about the layout for the OTV's controls. Thousands of engineers, pilots, and physicists worked to determine the launch sequence and how to operate the craft by Williams' memories of what the control's looked like.

The launch bay would be guarded, Williams knew that. He drew his weapon and allowed himself to skid to a halt in front of the vacuum proof doors that guarded its entrance. Whoever was on the other side of the doors, Williams had spent three years with them. He could well have trained them, evaluated them. It took a half a second for Williams to form the thought that he did not want to hurt anyone, and then for the Commons to evaluate it, disprove it (after all, Williams simply wanted to leave, whoever wanted to stop him was a captor not a friend), and extinguished the emotion. Williams quickly saw that the real issue was that he had forgotten his helmet in his cabin. It was a foolish oversight and one that wouldn't be repeated now that calm had been brought to the Commons. If the Galileo's crew realized his mistake and had depressurized the launch bay, he'd need a new plan. Two hundred military officers, L included, were considering the possibilities for him.

He was in luck. The bay doors opened without any protest, and he swung his MX-3 over the interior of the room as the doors revealed it. The Commons wouldn't leave anyone behind. They were one, as inseparable as a hand or toe.

The room seemed clear. Thousands of voices said that Captain Grey must have realized that Williams couldn't be stopped, called back the security, and saved lives. Williams was grateful for that for another half second.

The OTV's hatch opened easily with the twist of a steel wheel. Williams scanned the interior of the small ship. Aside from three large crates that had been used to ferry food from the planet's surface, it was empty. He entered the OTV and closed the hatch behind him. The simple mechanical system that held the door closed neglected a locking mechanism. That problem took the Commons less time than it took Williams to grab the ship's handheld fire extinguisher. Wedging the red steel cylinder into the door's mechanism jammed it closed.

He knew from security protocols that he could manually open the launch bay doors from the controls of the OTV. The ship was meant to double as an escape boat, and so would launch if ordered no matter what other systems had been destroyed or set in the wrong modes.

His armor made for a tight fit getting into the pilot's seat. The Commons had him carefully scan over the controls, read each label, and guided him through the power-up procedures.

His hands reached blindly behind him for the five-point safety straps which had proven vital in his previous descent. They had never done this before, he had never done this before, it was an active process that drew all of William's attention, thousands of voices wanting to see more of one thing or another, what one gage read or how another responded to the press of a button.

He didn't notice the sound of a crate opening behind him. Its hinges were plastic and did not squeak. The rubber soles of Mindy Arnold's boots were quiet on the OTV's deck. One step after another she came up on Williams from behind.

Williams worked on the five straps now in his lap as the Commons focused on the ship's launch sequence.

Mindy raised her sidearm.

He saw the flash of movement reflected in the canopy of the OTV, the Common's shouted for him to move, his body shouted for him to move, he simply didn't have time. The butt of Mindy Arnold's MX-3 connected with the back of his head, and he saw black.

"Dick in hand, sir."

***

THE GALILEO FLEW towards the edge of the system. As her engines warmed, power to them increased to the maximum rated amount. Systems were being checked and cross checked throughout the ship to make ready for faster than light travel. Technically she could transition to FTL inside the system, but transitions were considered dangerous. Many systems were designed to be turned off, or operating at a steady state, the process of getting form off to steady state was non-standard and as such had risks associated with it. Minimizing those risks meant doing things in as pristine conditions as possible, away from magnetic fields of planets and stars, away from intersystem dust.

With every moment of travel the Galileo increased the distance the Common's signal would have to travel. As a simple matter of physics this ought to mean the amount of information that could pass through it would decrease as a cubic function.

Major Williams, a bandage wrapped around his head, face slackened, lay centered on a gurney. Restrains kept him tight in place.

"Ben?" Grey asked.

The Major didn't move, didn't make any expression but his eyes tracked the Captain's and he answered. "Yes sir. And yes, I want to stay with the Commons."

Grey grabbed a chair and sat down beside his officer. It was just the two of them in the ship's medical bay. The thin plastic of the chair's seat flexed under his weight. "I'd feel a lot more certain about that if you didn't look like a damn zombie when you said it, Ben."

"No, you wouldn't, sir. No matter how I look or react you are going to doubt it's my own choice. At some point the Galileo will be far enough away from the Commons that you can be sure it is really me and even then you won't take me at my word because you won't like the answer."

"Ok. Let's say that's true. How about you explain it to me. Why are you and Dorothy like this? Why break off relations? Why the change?"

Williams didn't hesitate, the Commons guided his answer, "we simply realized the obvious. That when everyone has the same experiences, the same knowledge, individual variations amount to unsupportable opinions and the Commons has a duty to correct these in the name of truth, which in turn gives social unity, and a net benefit to all."

"The prisoners..." Grey whispered slowly.

"They were wrong. Their error led to harm to themselves and society generally."

The Galileo transitioned to faster than light travel, its shields activated. The Major's reaction was profound. His face tightened, and eyes began to dart around the cabin almost frantically.

"It's me, sir. Can we go back now?"

Grey tapped his gauntlet and confirmed the Galileo was moving faster than light, faster than any signal could be sent from the planet and reach Williams. He considered the Major. Williams had begun to tremble slightly, his body seemed smaller than it had only a few moments before. His eyes were fearful. "Ben. We need you. I am not going to accept that in a few days of being connected to the Common's you can't have the life you had before. So, no, you can't go back. But we are going to be here for you. We're going to help you get back to normal no matter how long it takes. We won't leave you behind. Understand?"

Williams reacted as though he had been stabbed in the gut, his body jerked gently. After a few minutes of trying to calm him, Grey left. Just outside the medial bay a guard stood, fully armored and armed. Grey tapped his shoulder, "it's him, but not, be careful."

***

A WEEK PASSED THAT WAY. Grey would often visit, but Williams consistently refused to speak with him. However, his condition did seem to improve. At first he was nearly catatonic but slowly he began to rise, even taking walks around the ship to exercise his legs.

A week to the day after being disconnected, Williams asked the Captain to take a walk with him and Grey gladly accepted.

Williams was freshly shaved, cleanly dressed, and looked as though he had just gotten through a long flu.

"Good morning, Major," Grey said, "feeling better?"

"It's hard to describe, sir. I'm certainly calmer, I suppose I've grieved and come to terms with things."

"Grieved?"

Major Williams led Grey through the ship's halls. After three years with nothing but routine tasks to do, the crew now had a wealth of sensor data, debriefings, and physical samples to analyze. Crewmen moved with purpose, making way for their commanding officers, but obviously eager to get to where they were going. Only a few still bothered to wear their armor.

Astrometrics had calculated a sixteen-month journey to the next system of note.

"Yes sir. The Commons isn't just access to the life and experiences of a civilization. On its own that is almost unbelievable. But that's just experiences. It's so much more than that. It's intelligence and wisdom. Having billions of people, hundreds of thousands of experts, to provide advice or answers to any question that ever crosses your mind."

The two men made their way around the port side of the ship and transitioned to starboard, "being disconnected feels as though I was Einstein and now I'm an imbecile."

"Free will ain't nothing," Grey offered.

"But what does that mean? Captain we, the Commons, discovered this last week and now I am too dumb to even put it into words properly. When you can see everything, from every point of view, and look at it with the knowledge of a world of experts in every area, why would anyone do anything differently than what was correct? Why would you overeat, why would you sleep longer than you need to, why would you react to a situation any differently than I would, except for a lack of a complete understanding?"

"Because our mistakes have value. They teach us, they take us on a journey for meaning in our own lives," Grey said.

The two men progressed forward into the ship until they reached the airlock Chetan Gonzales had died in. Katherine's painting still adorned the outer doors. A sea of stars and night, not a cold expanse but the warm embrace of the infinite.

Williams stopped and looked at the painting, "I won't try and convince you of the futility of that, sir. It would be too cruel to actually do, and I couldn't manage it the way I am now."

Captain Grey stiffened at that, "Ben. I'm your friend and commanding officer. As both I am telling you that this is for your own good. You have a valuable, important life to lead. You have a job to do on this ship that matters. You just need to get back into your routine again."

Benjamin Williams smiled at Grey, his shoulders slumping, resigned. "You are my friend, sir. I hope you know that." He took a step to his Captain and put a hand on his shoulder. "I just wanted you to know what this is like for me. Can you imagine what it would be like to be brilliant, to be important, to have everything imaginable from life, a world of people who truly understood you, accepted you, loved you. People you had no secrets from and had no need to hide any part of yourself from. Then to lose that? Imagine if you were suddenly crippled, your intelligence taken from you, your ability to be the captain of this ship or do any job you thought was important, taken away. But you could remember who you were, and knew you would never get that back. If that happened to you, honestly, what would you do?"

Major Benjamin Williams struck like a cobra. He shoved Grey, who was completely unprepared, square in the chest and sent him crashing down.

"You'd do the same thing, sir," Williams stepped back into the airlock, and with the push of the double center buttons, sealed the inner doors.

Grey gasped trying to draw a breath, the Major's hit had winded him, and he clawed his way towards the airlock to stop him. Even without air in his lungs Grey fought to his feet and hit the green button at the top of the airlock control. Nothing happened. He took a quarter of a ragged breath, blinked hard, and looked down at the airlock control panel.

He had hit the right button; the doors should have opened. It was a minor question, which side of the door had priority. With millions of systems, billions of lines of code, it hadn't been caught.

He tried to paw his communicator but couldn't get words out to activate it. Inside the airlock Williams calmly pushed the final three buttons on the console and the outer doors opened. Major Benjamin Williams was gently blown out the hatch by the residual air in the chamber, and into the nothingness of faster than light space.

CHAPTER 28

THE GALILEO DROPPED OUT OF FTL as soon as Captain Grey choked out an intelligible order; but there had never been any chance to save Williams.

After the funeral Grey sealed himself in his cabin and the Galileo sat idle in interstellar space. Even when a ship stops, life aboard her does not. There was still a long list of repairs to be done before another multi-month FTL trip would be prudent and the crew was busy. It was truly only the senior staff, now Katherine alone, who knew that this stop was a reaction, not a decision.

It took two days before Katherine decided to act and approached Captain Grey`s cabin. She had not been the first, and as she arrived Ensign Arnold, eyes red, exited just ahead of her. The Ensign didn't break stride when she saw Katherine.

For a moment Katherine considered stopping her, telling her it wasn't her fault. Yes, it had been Arnold's faith that started this. It could have been Arnold instead of Williams who had been connected to the Commons. But Katherine had the feeling things played out exactly as the Commons wanted. There had been several references to god and religion in the Galileo's initial message, and each of her crew had been questioned about faith when they were on the planet. Had the Commons wanted to orchestrate a crewman being connected, specifically to gain an understanding of religion they had played their cards exactly as she would have. But who could really tell the motives and plans of a global intelligence? In the end she said nothing and let Arnold leave the hall alone, then knocked on the Captain's hatch.

It took a long time for him to answer. When the hatch did finally open Grey, seeing her, simply nodded and stepped aside to let her in. The cabin stunk with the smell of grief.

Grey sat down at his small table as though he weighed a half a ton and turned his attention to his window. Katherine sat beside him and waited for him to speak.

It took nearly a half an hour, but it was Grey who broke the silence. "Did you know he had an estranged daughter back home? He'd written her a letter that he never sent."

The cabin window was filled with stars. They didn't sparkle, they didn't move slowly, they simply sat cold, bright, timeless.

"At least we can send her that much of him then."

Grey didn't acknowledge the comment, "before he did it... He told me that I had crippled him. Asked if I would want to live that way."

Katherine put her hand on Grey's knee and squeezed.

"He still could have had an amazing life," she said.

Grey kept his gaze fixed out the window a thousand miles away, "he said that they had cured wrong opinion, that it was for everyone's benefit. But without any wrong opinions, how is one person different from another?   A whole world Katherine. All those people and history, Dorothy, Ben, all gone. Maybe something new takes their place, but it won't be what we saw. I just don't know. And maybe it was my fault. We brought a disease with us as surely as Columbus did, it's just that ours was knowledge."

Katherine looked out the window and considered what her Captain had said.

"You see those stars; billions and billions of stars, even more billions of worlds around them. Even if this is an end, how much does the universe care that just one of those lights winked out? How much do we care; how much can we care?"

Grey took the small warm hand on his knee and held it tightly.

TO THE READER

Thank you for taking the time to read this book. The amount of thought, effort, and time that goes into a book like this is measured in years, not hours, and my one goal through it all has been for you to come to this page and wish there was more.

If you have enjoyed it please leave a review, it is ultimately the readers who decide a book's fate.

Visit www.AuthorNathanHGreen.com for my latest news, new works, and updates, or follow me on Instagram, @AuthorNathanHGreen.

OTHER BOOKS BY NATHAN H. GREEN

Treason's Temple

The United States of America fell, the Kingdom of America arose in its place.   But that's ancient history.   For Kuna Romeson what matters is that life isn't fair. It isn't fair for her: being a woman in the Kingdom of America stinks, unless you're as vapid as her classmates. Life isn't fair for her father: who deserved fame and wealth for completing a temple, but instead got shuffled into the back offices of a university. Life certainly isn't fair for her brother Lee: the constant target of bullies, eyes as big as moons at the thought of one day being a temple hero like their father, but born mundane.

When their father finds an illegal map the family has a choice: stick with the unfair lives they know, or become traitors in hopes of changing the world.

The one good thing about being a traitor: it frees you to do anything you can get away with.

Woe to the Victor – Coming Soon!

Captain Lewis Black drifts through space. Earth burns below him.

His wife is missing. The pilots under his command are dead. Air hisses into space from around the stump of his severed arm.

Now, a Maaravi landing ship approaches. He thanks God for that.   Torture him to death, throw him into a tank of formaldehyde, anything would be worth one last chance to hurt them.

Natasha Palmer owes a debt she can't pay. As lead engineer on the Reaper missile program it was her missile, and her failure, that cost humanity the war. When an abandoned Maaravi landing ship gives her a chance to save survivors she has to try. She doesn't have food, air, or a plan, and the first person she rescues doesn't even want to be saved.

But defeat is not always final, and some victories destroy the victor.

Made in the USA
Monee, IL
01 February 2022

90429742R00167